**"Dr. Magnusson is very important
to the balance of power, Tara."**

"The powers he is working with are truly immense . . .
gravity, time, the void . . . technology beyond imagination. And this power would be very, very dangerous if it
fell into the wrong hands. The Pythia thinks—"

"I don't care what the Pythia thinks," Tara snapped.

"The Pythia thinks this technology could be misused
and result in vast devastation, even global war. He must
be found."

Tara leaned back in her chair. She wanted no part of
this. "Sophia, I . . ."

Sophia looked down at her hands. "I would not ask
this lightly. We would have asked your mother for her
assistance."

Tara bristled.

Sophia continued, "But she is gone, and you are the
only one left in her line who has her particular knack for
finding people."

Tara glanced down at the picture of the scientist.
"Even if I wanted to, I'm so far out of practice, I would
be of very little use."

Sophia grinned at her. "No one ever falls out of practice in your art."

"I can't."

Sophia slid the file across the table to her. "No one
will make you, and I won't come knocking again. All I
ask is that you think about it."

Tara could not refuse her that much.

Dark Oracle

Alayna Williams

POCKET BOOKS

New York   London   Toronto   Sydney

Pocket Books
A Division of Simon & Schuster, Inc.
1230 Avenue of the Americas
New York, NY 10020

This book is a work of fiction. Names, characters, places, and incidents either are products of the author's imagination or are used fictitiously. Any resemblance to actual events or locales or persons, living or dead, is entirely coincidental.

First Juno Books/Pocket Books paperback edition June 2010

JUNO BOOKS and colophon are trademarks of Wildside Press LLC used under license by Simon & Schuster, Inc., the publisher of this work.

POCKET and colophon are registered trademarks of Simon & Schuster, Inc.

For information about special discounts for bulk purchases, please contact Simon & Schuster Special Sales at 1-866-506-1949 or business@simonandschuster.com.

The Simon & Schuster Speakers Bureau can bring authors to your live event. For more information or to book an event contact the Simon & Schuster Speakers Bureau at 1-866-248-3049 or visit our website at www.simonspeakers.com.

Designed by Jacquelynne Hudson
Cover illustration by Chad Michael Ward

Manufactured in the United States of America

10 9 8 7 6 5 4 3 2 1

ISBN 978-1-4391-8279-6
ISBN 978-1-4391-8282-6 (ebook)

Acknowledgments

Thanks to the ladies of the Ohio Writers Network for their unflinching support: Michelle, Linda, Rachel, Melissa, Emily, and Faith.

Thank you to the folks at National Novel Writing Month, who continue to celebrate literary abandon.

Thanks to my husband, Jason, who has suffered through my fetish with commas.

And thanks to my editor, Paula Guran, for the opportunity and guidance.

Chapter One

THE AIR seethed, like a living thing disturbed.

Dust settled from the sky as the roar of the explosion rolled away into the desert. Gradually, the sky cleared, revealing stars. In the sandy haze of dust, a building had blistered open, like an empty shell too weak to hold a great and terrible seed. Chunks of concrete littered the ground, illuminated by weak sparks and fizzles from the severed legs of ruined machinery.

Swimming through the wreckage, dozens of tiny lights milled like fireflies, winking in and out. Unlike fireflies, they burned dark violet, wandering in wayward paths. Undisturbed by the remnants of walls, they glided through twisted I beams as easily as smoke. In bright flashes of light, some flickered out. Others swarmed together, levitating before they vanished with the rushing sound of air, leaving spirals of dust in their wake.

They came from the machine. The hull of the massive mechanism lay open in the darkness. Its skin ripped open by the force of the explosion, wires dangled in heavy tentacles over ruined copper tubing warped into blossoms by the sound. A solenoid switch clicked on and off, on and off, with no circuit to complete. The violet particles rimmed the interior skin of the machine, seething over the steel like the surface of an indigo sun. The machine was like an egg cracked open, pouring life into the night.

But it was not life. The particles drifted away, blazed out, sucking bits of air and time as they disappeared. The faint light illuminated a trace of human wreckage in the debris: a silver watch.

Its face gleamed smooth and unbroken, but the time its hands had measured had stopped. There was no trace of its owner, the man who had keyed the last operating procedure into this apparatus.

No life; no life, at all.

Yet, something more than life. Dim violet sparks crept out into the darkness toward the sounds of distant sirens.

TARA HAD ONCE BEEN ACCUSTOMED TO AWAKENING TO STAC-cato knocks on her door in the middle of the night. She had always answered that summons to roll out of bed in razor-sharp readiness back then. She could dress and launch herself beyond the door in less than ten minutes, her case full of notebooks, guns, and more arcane tools of her trade. Sometimes, she could even squeeze feeding the cat into those preparations.

That was a long time ago, but old habits never really went away.

This knock was different, softer. Tara rolled over in bed, her bare feet skimming the floor. Automatically, she reached for the holstered .38 revolver hung behind the headboard, just out of sight, but close at hand. The cat leaped down from the pillow beside her to hide under the bed.

Found. Here. How? Tara's brow wrinkled. She'd never been disturbed in this place by anything but her own dreams.

The shadows of tree branches stained the floor in abstract chiaroscuro shapes. Melting snow rattled through the forest beyond the exterior walls of the cabin. Tara had hoped to feel the thaw in her bones for weeks now, had watched the ice slip and break under the late-winter sun. Though it was nearly March, the ice would be treacherous to most visitors, and would dissuade them from traveling the hidden dirt road to Tara's sanctuary. There wasn't even mail delivery this distant from civilization. For all intents and purposes, the little cabin didn't exist, forgotten in the buzz and shuffle of the outside world. Tara had hoped some of that forgetting extended to her.

Tara walked noiselessly over the pine floorboards. She knew the location of each squeak, sidestepping them in the dark as expertly as a dancer with an invisible partner. She crossed the cabin's living area, illuminated only by dull embers in the fireplace worming into the sweet-smelling apple wood.

Again, the knock. Tara touched the door, feeling the

vibration echo through the surface. She could close her eyes to it, crawl back into bed. She could pretend she wasn't here, had never been here, that she hadn't heard.

But the knock rang with a quiet authority that could not be ignored.

Tara slid back the dead bolt and cracked the door open as far as the chain would allow. She held the gun in her left hand, behind the door, invisible to the caller. She thumbed back the well-oiled hammer with an echoing click. In the dark, the ratchet of a shotgun would have been a more effective deterrent to unwanted visitors, but the sound was still unmistakable. Her hand sweated against the rubber grips, her index finger grazing the stainless steel trigger guard.

"Yes." Her voice felt rusty. It had been a very long time since she had used it, other than with the cat.

"Tara. It's Sophia."

Tara swallowed, peered through the gap in the door. The wan porch light illuminated a woman with brilliant silver hair standing outside, her breath making ghosts against her lined skin and dark coat. The woman smiled reassuringly, the expression rumpling pleasantly around her gray eyes.

The smile chilled Tara, tightened her chest. She closed the door, inhaled a deep breath. Slowly, her fingers worked the chain free, then opened the door wide.

"I'm sorry to have come at such a late hour," Sophia said. "It couldn't be helped."

Tara only nodded and stood aside as Sophia stepped into the dark room. Tara reached for the light switch.

Though she was accustomed to seeing in darkness, she was certain her guest was not.

When she turned back, Sophia looked pointedly at her gun. "My dear, you won't be needing that." Sophia shrugged out of her coat. Tara knew this was all Sophia would say about the weapon.

Tara released the hammer on the gun. The heat from her fingers fogged the stainless steel. She placed the .38 on the kitchen counter, leaned against the sink with her arms crossed. "Why are you here?"

Sophia fixed her with her Athena-gray eyes, serious and piercing. "Your mother—"

Tara made a cutting gesture with her hand. "I don't want to talk about my mother."

Sophia did not look away. Tara knew Sophia had been the last person to see her mother alive. And Tara hated the jealousy and anger she felt, thinking about that.

Sophia continued. "Your mother would not have wanted this for you."

Tara narrowed her eyes. "What would she not have wanted?" She sketched the cabin and the forest beyond with her hand. "I have peace. And I *did* have solitude."

Attracted by the light and the voices, Tara's cat drifted into the kitchen. He blinked his golden eyes at Sophia. She rubbed her fingers together, and Oscar trotted over to her, tail up. Much to Tara's irritation, he began rubbing his face on Sophia's black pants, leaving trails of charcoal fur. He was far too comfortable with her.

Unbidden, Sophia pulled out a kitchen chair and sat down. Reluctantly, Tara slid into a chair opposite her.

Oscar leaped into her lap, purring like a diesel engine. Her silver hair hung in a tantalizing braid over her shoulder, and Oscar took a swipe at it. Sophia let him bat at it until his claws became tangled, and she gently worked them free. "She would not have wanted this isolation for you, especially after what happened."

Tara bit back her anger, leveled her voice. "My mother is gone. I make my own choices."

"Dear child." The older woman reached for Tara's hand. Sophia's touch was surprisingly warm. Tara remembered those hands from when she was a child, warm as sunshine, brushing her hair. "You've lost much."

Tara's jaw tightened. "And you and your sisters would probably blame me for following . . . what was it, you called it? The destroyer's path?"

Sophia shook her head, quivering her crescent-shaped earrings. "Not that. The warrior's path. And we would never blame you."

This old argument, again. "I became a profiler because I wanted to help. And I did." Tara's fingers traced a scar disappearing under her sleeve, and she shrugged. "Besides, that's over now." She didn't mask her wry expression, disappointed in herself that she still sought Sophia's approval. "I would have thought you would have approved of me leaving that life."

"Leaving *that* life, yes. Not leaving life altogether."

Tara rubbed her temple. "Sophia, what brings you here? Did you want to see me? Or do Delphi's Daughters want something?" She pressed her mouth in a grim slash. She'd not spoken of Delphi's Daughters in a long time, and the name of that secret society was foreign on her tongue. She would not be their tool.

Tara had been a tool for the Feds for too many years, summoned out of sleep to solve unspeakable crimes. Like a doll, she would be taken out of her box, wound up, and set upon a case. When she wound down, drained of all insight, they'd put her back in the box, only to come knocking again. She would not allow herself to be used that way, not again. Not by her government, and not by Delphi's Daughters. Delphi's Daughters had existed since the beginning of recorded time, and she was sure they could exist without her.

"Both," Sophia said, her face honest and open. "Something has happened, and we need your help."

"I'm all helped out. Sorry."

Sophia pulled a manila file folder from her bag and set it on the table. Tara did not touch it. Sophia pulled a photograph out of the file and slid it across the table. Still, Tara refused to touch it. But she could not help looking. The picture was of a man in his fifties, dressed in a wrinkled lab coat, with his hands jammed in his pockets. His posture was of one who spent a great deal of time hunched over computers, and his stringy body suggested someone who often forgot to eat. His expression felt intense, even through the photographic ink. She could practically see the gears of his thoughts working behind that blue . . .

Tara shoved back from the table, as if the photo was too hot to touch. She didn't want to fall into it, didn't want to have to fight to claw her way back out. "Sophia. I can't."

The older woman did not remove the photo. "He's

very important, Tara. His name is Lowell Magnusson. As I understand it, he was involved in some very powerful technology. Dark matter and gravitational fields. There was an accident earlier this evening. His atom smasher blew up. He's gone missing."

Tara frowned. "Why is he important to you?"

Sophia laughed, a sound like bells. A sound that reminded Tara of her mother. "Strange, isn't it? He's a man, and he has no ability to see into any future beyond what his own imagination can create . . . One would *think* that would land him far outside of the purview of Delphi's Daughters."

"One would think that, yes." Tara waited for an explanation. Delphi's Daughters dedicated themselves to salvaging hidden things, to preserving the intellectual and physical lineages of esoteric knowledge since the time of the Oracle of Delphi. In all the time she'd observed her mother's association with the secret society, she'd never seen men involved. It was always the women, whispering their arcane and alchemical lore from mother to daughter in unbroken chains spanning centuries. They trafficked in information and secrets, building empires of influence and knowledge, manipulating world events to their liking. And Tara, who had inherited her mother's talents, remained a stubbornly broken link. She had refused to follow in her mother's footsteps and join them.

Sophia's laugh trickled away, and her eyes darkened to the color of winter storms. "Dr. Magnusson is very important to the balance of power, Tara. The powers he is working with are truly immense . . . gravity, time, the void . . . technology beyond imagination. And this technology would be very, very dangerous if it fell into the wrong hands. The Pythia thinks—"

"I don't care what the Pythia thinks," Tara snapped. The Pythia was the strongest of modern oracles; surely she could see Tara wouldn't help her.

"The Pythia thinks this technology could be misused and result in vast devastation and global war. He must be found."

Tara leaned back in her chair, balancing on the back legs. She wanted no part of this. "Sophia, I . . ."

Sophia looked down at her hands. "I do not ask this lightly, Tara. We would have asked your mother for her assistance."

Tara bristled.

Sophia continued, "But she is gone, and you are the only one left in her line who has her particular knack for finding people."

Tara glanced down at the picture of the scientist. "Even if I wanted to, I'm so far out of practice, I would be of very little use."

Sophia grinned at her. "No one ever falls out of practice in your art."

"I can't."

Sophia slid the file across the table to her. "No one will force you, and I won't come knocking again. All I ask is that you think about it."

Tara could not refuse her that much. That much would, at least, get her out of Tara's house.

• • • •

THE FILE FOLDER LAY UNDISTURBED ON THE KITCHEN TABLE for many hours after Sophia left. Tara moved around it, trying to pretend it didn't exist. But she found herself orbiting it unconsciously, like a star around a black hole. Unable to return to sleep, she made herself a cup of hot chocolate and paced the kitchen, chewing on her thoughts.

It would take a great deal of desperation for the Pythia to send someone to her doorstep. Delphi's Daughters and Lowell Magnusson obviously needed her help, but she resisted. Altruism warred with her desire to stay clear of the business of profiling again. Absently, she scratched at the scars crossing her belly. The last time she'd gone tracking in men's minds, she'd nearly lost her life. It was not a risk she was willing to take again, even for an innocent like Dr. Magnusson.

Oscar leaped up onto the kitchen table and sat on Magnusson's picture. He parked himself on his butt and splayed his toes to take a bath.

"Oscar." She pulled the picture out from under his furry bottom. She glanced sidelong at the bathing beauty. "She whispered something in your ear, didn't she? You're in cahoots with *her*, aren't you?"

Oscar nonchalantly ignored her, passionately cleaning his paws.

"Traitor."

As far as Tara knew, Sophia's particular talents lay in scrying, not in manipulating animals. That didn't mean she couldn't. No one but the Pythia ever knew the true extent of the power of Delphi's Daughters.

Hesitating, she touched the picture. She held it at arm's

length, reluctant to allow the image to creep too far into her head. Lowell Magnusson stared back at her. He was wearing a truly awful navy blue tie patterned with cartoon planets, comets, and stars. It was the kind of tie one would receive as a gift for Father's Day. No one would ever pick a tie like that out for himself.

Tentatively, she flipped open the folder.

The file didn't belong to Delphi's Daughters. As far as Tara knew, the secret society didn't keep files. They were dreadfully old-fashioned that way. Rather, they seemed to gather information volunteered from unusual places. Judging by the form titles and letterhead, this file had come from the State Department. The Daughters of Delphi had money, stashed in accounts around the world. Old money. And money could buy a tremendous amount of information and influence.

Lowell Magnusson, age fifty-three, was a quantum physicist on contract for the Department of Defense. He was currently on sabbatical from teaching at Cornell. Tenured. Nice gig. Divorced, with a daughter, Cassie, age twenty-three. He'd been cited by the city of Albany twice for failure to mow his lawn, and his vanity license plates read QUARKY. He'd been raised in a small town in Ohio, which had named a reading room in the county library after him. Neither of his parents was still living, and he had no siblings.

His interest in astronomy had begun when he was twenty-one. As a graduate physics student working as a research assistant at Ohio State University, Magnusson had the good fortune to be present when his mentor, Dr.

Jerry Ehman, received the famous Wow! radio signal. Ehman and Magnusson had been involved in the SETI project at the Big Ear Radio Telescope at Ohio State University in 1977, when the Big Ear caught a seventy-two-second burst of odd radio wave activity. The signal strongly suggested the existence of extraterrestrial life. It had never been replicated.

Tara flipped through a series of ID badge photos of the subject. Magnusson took a bad ID photo. He was squinting in half of the shots. His driver's license also displayed the same blink reflex. She paused at a picture of him standing with a young woman who Tara assumed to be his daughter. They stood together in front of a string of lush green mountains, smiling under a bright blue sky. Magnusson was wearing a lurid yellow floral Hawaiian shirt that showed off a spectacular case of blistering sunburn. His daughter stood with her arms behind her back. She was her father's daughter: dark hair, lanky frame, with her dad's deep blue eyes. In the background stood the white dome of a large telescope facility. Hawaii, Tara guessed.

She thumbed through the file, reading paragraphs at random. Several papers Magnusson had written were included, and she read abstracts of articles dealing with the theoretical properties of dark matter and dark energy, describing neutralinos and super-dense particles, gravity wells and the bending of light around unseen objects in space. Magnusson was fascinated by the big cosmological questions of the universe: If only thirty percent of the universe was made of conventional matter and energy—

things that could be touched and measured—where was the rest? How can we detect this so-called dark matter and dark energy, which is virtually undetectable?

Tara closed the folder on Magnusson's questions, leaving out the picture of the physicist and his daughter. She was certain Sophia had included it to tug at her emotions.

Beside it, Oscar snored softly.

Tara pushed away from the table, padded to the bedroom. The gray light of dawn lightened the windows, casting a soft glow over the worn quilt covered in a frost of cat hair. She stood before the dresser, bare except for a closed jewelry box and a framed photograph of her mother and her when Tara was a child. Her mother, dressed in a paisley dress and straw hat, dark hair flowing over her shoulder, had flung her arms around Tara. Her smile was broad as a bow, unself-conscious. Tara was barefoot, wearing a yellow dress embroidered with ducks her mother made for her. Sunlight shone through tree leaves. Tara gently held a salamander in her dirty hands, joyously displaying the newly captured creature to the camera.

Out of the corner of her eye, Tara glimpsed her reflection in the photo frame's glass. There was no mirror above the dresser or anywhere else in the cabin; Tara had removed all those when she'd moved in. The indistinct image illumined by the dim light of dawn showed the resemblance to her mother. Blue eyes, chocolate hair, skin pale as porcelain. But a truer looking glass or even turning on the light would reveal where the similarities ended: with the scars on her throat, the dark circles under her eyes—the haunted look that never completely left her visage. For a moment, she fingered a raised scar on her collarbone, then let her hand fall. She was not her mother's daughter, after all. Her mother's daughter would not be so reluctant to follow in her maternal footsteps.

Tara knelt to open the bottom drawer of the dresser, a drawer that had remained firmly closed for a very long time. She withdrew a small bundle wrapped in a red silk scarf. It had been her mother's scarf. It still smelled a bit like her, jasmine and orange, fragrances that seemed out of place in this dull gray season. The bundle felt weighty in her hands as she carried it back to the kitchen. She spread the embroidered cloth open on the kitchen table, smoothing the fringe out.

A deck of Tarot cards and a small brown leather notebook lay on the table. The notebook had most of the pages torn out of it; the few remaining leaves were blank. The cards were well-worn with use, small nicks marring the art on the back of the cards: a tree, outlined in gold, branches reaching toward a night sky and roots reaching into the black earth. The black had faded with time. Tara had never really known the provenance of this particular deck. As much as her mother had tried to encourage her to find an affinity with another deck as a child, Tara had latched on to this particular one. It had belonged to her mother but, along with several other decks in her possession, wasn't the one she used daily. Tara had suspected the cards were much older than her mother. She'd never seen another deck like it. The cards had spoken to her the first time she touched them, seeming to warm to her hands and buzz when she shuffled them like the wings of humming-birds. She'd bonded to them right away.

But the cards spoke to her no more. Since the terrible incident that had scarred her and sent her into hiding, Tara had sealed them away and silenced them. Still, she'd never been able to destroy them.

Tara rested her chin in the palm of her hand, hair tricking over her wrist, reluctant to touch the deck. Her gaze brushed the picture of Lowell Magnusson and his daughter, smiling at her from glossy paper.

She feared opening the door to her intuitions again, to the synchronicities that would wake her from sound sleep. But Sophia had opened the door for her, and there was no silencing the clarion of the knowledge that someone needed her help.

Tara sighed, reached for the deck. Just one attempt at a reading and she'd put the cards away again. Then she'd tell Sophia she couldn't help.

She centered herself, putting her feet flat on the floor and her hands palm up, open in her lap. She listened to her breath. Tara could also hear the whirr of the refrigerator, the cat's snores, the splintering of ice outside, a crackle of a last ember in the fireplace. But she focused on her breath, and that sound drowned out the others. She emptied her thoughts and concentrated them on Lowell Magnusson. When she felt calm and still, she reached for the cards. The deck flexed in a familiar rhythm as she shuffled. Her hands still remembered.

The idea of the Tarot was centuries old. Predecessors to the modern deck of playing cards, they retained the archetypical imagery of the hero's journey through two series: the Major and Minor Arcana.

The twenty-two images of the Major Arcana depicted ideas and archetypes that had existed throughout time: death, rebirth, life, justice . . . all abstract ideas embedded in the soul from the beginning of time. They could represent major events or pivotal people in one's life. In the modern deck of playing cards, only one of these cards survived: the Joker. It was the analogue to the first card of the Major Arcana, the Fool, representing innocence. Somehow, it was ironic that innocence would always survive through the ages.

The fifty-six cards of the Minor Arcana were divided into four suits: cups, wands, swords, and pentacles. Their modern analogues of hearts, clubs, spades, and diamonds lived on in every poker room, casino, game of solitaire, and senior citizens bridge group in the world. Each suit was associated with an element and an affinity: cups to water and feelings; wands to fire and action; swords to air and realms of thought; and pentacles to earth and prosperity. The Minor Arcana most often represented the attitudes and feelings of the questioner, where the court cards of each suit—the kings, queens, knights, and pages—could often represent people met along the questioner's journey.

Together, these enduring images of the Tarot were intended to trigger the questioner's imagination. They used symbols to bring hidden information into the conscious mind, by creating associations and emotions. Each individual's reaction to a symbol would be unique, colored by experience, memory, and situation. These unique reactions yielded an association meaningful to the questioner. Jungian psychologists believed that the Tarot provided a pathway of connections, a means for the conscious mind to reach into the subconscious using symbols as a tool. But Tara knew Tarot could access much, much more.

"What do I need to know?" she thought aloud, working the deck. She shuffled until her mind felt blank and the cards seemed to stick together. She placed the deck to her right and began a Celtic Cross reading; although differences in placement varied among readers, it was the oldest and most common pattern of laying out the cards—the spread. A spread was a way of asking a question, a framework for a story to develop. The Celtic Cross was a broad reading, touching on past, present, future, and the querent's place in the environment. This version had been her mother's favorite, and one of the first spreads Tara had learned.

She drew the first card and laid it faceup on the center of the scarf. This card represented the present situation: the Four of Swords. A knight lay in effigy in a church. Light streamed through stained-glass windows, illuminating four swords hanging over his head, and a wreath of white roses lay on the effigy's hands. Tara's mouth twisted. It signified enforced solitude, respite to heal . . . but could also suggest fear of facing the world.

She drew the second card, laid it crosswise across the first. This represented her immediate obstacle or support. The High Priestess stared back at her with a direct, serious expression. The Priestess held a sheaf of paper and was crowned with a silver moon headdress, representing spiritual mystery. Tara's attention drifted to the file folder, and she thought of Sophia's silver moon earrings. Sophia both opposed Tara's solitude and supported her leaving it. Beyond Sophia, Tara thought of the Pythia, the Priestess of her own secret order.

She drew another card and laid it vertically above the others, directly below Magnusson's picture. This card crowned the first two and represented the highest destiny that could be hoped for in the situation. The card depicted the Magician, the inventor, the alchemist . . . the source of vital creativity. A man in a violet cloak stood holding a wand to the sky, with symbols of the four elements spread on a table before him: a sword, a pentacle, a wand, and a chalice . . . air, earth, fire, and water, made one. Above the Magician's head was the figure-eight shaped lemniscate, the sign of infinity, glowing golden against a background of lilies. Tara's gaze flickered up to the scientist's photo.

Tara steepled her hands before her. The fact the Magician was in the destiny position suggested Magnusson could be found. The two last cards laid out before her worried her. Both were Major Arcana, large archetypes cycling through life. This question was important, of great weight, heavy as lead.

She drew the fourth card and placed it below the first three to symbolize the distant past influencing the situation. The Two of Swords. The card depicted a blindfolded woman sitting on a beach, balancing two swords in crossed arms, one on each shoulder. The ocean roared behind her.

Tara tipped her head, absorbing the card. The card could denote the deliberate closing of one's eyes to the truth of the ocean, a closed heart, or unwillingness to choose sides. A precarious situation, to be sure. Tara couldn't tell if this referred to Magnusson's experience, or to her own. It seemed her experiences and feelings were bleeding over into the reading.

She placed the next card to the right of the Priestess to represent the recent past. The Eight of Pentacles was reversed, its image upside down from Tara's point of view. A man worked at a bench, meticulously tooling disks of pentacles, absorbed in his work. In the upright position, this would have meant pride in one's work. Reversed, it suggested unsatisfying work, professional envy, jealousy, or covetousness.

This was the second eight she'd drawn. Her thoughts drifted back to the lemniscate, the infinity sign gracing the Magician's head. She was certain these last two cards referred to Magnusson's situation.

She drew a sixth card, placed it to the left of the other cards. This card would describe the near future and near influences. The Knight of Pentacles brooded over a disk engraved with a star cradled gently in his hands. He was dark haired, sitting astride a black horse. A practical man. A man of action, deeply rooted in the physical world. Tara mentally filed this image away for later. She did not know this person, and he did not seem like an aspect of her own personality. Perhaps he would figure into the investigation.

She placed the seventh card on the lowest right-hand

corner of the table. This represented Tara, as the questioner. The Queen of Swords, the snow queen. The card showed a crowned woman sitting on a throne before a gray sky. Wind and snow tangled in her hair and cloak, and she held a silver sword upright. She held the sword in her right hand, but held her left hand as if the sword of her intellect had cut her. She looked at a horizon Tara couldn't see, and her expression was one of sorrow. The traditional meaning: sadness, sterility, mourning. After Sophia's visit, it wasn't hard for Tara to imagine herself in that context.

Enough about her. Tara quickly drew the next card from the deck. The eighth card represented the environment. She drew the Tower, the card of disaster, of revolution. It depicted a tower, struck by lightning, from which two people fell to the ground. A powerful image, and a powerful event of upheaval, betrayal, chaos. Sophia had said there had been an explosion in which the scientist had disappeared. Tara looked carefully at the figures falling from the tower, wondering if they would survive.

She placed the ninth card above the Star. This represented inner emotions, hidden things. The Star. A maiden bathed in a starlit pond, gazing up at a starry sky. She poured water from two cups, pouring energy back into the universe. This was a softer release of power than the Tower, a subtle transmutation. It represented hope, truth.

Tara pulled the last card and put it on the table above the Star, finishing the vertical column. This card, the Six of Swords, represented the final result. A ferryman rowed a boat carrying six swords over water to a green, distant shore. It was a card of movement, of travel, but of carrying a precious burden.

Tara leaned back in her chair. The reading was mixed. She felt sure some of the cards called to her personally; others reflected the larger situation of the missing man. The reading was heavy on swords, which symbolized the element of air but, of the Minor Arcana suits, involved the most conflict. A large number of Major Arcana cards suggested the situation involved significant forces in play.

Oscar rolled over dramatically, his tail twitching the deck she'd laid to the side. She reached over to rub his speckled belly with one hand as she jotted down the spread and her impressions in the little notebook. She wrote down the date, the question she'd asked, and the cards she'd drawn, in order. Below each card, she jotted her thoughts of how they interacted with the situation, what details stood out, which associations she made in her mind. She left plenty of blank space, especially for those cards she didn't understand fully now. Perhaps their meaning would become clear in the future.

She knew Dr. Magnusson had little time. Most missing persons had to be found within the first hours or days of their disappearances, or risk being lost forever. In her head, a mental clock was set, ticking softly. Sophia had said he'd just disappeared. Perhaps there was still time. She grimaced inwardly. She hated the idea of getting involved, but the photo pulled at the rusty wires of her heartstrings. If that young woman was left without parents, as Tara had been . . . Tara didn't think she would be able to set aside the guilt. The cards had come alive to her, at least in part. She knew she could help.

Her gaze lingered on the last card, the journey card. That card, at least, was very clear to her rusty senses. She sighed and reached for the phone to ask for Sophia to reserve her a plane ticket and arrange for someone to feed the cat.

Chapter TWO

THE DESERT wasn't what Tara had expected.

She'd thought it would be shades of brown and gray, not awash in color. As she peered out the plane window, gray sky contrasted with the soft violet of the mountains, capped in snow. Cloud shadows played over the mountains like water, seeming to gather close to the rust-colored earth. The mountains washed down to sand, rimmed in green and studded with pine trees.

The greenness of the landscape surprised her as the small plane circled in a tightening landing spiral. The Los Alamos County Airport tarmac spread in a short, black ribbon below the mountains, set in a patchy sage and brown lawn. The plane descended sharply to approach the runway. Tara couldn't hear the voice of the pilot beside her over the roar of the Cessna 172's propeller. She was the only passenger, occupying the copilot seat. She sat on her gloved hands to keep them warm. The cold of the long trip at high elevation had seeped into her bones.

The wheels bumped the tarmac, and the pilot expertly reined the light plane in to a landing. Still, Tara's heart crawled into her throat as the end of the runway neared. The pilot pulled the plane into a graceful turn and taxied gently toward the terminal: a low concrete building capped with a turquoise roof. The buzz of the propeller slackened as the Cessna pulled into the run-up area adjacent to the terminal.

The propellers slowed to a stop. Tara reached back to the baggage area for her single bag. Old habits died hard, and Tara always packed light. She released the latch and hopped onto the asphalt. The wind gusts pulled at her hair, which—hours ago—had been neatly tied back. Self-consciously, she smoothed her coat over her black pantsuit. The suit was many years old. Probably not the latest cut, but she wasn't here to impress. She was here to work.

A man briskly strode across the run-up area toward her. Tara immediately sized him up. Federal agent, to be sure. He was an Asian man in his mid-thirties, a serious set to his jaw. His tailored coat very nearly hid the bulge of a shoulder holster. The charcoal suit was practically government-issue. Tara could see the knife-sharp creases in his slacks from yards away. Well-shined shoes spoke to seriousness and attention to detail.

"Dr. Sheridan?" he asked over the ringing in her ears.

"Yes."

The agent offered his hand in a brusque handshake.

"I'm Agent Li. Welcome to New Mexico. This way, please."

"Thank you." Tara slung her bag over her shoulder and trotted off after Li. She noted he didn't look back to see if she followed him. He skipped the terminal entirely and headed to the parking area, flashing FBI credentials at a guard. Tara glimpsed them as he tucked them back in his coat pocket.

They weren't real.

Tara had seen credentials of all descriptions. She knew what to look for, and the way Li had hesitated for an instant before he chose a pocket to reach into suggested he had more than one set on his person.

Bemused, she followed him to his car, a nondescript dark sedan with blue and white U.S. government plates. As she took her time unloading her bag into the backseat, he scanned the parking area. He jingled coins in his pocket, an unconscious gesture of impatience.

"So," she began conversationally, as Li climbed behind the wheel and put the car in gear. "Who do you really work for?" She kept her tone light, as if she asked about the weather.

Li had stretched his arm behind her seat as he backed out of the parking space. He paused, and an eyebrow crawled up his forehead. He answered carefully, "My creds say I work for the Bureau."

Tara smiled. The evenly parsed answer wasn't a lie. It suggested Li was uncomfortable with lying. And that was a good thing. "I've held all kinds of creds, myself. Some real, some not. Which ones of yours are real?"

Li pulled out of the parking area, glancing sidelong at her. "Department of Justice, Special Projects Division."

Tara nodded, willing to accept that vagary for now. "You didn't seem the military type."

Li frowned. "Your investigative skills are still sharp, Dr. Sheridan."

"I try."

"Your file's been heavily redacted." Li took a left turn onto a two-lane highway. His tone was direct, matter-of-fact. "What remains describes your academic background . . . PhD in psychology, though you never practiced. Several academic articles on Jungian psychology, Gestalt therapy, and synchronicity. A short stint profiling with Special Projects, in behavioral science profile investigation. What is it, exactly, that you do?"

She shrugged. "I find people. As you said, I was a profiler."

"And now?"

"And now, you could say I'm a consultant."

Stalemate. Neither one wanted to give up information that wasn't need-to-know. Tara changed the subject. "How did you draw babysitting duty?"

Li paused. She'd hit the nerve of his impatience.

"I'm not in charge of this investigation." Tara saw by the tightness around his eyes he was doing as he was told to do, and he didn't like it. But he conformed to the rules.

Tara reached over, hit the power button on the car radio. Unexpectedly, the sounds of death metal rattled through the car, shaking the glass in the windows. Tara lifted her eyebrows and looked at Li. *Interesting.*

Li gripped the wheel with both hands and stared resolutely into the distance.

She turned down the volume, but just slightly. "Where are we going?"

"The last location Lowell Magnusson was seen." He stabbed a thumb at the backseat. "Your radiation suit's in the trunk. I brought extra duct tape."

THE CRIME SCENE WAS STRAIGHT OUT OF A SCIENCE-FICTION film. In an ancient caldera nestled in a plain between the mountains, grasses drenched with ash twitched in the chill breeze. A concrete ring looped in on itself in a figure eight, curving around a half-destroyed structure at its heart. It reminded Tara of aerial photos she'd seen of crop circles. A hastily erected tent covered the plain concrete block building, white plastic snapping like a surrender flag in the wind. People wearing hazmat gear streamed in and out of the tent, carrying metal scraps and radiation detectors. Long plastic hoses connected to trucks on the remote dirt road snaked into the tent like tentacles. It seemed as if a giant alien jellyfish had descended from outer space upon this sere place, and was busily consuming and regurgitating spacemen. Fire trucks parked beside it seemed like small toys seen from this distance. A fine dusting of snow had begun to filter down from the gray sky, frosting the scene with an otherworldly gleam.

Military police rimmed the perimeter, checking cars at the gate. When Agent Li pulled up, the MP was apparently unimpressed with his credentials, handing them back with white gloves that smelled like gunpowder. Tara sat back in her seat, arms folded. Territorial bickering. This could take a while.

"Sorry, sir. Essential personnel only."

"We're here with clearance from DOJ Special Projects Division." Li handed over a sheaf of papers the MP frowned at.

"This isn't a DOJ installation. This facility is under the jurisdiction of the U.S. Army."

"I understand that. DOD asked us to be here."

"I'll have to check with my CO."

"You do that." The MP walked back to the gate, speaking into a staticky radio. Li glared through the windshield at him, fingers drumming out an impatient rhythm on the steering wheel. Tara glanced at the chain-link fence, eying the ribbon razor wire curled over the top. Interesting. The top segment of the fence was slanted inward, a design typical for prisons: it made it more difficult to climb up the slant. Contrary to the MP's behavior, this installation was apparently just as concerned with keeping people *inside* the fence as it was with keeping people *out*. Perhaps the people who worked inside were less than enthusiastic about being there.

"Is this part of Los Alamos National Laboratory?" she asked, watching the snow spiral over the fence.

"Officially? No. It's technically farmland."

"Nice crop of spacemen down there."

"It does belong to them." Li blew out his breath in frustration. "As such, our jurisdiction is limited. Special Projects is here as a formality, to do any civilian legwork off-site and bless the findings of the military investigators." His mouth twisted, as if the words tasted sour.

"This isn't your usual area of expertise, is it?"

Li glanced at her. "White-collar crime. Embezzlement. That sort of thing. Shady balance sheets and stock market manipulation."

"So what did you do to get sent here?"

Li shrugged, glared at the MP. It seemed they would be here a long time. "Once upon a time, I caught a senator doing a very bad thing with campaign finances."

"Hookers and beer?" Tara guessed.

"Hookers and cocaine." Li gave a half smile that crinkled his face. Tara liked the expression . . . a crack in the official façade. "And clown porn."

"Clown porn?" Tara wrinkled her nose.

Li shuddered. "Clown porn. That stuff's surprisingly expensive."

"Didn't end well, did it?"

"Evidence miraculously disappeared before I could get it to the grand jury. Let's just say I'm in purgatory until Bozo the Senator's term runs out."

The MP had finished talking to his radio. A Jeep rolled up, and a familiar figure swung out of it and strode to Agent Li's car. He was dressed as a civilian in an overcoat and tie: no military uniform, no spaceman suit. Closely cropped gray hair framed a sharp-edged face, punctuated by nearly invisible glasses with weightless frames. He bent to look in the car window, cocked his head.

"Dr. Sheridan," Agent Li began, "this is my case supervisor, Division Chief Corvus."

Corvus kept his hands in his pockets. "Tara. Nice to see you're well." His gray gaze seemed to disassemble her, molecule by molecule, for evidence to the contrary.

Tara's mouth felt dry as lint. "Richard. Congrats on the promotion."

"Thank you. The Division was never the same without you. We were sorry to see you go. And even sorrier to have lost track of you." His solicitude was plastic, obligatory. "I have to admit to being rather . . . startled to learn from the powers-that-be that you'd decided to rejoin us."

Tara smiled, though it did not touch her eyes. He didn't want her here. The order had come from above. She had no idea *how* far above, had no idea how far the Pythia's reach extended, but it had been far enough to annoy Corvus.

Tara gestured with her chin to the scurrying white figures in the caldera. "What's going on down there?"

Corvus's eyes flickered past the fence. "Magnusson's particle accelerator blew up, and they're checking for residual radiation from the accident."

Tara's mouth twisted. Corvus called it an accident. He'd already made up his mind. "Have you been down there?"

Corvus smiled. "I thought I'd let you two look around." He gestured for the MP to reel back the gate. "Get back with me when you're done."

Agent Li put the car in gear and coasted past the gate. "I didn't know that you knew Corvus."

Tara frowned. "He and I were assigned to the same unit, several years ago." She stubbornly refused to elaborate.

"Is it normal for him to be so . . . hands-off?"

"What do you mean?"

Li gestured to the plastic bubble and frustration shone in his voice. "He hasn't even looked around. I haven't worked with him long, but . . ."

Tara smirked. "Small piece of advice, Agent Li. Richard Corvus never gets his hands dirty, nor is he in the habit of putting himself in harm's way. He doesn't want to get any glowing particles from the atom smasher on his new suit."

Li's eyes widened at her directness. "I, uh . . . Thanks for the tip."

"Sure." Troubled, Tara turned away and looked at her reflection in the window, a pale ghost against the desert landscape. She'd half expected Li to jump to his supervisor's defense. She'd said what she did to both provoke him and warn him. Li seemed a decent enough guy, and she didn't want what had happened to her to happen to him.

TARA'S BREATH FOGGED THE PLASTIC SHIELD OF THE RADIA-tion suit helmet, obscuring her vision. The white disposable Tyvek suit was too large; it pooled around her wrists and ankles, cold and sticking to her skin. A suit like this wasn't intended to prevent direct touching or inhalation of radioactive particles, and was nowhere near as safe as a dense material like Demron or a vapor-sealed Level A encapsulation suit. Although Li had double-secured the seams with duct tape to try and make it vapor-tight, Tara knew that a thin suit like this didn't provide a complete barrier against radiation. The military wouldn't have enough encapsulation suits on hand for a disaster like this. The suits at least offered some protection and, maybe more importantly in military-think, they made people *feel* safer.

She could hear her breath rattling in the flimsy respirator helmet, swirling, making fog-ghosts, and being sucked back through her mouth and the filter. It seemed like a walking meditation, as she could not escape her own breath. She tried to focus on it, even it out, while ignoring the zing and panic of thoughts that buzzed between her ears. At this elevation, her inhalations felt shallow in her lungs. She smelled chemical fire-retardant foam, and it made her eyes itch.

As soon as she'd donned the hood, she'd felt trapped. The air, thin at this elevation anyway, seemed entirely too close and stale. She had to be careful to control her breathing. Her chest tightened. Tara had the sense of being suffocated in a plastic bag. If she breathed too quickly, the plastic crackled. She tried not to envision sucking the plastic into her nose and mouth, choking her. Tara took deep draws of air, trying to compensate for her fear and the weak oxygen.

Breathe. Just breathe, she reminded herself, trying to resist the urge to rip the mask off her face.

She turned her head, and the hood did not move with her. Agent Li had carefully duct-taped the hood to her shoulders and the gloves to her sleeves. The suit was one piece, footed like children's pajamas, crinkling as she walked. She held her small digital camera wrapped in a plastic storage bag concealed in her palm. She always took a camera to every crime scene: the lens of a camera could capture details that were easily missed but could be detected and dissected later. She paused to catch her breath under the guise of snapping a few photos.

Breathe.

As she trudged behind Li into the caldera, the black grasses whipped snow in their wake. Snow spat from the sky, dusting the ground. Glass particles strewed the snow, like sequins on a wedding gown, crunching underfoot. The footprints they made were uneven, the plastic booties shifting in shape with each step. They stepped over the shallow concrete tracks spreading over the caldera. They reminded her of pipes, and her feet rang hollow against the surface as she clambered over. Based on what little she knew about the technology, she supposed these were the conduits through which the particles were accelerated, to be crushed together at the nexus where their paths crossed in the now-destroyed building.

Seeing the other suits milling about, she realized they were all entirely indistinguishable from one another. Anyone could be here; she had no way of measuring rank or looking anyone in the eye, a true handicap to her work. It would be like working blind.

Her heart hammered, and cold sweat trickled between her shoulder blades. She closed her eyes to center herself and listened. The wind rattled plastic, sliced through the grasses, cut through the zing of Geiger counters and the low murmur of voices. As barren as this place looked to the eye, it seethed with something that made her skin buzz.

Perhaps it was the altitude. Or the residual radiation.

Breathe.

Breathe.

She followed Agent Li to the massive tent, and he drew the veil-like plastic aside. Her breath snagged in her throat as she stepped into an entirely different world.

CHApter **THree**

WHILE THE caldera had been pristine white, nearly peaceful in its sterility, the inside of the shell of the tent seethed black and chaotic and filthy. Like a crushed beer can cast aside by a hungover god, the peeled-open particle accelerator was ripped apart from its moorings. It lay on one side, steel skin sheared back to reveal blackened guts of tightly spiraled copper tubing, wires, and ash. It was massive, at least two floors high, laced by the remnants of ladders. Carbon dusted the scene in a fine blanket of sticky black, obscuring the hazard signs still remaining on the walls and filtering like silt from the twisted ceiling beams. Above, the roof had dissolved, revealing an artificial white plastic sky. Two exterior walls were similarly missing, concrete blocks shattered and strewn on the ground. Like ants searching for food, workers vacuumed up debris with long hoses, carrying it away in handcarts.

The spacemen-ants precisely and quickly swarmed over the machine. There was no indecision, no hesitation or flinch; these were soldier ants. Soldier ants with special expertise in these types of cleanups.

Other workers sealed charred electronic components in plastic bags, cataloguing the remains in the autopsy of this monster. Tara surreptitiously snapped a few photos with the tiny camera in her hand, hidden in the too-large folds of the glove.

"They're destroying the scene," Li muttered. "There'll be no evidence left by the time we get to it."

"We'd better work quickly." As she breathed, Tara could feel the plastic sticking to her back like an ever-shrinking second skin. She would like nothing better than to get in and out quickly. She wanted to see the scene, to get some feeling for the place Magnusson had spent his days, to get a sense of the invisible fingerprints he'd left on his corner of the world.

"Who's in charge here?" Li asked a passing worker-ant, but was ignored. He caught the sleeve of another, repeating his demand, and was shrugged off.

"There." Tara pointed to a suit tapping away at a bright yellow laptop perched on a wheeled cart, covered in a clear plastic bag. She'd seen how the other people diverted their paths around this person, like water around a rock. A man, Tara guessed, by the build and height. Clearly, he was someone important.

Li strode to the white-wrapped figure. "Are you in charge?" His voice was muffled by the plastic and filters, but sharpness still crackled in his tone.

The figure turned. Through the plastic shield, she could see the burn of blistering blue eyes. No verbal acknowledgement, only that scalding glare.

"Are you in charge?" Again, the test of wills.

"Who're you?" A voice like gravel. He sounded as if he smoked steel wool.

"Agent Li, Special Projects Division. Who are you, and why are you dismantling my crime scene?"

The blue eyes crinkled in amusement. "Major Gabriel, Defense Intelligence Agency. And let me clarify a couple of things for you, Agent Li." Gabriel stepped close, towering a head over Li. To his credit, the agent didn't budge.

"First, this is a U.S. Army installation. This is not 'your' playground. This is not 'your' *anything*." The major's forceful breath mushroomed the hood of his suit. "Second, this is not a crime scene. It's not a crime scene until *I* decide this is a crime scene. Are we clear?"

"Absolutely, sir." Tara stepped forward, letting her fingers rest lightly on Li's sleeve in warning. She could feel him glowering at her, and sweat glossed her brow. She extended her sticky-gloved hand to Gabriel. "Tara Sheridan. We just need to do a quick look over. Standard procedure, fill out some forms, and we'll be out of your hair."

Gabriel took her hand, and she felt the tension in his grip. "Ms. Sheridan." He flipped his gaze, bright as cornflowers, to Li and back to her. His weathered skin looked sunburned beneath the plastic shield. He wasn't assigned here; he was too much brass. Someone had gone to considerable trouble to bring him in from somewhere distant, some latitude that had enough sun this time of year to burn flesh.

"We'll file our report with your office." She nodded at him as she spoke (*yes-yes-yes*), giving him the impression of agreement. "Formalities." She kept her posture low, looked up at him with an expression she hoped he took as submission.

He squinted at her. "Fine," he snapped. He gestured, and a petite woman in another white suit materialized beside him. "Dr. DiRosa will assist you. She worked with Magnusson. Keep it short. We have work to do."

"Thank you, Major."

"Ma'am." He turned away from them, back to his laptop. She and Li were dismissed.

DiRosa gestured and walked back toward the ruined machine. "This way."

Li let DiRosa get a few steps away. Seething, he yanked Tara's elbow, started to say something, but she held up her hand.

"You can chew me out for emasculating you and kissing Gabriel's ass later," she hissed. Her fear made her impatient, and she could feel her empathy draining right out of her, with the cold sweat trickling down her shoulder blades. *Breathe.*

"They are taking our evidence," Li snarled.

"And you can either be quiet and gather *some* information, or throw a tantrum, and get nothing." Tara's eyes narrowed. "Now, promise to play nicely with the other kids, and perhaps they'll let us play with their toys."

Li's brown eyes blazed in wrath. She'd pushed his buttons, and he was ready to ignite. She didn't have time for this kind of rigidity. She trotted off after DiRosa, letting Li stomp along in her wake.

"Dr. DiRosa." Tara kept her expression soft, neutral. "What can you tell us about this?" Her gloved hand sketched the hulk of the particle accelerator.

"It blew up yesterday night at 2343, ma'am. Security logged Dr. Magnusson entering the site at 1945." Though she had been introduced as Magnusson's colleague, DiRosa's speech cadences were pure military. Gabriel had turned them over to someone who would handle them perfectly. Tara looked at her sidelong through the shiny plastic mask. Her almond eyes were bloodshot and puffy beneath the careful makeup and salon-highlighted blonde hair. She knew Magnusson. She liked Magnusson. Despite her words, his disappearance had rattled her. Tara could use that to her advantage.

"Was he alone?" Li's voice strained through gritted teeth. To his credit, he was swallowing his anger and moving forward. Good man.

"Yes."

"Where was he last seen?"

"Security cameras caught him entering the accelerator room at 2210. He stayed in frame until approximately 2330."

"Did he turn on the machine?"

"Yes."

"We'll need a copy of the tape."

"Of course."

Tara didn't hold out hope they'd get it. From what

Tara could discern beneath the white suit, DiRosa's body language was tense and unyielding.

"What was Magnusson working on?" Li asked, forever direct.

"That's classified, sir. I'm sorry."

Tara's eyes roved over the remnants of the machine. "What exactly do machines like this do?" That was a broad enough question that DiRosa should be able to answer.

"It's a particle accelerator. An atom smasher, colloquially. The idea is to force an atomic particle, like an electron, to collide with the nuclei of other atoms at nearly the speed of light."

"Is this a typical device for this purpose?"

"No. Most accelerators are linear or circular, which require substantial real estate to accelerate the particles. This variety is . . . was . . . an experimental type, a spiral accelerator based on an infinity loop design. It accomplishes appreciable amounts of acceleration, but in a much more compact space. Essentially, it uses a three-dimensional array of electromagnets to spiral particles to the collision at the center." Tara could see her posture loosening as she talked about her research. The cadence of her speech quickened and became more fluid as she spoke. "The drawback is an excess amount of synchrotron radiation, which is difficult to filter out, but the advantages in design and material elegancy render that a manageable issue."

"Have there been any other accidents with these types of devices?"

"Not at this site."

"And other sites?"

"That's classified."

Tara stuck to the topic. "Do you know what caused the explosion?"

"That's unknown. The off-site recorder recorded normal power-up, but an unusual power surge crashed the instruments. We expect it was an accident." Her voice was firm, but she bit her lip, telegraphing her unease with the decision "we" had made.

"Have you found any remains?" Li's voice was expressionless, but he leaned forward to hear the answer.

DiRosa hesitated before she shook her head. "We found a contact lens and some textile evidence. We're looking for DNA. As you can see, much of the structure is destroyed. If Magnusson was standing behind the radiation blast shield . . . here . . ."—she pointed to a blistered pile of rubble—". . . there may be very little to find."

It was then Tara realized there was very little actual debris. She'd seen the aftermath of car bombs and IEDs. There was always wreckage left equal to the amount of the original structure. Nothing ever disappeared completely. That was simply a basic fact of the universe.

Tara's brow wrinkled. It seemed wrong. Half a building was destroyed, but there weren't enough bricks, dust, and scraps of metal to make up the difference. Very little was actually vaporized in an explosion. Here, there was very clearly missing mass, tons of it, which meant missing evidence. She thought of the ants combing over the wreckage. The material had to have gone somewhere. Did they take it? Why?

Li and DiRosa continued the interview dance, and Tara walked to the rubble she'd pointed to. The camera clicked in her hand, as she aimed it toward the ruined particle accelerator. She looked up at the hole in the roof open to the plastic sky. She imagined sky, imagined escaping this prison of plastic, then forced her thoughts back to earth.

Breathe.

This could be the last spot Lowell Magnusson had stood. Tara turned on her heel, trying to imagine what this place would have seemed, humming and whole, orderly. This place would have been close to him, familiar as his own home. The machine must have been sterile and imposing; he would have needed an office area. She saw no wood debris, no suggestion of file cabinets, no broken chairs, no detritus of computers. He must have had somewhere to analyze his data, some space for him to sit in a chair and think, to spin out his theories and compare them with the invisible realities he set in motion in the heart of the machine.

"Did Dr. Magnusson have an office in this building?" she asked.

DiRosa hesitated. "Yes. But there's not much left to show you."

TARA FOLLOWED LI AND DIROSA THROUGH THE ARTERIAL halls of the structure, through the haze of dust and dim emergency lights. Only part of the power seemed to have been restored to this area of the complex. Flashlights shone under doors, and silent strobe alarm lights cast harsh, angled shadows along the walls. Where they walked, industrial green tile was speckled in dust and footprints, illuminated by caged utility lights daisy-chained to orange extension cords. In the churning darkness, Tara could hear the buzz of a generator, the snap of plastic, and the filtered echo of voices. Her heart still trip-hammered in her mouth. She hoped the other two would not see how tightly her fists were clenched. The darkness served only to amplify her claustrophobia, stirring it with dark, unseen hands. She walked behind Li and DiRosa, the plastic of her helmet squeaking like a dog's toy as she hyperventilated.

This was too much like *before*. Like suffocating.

Breathe.

Breathe.

Breathe.

Card readers glowed with dull green eyes studding each door still important enough to be fed by sparse emergency power. DiRosa slid an ID badge through one reader, keyed in a code on the door lock. The stainless steel lock whirred and opened, suggesting some heavy machinery at work in the walls.

"That seems pretty low-tech for this kind of installation," Li commented. "I would have expected biometrics—palm and retina scanners, that kind of thing."

DiRosa's bow mouth twisted in a frown. "We don't have the electricity to run them now. That part of the grid's toast." She gestured them through the door, unhooking a utility light and snaking its orange tail behind her.

"This is it?" Li stared at the blank white room. It

looked like a set piece from an existential film: white walls, steel desk, ergonomic office chair on wheels neatly tucked under the edge. The blotter stretched pristinely blank across the desk, unmarked with any notes, phone numbers, scribbles.

Li yanked open the industrial green file cabinet. Drawer after drawer gaped empty. He turned to the two large flat-panel computer monitors perched on the desk. He reached under the desk to power the computer on, only to grab a handful of dangling cords. The PC case itself lay strewn in pieces on the cold floor, shattered open in a broken mass of technological spaghetti.

Li yanked at its green guts, pulled out the cracked motherboard. "The hard drive's gone." He looked up at DiRosa accusingly. "This was your people."

DiRosa shook her head. "We found it that way."

"You have backups somewhere?"

"We're trying to pull them now."

"I need copies of all his correspondence, reports, memos—"

"We'll give you the ones we can, after they've been cleared."

"So you're going to give me a pile of paper covered in Magic Marker redactions?"

"Agent Li—" DiRosa began, and Tara heard the crack in her voice. "Please understand we must follow procedure."

"I *understand* that you want us to look, not touch."

"What I want doesn't matter." Her voice tremored.

Li leaned on the edge of the desk. Now that DiRosa

was outside Gabriel's earshot, perhaps she would open up. Tara heard his tone soften as he switched tactics and tried to dig into the soft flesh of the man's personal life. "How long did you know Dr. Magnusson?"

"I'd worked on this project with him for six months."

"Tell me about him."

DiRosa blew out her breath, fogging her visor. But not before Tara could see her blinking back tears. "He's . . . brilliant. And entirely aware of that fact." She tried to rub her nose through the radiation visor, succeeding only in smearing a string of snot around.

"He was your mentor?" Tara drew the conclusion based on their ages.

DiRosa nodded. "It's like trying to run after a racehorse. You know you'll never catch him . . . but you surprise yourself by how fast you can run, trying to keep up." Tara noted her unconscious use of the present tense. DiRosa didn't believe Magnusson was gone. It was too early to tell if it was denial.

"Had Magnusson changed his behavior lately? Any changes in his hours or habits?"

"He'd seemed preoccupied. I thought . . . I thought maybe he'd finally climbed out of his shell and found himself another . . ." She stopped herself, corrected. "A girlfriend. Or discovered the internet."

"How long has he been out here?"

"Six months."

"Any friends or associates you know of?"

"He kept his personal life separate from work."

"Introverted?"

"You could say that. The word I would use is *intense*."

"*Intense* . . . Did he make any enemies?"

DiRosa paused. "Magnusson had some issues with working within the chain of command. He was more . . . accustomed to working as he had in academia, without such close supervision."

"He didn't play well with others?"

"Not really. He could be pretty damn abrasive. He could be . . . impatient with people who couldn't keep up and see his vision. I think . . . I think he wanted more freedom in his work, and I would have been surprised to see him stay much longer."

"Why did he come, then? I can't see an academic playing nicely with guys like Gabriel."

"The government has the deepest pockets for the best toys. Ours are shinier, faster, and more expensive than the ones even Cornell can buy. He wanted to get his hands on them, pursue some of his own interests."

"I can't imagine you're too amenable to that, here."

"We're not." DiRosa's voice tightened.

Tara listened to Li work on DiRosa while she rummaged through the desk drawers. She hoped the activity masked her shivering; the sweat had begun to dry, and she could hear her suit rattle if she held still. Her fingers riffled through blank notepads, unused pens, sets of screwdrivers still in their blister packaging. If not for the destroyed computer, the scene looked like an advertisement for an office supply store. None of the lead in the pencils had been worn down to an angle. All the erasers were perfect. She thumbed through a yellow legal pad, one after another. All the perforations were still intact.

She ran her fingers over the keyboard. There were no crumbs, no worn letters on the keys, no residue of spilled coffee. It looked new.

Whatever Magnusson wanted others to think, he did no work in this office . . . if it was truly his, and not a set piece provided for their benefit.

She knelt down in the debris of the computer, felt the USB ports. They were loose with wear. Bringing them out from under the desk, even in the weak lighting she could see scratches on the terminals.

She smiled. Magnusson *had* worked here. He'd just taken his work home with him, probably on a portable drive. He wanted no traces of himself, or his work, to linger here. No photographs, no decorated coffee mugs. No substantial part of himself.

She and Magnusson had something in common. Magnusson didn't want to be here. The realization of it suddenly lit her brain like a struck match. It meant he'd hidden his knowledge someplace else.

It was dusk by the time the alien jellyfish spat Tara and Li out of its plastic gullet. Late-winter sun shone coldly over the brittle grasses as they trudged across the caldera to the access road and the distant line forming at the decontamination center. The low gray clouds had reeled back, spitting a few flakes that drifted through the field. Dust and ash motes glistened in orange light, suspended in the air like dandelion fluff. Tara wished she could feel the saffron sun on her face directly. The plastic visor seemed to warp everything she saw in a circular pattern of fine, rainbow scratches.

Once they were out of earshot of the jellyfish, Li grabbed Tara's arm, turning her to face him. "Let's clarify a few things." Through the glare of his mask, she could see the anger shining in his expression.

"This is the part where you tell me this is your investigation, and not to cut you down in front of the enemy?" Tara tried to cross her arms, but Li gripped her elbow too tightly. She narrowed her eyes, gulped in air. Her hands were balled into fists. She couldn't take any more of feeling *trapped*.

"Yeah. This is that part." Li's breath fogged his mask. "Don't you *ever* undercut me like that again."

"Look. I'll be brutally honest. I don't particularly care about your ego, your feelings, or your rules. I'll do whatever it takes to get the job done. If that means eating some crow or petting Gabriel like a purse dog, then that's what I'll do." She snarled the last sentence at him.

She shook off his arm, hearing a rip in the shoulder of her suit. She stalked away. She'd gotten sick of this kind of ego-driven territory surfing long ago. She didn't realize how incensed she was until the cool air crawled up her neck and into her face, bracing her.

Breathe.

"Oh," she exhaled. It was the most glorious feeling. She could smell the sunlit ash purely, now. The chill air wrapped its hands around her neck, caressing her face and freezing the sweat on her skin.

In the corner of her eye, she glimpsed something shining on the ground, a spark of violet and chrome. She bent to look, but the glare from the setting sun obliterated everything in her vision through the damned mask.

She opened the collar of her suit, pulled off the hood. Cold air washed over her, flash-freezing the sweat glossing her face. Her hair was drenched, and she shivered as the wind tore through it. She breathed deeply, slowly, of the ash and sun. A snowflake brushed out of the molten light and landed on her cheek, dissolving instantly. She felt like she was an incredible heat, meeting cold, pure air. Vapor steamed from the face, as if she'd just stepped out of a hot bath. She reached down for the glint in the grasses. Her gloves felt clumsy, and she was unable to feel anything through the thick plastic. She stripped off her glove, let her fingers comb the grasses, searching . . .

She could hear Li running up behind her, yelling at her, his voice muffled by the filter. He grabbed her shoulder as her hand grasped the shining thing on the ground. She gasped when her hand closed around it and metal and static electricity bristled through her bare hand.

She opened her steaming hand to show it to him, as her breath frosted the face of the stainless steel watch, its hands frozen behind the glass.

THROUGHOUT TIME, ORACLES HAD ALWAYS GATHERED AROUND the four elements. Whether it was the original brazier in the Temple of Apollo burning over the sea, or bonfires before caves through which shamans tossed sparkling powders and cast shadow figures of animals with their hands, the elements always tugged at invisible lines drawing them together. The Daughters of Delphi were no different.

Her sandals tied together and slung over her shoulder, Sophia walked into the darkness of the dunes. Sand squished between her toes and swirled around the rolled-up cuffs of her jeans. Arthritis creaked in her right knee, but she ignored it. She'd parked her car a mile back on the road, coming to this inaccessible place by foot, climbing dunes and wending her way around the sharp roots of sea oats.

Sophia breathed deeply of the coastal air. The salt seemed to settle deep in her lungs. She could smell the sea long before she climbed down the last rise of dune to the black ocean. Wind drove the smoke from a bonfire over the sea. Around the fire, she could see the other Daughters of Delphi gathered . . . at least, those able to travel to this hemisphere on short notice. It seemed to her, over the time she'd been in the order, their numbers had shrunk. When she was a child, she remembered dozens of women ranging around fires in groves. Today, there were less than thirty. And most of those women were nearing her age.

They needed fresh blood. More priestesses. But there were so few willing to undertake the discipline to cultivate the powers of an oracle. Power had a price, and fewer women were willing to pay it.

As she neared, the fire burned so bright it obscured the stars in the sky. Fire was the current Pythia's element. Each of Delphi's Daughters possessed her own unique divinatory talent. This Pythia's talent was pyromancy. Fire loved her, and it showed.

The Pythia stood barefoot before the fire, seemingly impervious to the chill. Dressed in orange silks, she was a short, rounded Arabic woman with glossy black hair blowing loose over her shoulders. Gray hair streamed from her temples. Her almond eyes were rimmed with kohl, and golden earrings shivered behind her jaw. Her rounded figure moved with the sinuous grace of a dancer.

Sophia bowed her head, feeling the heat on her face and shoulders. "Pythia." Once, Sophia had known her true name. But now she was simply the Pythia.

"You spoke with her. With Juliane's daughter." Her contralto voice was low, melodious, but it was a melody wrapped around steel.

"Yes."

Obsidian eyes took Sophia in, and Sophia knew they absorbed the sum total of truth of her experience. There was no use lying to the Oracle of Apollo.

The Pythia frowned, arms crossed. "You did this on your own, without my blessing."

"We need her."

The Pythia's eyes narrowed, and Sophia could see the shadows of the other women shifting uncomfortably in her peripheral vision.

Sophia stood her ground. She was an old woman, and there was little the Pythia's wrath could do to her. She lifted her chin. She would take whatever punishment the Pythia would mete out.

One of the other women in the circle stepped forward. Sophia's eyes narrowed. It was Adrienne, the youngest Daughter. Dressed in motorcycle leathers, carrying a helmet under her arm, Adrienne stalked into the firelight. Straight blonde hair spilled over eyes the color of frost on flint. "We don't need her. We don't need an interloper."

Sophia glared at her. But Adrienne was young. Impetuous. And she'd made no secret of the fact she wanted the title of Pythia. Rumor had it Adrienne was engaging in some shady work outside of Delphi's Daughters, and some of that darkness seemed to cling to her. "Tara is not an interloper. Her mother was the successor to the Pythia. Tara is her mother's daughter. She is strong."

"Juliane is dead. Her weak daughter will do no better. An outsider should not be chosen." Adrienne paced around the fire, glossy leather gleaming like the skin of some reptilian chimera that had not bothered to completely take human shape. "Surely the great Pythia, the Oracle of Apollo, can see what I can: the terrible future even an old woman could read in her morning tea leaves. Magnusson's technology could revolutionize the world, bring limitless energy. Or someone—some madman or religious fanatic—could use Magnusson's new technology to commit a terrorist act. It's too powerful, and too easily hidden. And the reaction by an aggrieved state would lead to war, perhaps even global conflict." Adrienne snarled, "A successor to the Pythia must be chosen who can fight. Not a used-up relic."

A whisper rattled like dry leaves around the circle. Sophia put her hands behind her back so the Pythia could not see them shake in fury.

The Pythia stared, and the fire before her roiled. When she spoke, it was with the voice of a queen, strong and commanding. "You forget your place, Adrienne. You are one of Delphi's Daughters. Not the Pythia."

"I'm not the Pythia. I'm only a geomancer." Adrienne's hand sketched around the other women in the circle. "But I see your time is short. I see the sight is leaving you, that you are fading. All the glamour in the world cannot hide it."

The Pythia's chin lifted, and her Cleopatra eyes narrowed. Sophia's breath clotted in her throat. They all knew this to be true, but none had spoken of it. None of them would dare.

The Pythia's ruby lips curved upward. A fracture of light blistered through the apple of her cheek, as if her skin was a paper-thin vessel holding a great and terrible light. The light cast shadows of her eyelashes below her brow, giving the illusion that a spidery creature clawed through her eye socket, trying to escape that burning within.

The fire blazed out and stung Adrienne. With a crackle, it licked and bubbled the skin of her jacket. The smell of scorched flesh filled the air; Sophia couldn't tell whether it was all leather or partly living skin. Adrienne snarled and fled to the waves to quench the burn.

"Very good, Sophia." The Pythia smiled serenely, as the fire subsided. "You did exactly as I expected you would, as I foresaw. You are bringing Juliane's daughter back to me."

Sophia's eyes slid to the waves, where Adrianne held her arm, hissing, in the whitecaps. Such hatred in the girl's glare . . . Sophia knew Adrianne would not give up the role of Pythia without a fight.

And she feared what that meant for Tara.

Chapter **Four**

Tara rubbed her wet hair with a thin motel towel. Her hair felt dry as straw, and her skin was scrubbed beet-red. The army had decontaminated her within an inch of her life before she'd been cleared to leave the site. She felt raw all over from the humiliating experience of being scrubbed with a cold car wash brush in the decon tent. She'd emerged smelling like lemon dish soap. Though it hurt, her first impulse when she'd gotten to the motel was to scrub that artificial smell from her body with a warm shower.

Through the steam in the mirror, she could see the scars traveling up over her collarbone like lightning, across her chest, where they puckered beneath her left breast. They crossed over her hipbone like a vine, clawed up her right arm. One thigh was dotted in a rippling white scar, as if a stone had been cast on a still pond, disturbing the surface. The scars went deep; Tara had been told she would never have children. Though that had never been in her life plans, she still hated the Gardener for taking that right away from her.

Tara never really looked closely at the scars. Looking brought too many feelings: helplessness, anger, fear. The wounds were long past the point of hurting. They simply felt stiff, as if there were laces wound around her ribs she couldn't take off.

The decontamination officers had looked at her with pity when they asked her to strip out of the white Tyvek suit and get into the shower. Tara did as she was told. There was a moment of silence as she stepped into the orange tent, teeth chattering from the cold. The decon officers surrounded her like plastic-swathed ghosts, but one of them worked up the nerve to ask.

"What on earth happened to you, hon?" The woman tried to be gentle as she ran the plastic brush over her back.

Tara had stared forward, had considered refusing to respond. But she did answer, shivering, teeth clattering as the hose blasted her, summoning all the false bravado she could. "You should see the other guy."

They took her camera away from her, but not before she'd had time on the walk back from the field to tuck the sliver of a memory card inside her cheek. The decon officers (the "doffers," they called themselves) didn't even suspect her of chewing gum.

She did have to put up a fight about the watch. Tara had slipped Magnusson's watch on her wrist, insisting it was hers. Her father's watch. An heirloom. The doffers took it away from her, but the woman who had asked her about her scars slipped it back to her on the way out. Pity did have its currency.

They kept the rest of her clothes and sent her out in a blue paper suit that zipped up the front. In her peripheral vision she thought she spied Corvus, but he walked away too quickly, probably imagining synchrotron radiation crawling up his pant leg and burrowing into his well-sunscreened flesh. Corvus hadn't changed much since her time with him.

Li had been waiting for her at the other side of the decon tent. They'd given him back his clothes, but he looked deflated, much less in control of things than he had when she'd first met him early in the day.

"You okay?"

She nodded. "Yeah."

But they both knew the decon procedure, for all its official aura, didn't do much other than make people feel better. It was to make the military appear useful. Whenever you were doing *something*, you were solving the problem, and the decon made the subject of its gentle ministrations feel as if something was being done. It was a flurry of action intended to give some blanket of security.

Tara knew she should be worried about whatever radiation she had been exposed to, what damage it may have done to her cells as it silently worked throughout her body. Yet, she couldn't summon any fear. Instead, she felt numb to the possibility of further harm to her body, indifferent. Maybe it was because a few unseen synchrotron particles bouncing under her skin seemed so much less hazardous than the scars crisscrossing it. She'd survived the reality of those; the invisible force of radiation didn't seem real in comparison.

Involuntarily, she thought of her mother, of the radiation she'd been bombarded with to stop the spread of cancer. It seemed difficult to fear anything that couldn't be seen, and even harder to expect that something so invisible could cure cancer.

Tara shrugged into sweats and tucked her feet under the bedspread. It smelled vaguely like mothballs, but anything was better than freezing and smelling like dish soap. A portable printer whirred on the nightstand, connected to her laptop computer. She'd worried spit had damaged the camera's memory card, but the card reader had managed to pull all the images she'd captured from the scene. She pulled a sheaf of papers out of the printer and began to page through them.

They weren't her best work. Taken from bad angles, with the camera covered in a plastic bag, some details were indistinct. The seams of the bag sometimes got in the way, creating glare and blur. But she had managed to get several decent shots of the caldera, the ruined accelerator, and Magnusson's office, though the lighting was very poor. She scanned them from margin to margin, looking for details she'd missed in her distracted state of claustrophobia.

She drew one from the pile, a decent shot of the caldera, spreading from end to end of the shot. A white-garbed figure was walking away from the camera. Something about the landscape, the ebb and flow of the jagged edges of it, seemed familiar. Her intuition prickled, and she climbed out of bed to open her luggage.

Her Tarot cards, still tied carefully in her mother's scarf, were tucked in the lining of her bag. Her Tarot journal and pen were safely wrapped beside it. She took them to the bed, the cards still cold from being in the back of Li's car all day. They warmed as she flipped through them, faceup, searching for the image that seemed familiar. She wiped her mind clean of thoughts, fanning the intuitive flash that had begun to take root. Some bit of information was lodged in her subconscious, and perhaps the cards could shake it free for her.

There. She pulled out the Eight of Cups, placed it beside the photograph of the caldera. The card depicted a cloaked man, his shoulders slumped in despair, leaving behind eight stacked chalices. He fled into the night across a desolate landscape, leaving those golden treasures behind. The jagged edges of the gray landscape appeared very similar to the edge of the caldera, and the man walking away from the camera had much the same set to the shoulders as the man in the card.

She contemplated the card, jotted it down in her notebook:

Eight of Cups . . . disillusionment, abandonment of unfulfilling efforts.

She thought about Magnusson, about his careful abandonment of his office. He had taken everything with him. Perhaps Magnusson had chosen to disappear. Perhaps, as DiRosa had suggested, his goals were at cross-purposes with those of the government lab, and he had chosen to destroy his work and vanish.

Frowning, she flipped back through her journal. The card she'd originally chosen for Magnusson was the Magician. The Magician was a creator, not a destroyer. It would take extraordinary pressure for him to destroy his own work. What had happened to cause him to take such steps? What had he been asked to do?

A soft knock at her door startled her. She jerked her head up, that involuntary reaction from years of being summoned out of sleep. Tara blew out her breath in frustration. She was too jumpy, and furious with herself for letting her anxieties get the best of her today. She wrapped up her cards and notebook, stowing them back in her travel bag.

Padding to the door, she peered into the peephole. It was Li, dressed in a leather jacket and jeans, holding a pizza box.

Hmm. Pizza.

She opened the door partway, smelling pepperoni.

He lifted the lid of the box, gave a guarded half smile. It was a nice smile, sheepish and open. "I come in peace?"

Her stomach gurgled loudly, and Tara's cheeks flamed at the sound. "Peace offering accepted."

"Look, I'm sorry about the radiation thing."

Li and Tara sat cross-legged on the floor, the pizza open box between them and photos spread out on the green carpet. They'd been scribbling out their interview notes from the day on yellow legal pads.

Tara looked up from her slice, pen still. "It's okay, really. It wasn't your fault, Agent Li."

"Well, it was." Li looked down, and Tara could see he was deeply embarrassed. "I don't make a habit of tearing colleagues' radiation suits and exposing them to renegade quarks."

Tara shook her head. "I was not on my best behavior today. I'm pretty claustrophobic," she confessed, "and I let that get in the way."

Li stared down at his hands. Dressed in a T-shirt and jeans, he seemed much younger than he did in a suit and tie. She liked this version of him better: he seemed more natural, at ease. "I know I can get overly, um, inflexible in my thinking."

"Forgive and forget?"

"Okay. Forgive and forget." Li reached for one of the photographs she'd taken. "I still can't believe you got these out of there. You're much sneakier than I gave you credit for."

"Thanks, Agent Li. I think."

"I think we can be on a first-name basis, since I tore up your radiation suit. It's Harry."

Tara inclined her head. "Harry," she repeated. It was a nice name. Practical and gentle. It didn't seem like the name of a federal agent.

"What do you think of this?" She reached up on the dresser and handed him the watch she'd found at the scene.

"Correction . . . you're beyond sneaky. I'm not sure I want to know how you got this out of there."

Tara made a face. "I wore it on my wrist."

"Very persuasive of you, then." He cocked an eyebrow.

She watched him closely as he turned it over in his hands. The crystal was unmarred, which seemed unusual under a high-impact situation. But the hands and case had warped, twisted, stretched to a shape that was a bit off-center. The hands suggested some time after two o'clock, but the distortions made that a guess. It looked like a watch designed by Dali.

"It's not melted," he observed, running his fingers over the crisp edges of the case. On the back, it had been engraved with the number eight or the symbol for infinity, depending on one's vantage point. Tara was reminded of the echo of that shape in the loop of the particle accelerator. The engraving was sharp and untouched. The links were stretched out a bit, and it seemed the metal was softer in some places than in others.

"I have no idea what to make of this," he said at last, handing it back to her.

She turned it over in her hands a few times before she returned it to the dresser. Perhaps some bits of radiation still clung to it, but it felt odd. Warmer in some places, cooler in others, and it buzzed when she touched it.

Harry picked up the same photograph Tara had been contemplating earlier, the one she'd intuitively linked to the Eight of Cups. "Hey, look at this." He pointed to a glimmer of light on the horizon.

Tara squinted at the glimmer he'd pointed out. "I don't know what that is."

"A light artifact from the camera being in the plastic bag?"

"Maybe."

She grabbed her laptop and called up the digital photograph. Under magnification, she could see it looked much like a star, as seen by a telescope. To the naked eye, it appeared to be one point of light. Resolved by enlargement, it split into two white lights.

"Headlights," Harry said. He riffled through his papers, spread out a county map. "There isn't supposed to be a road there."

Tara summoned up an internet satellite map and zoomed in to the area in moments. To her disappointment, no road appeared on the map. But the installation they had just visited in the caldera didn't appear, either. She double-checked her coordinates against Harry's map. It was the right place, wiped blank by the order of someone in power and shaded into digital obscurity by an artist.

"Maybe someone saw something," Harry mused. "I want to check that out tomorrow to see where it leads."

"Agreed." Tara hunched over the laptop on the floor. She realized her sweatshirt had slipped a bit over her shoulder, and the white weal of a scar was visible over her clavicle. She noticed Harry's eyes had followed the line of it. She sat back, embarrassed, and pulled the neck of the sweatshirt up.

Mercifully, he did not ask. Harry leaned back against the dresser, stretching his legs out before him. "The way I see it, there are several possible answers to Magnusson's disappearance."

"Which are?"

"It was a pure accident, and he was killed in the explosion. That seems to be what Corvus is thinking."

Tara kept her face neutral. "And that also seems to be what Gabriel is thinking."

"It could have been sabotage, by himself or another person, and he was killed."

"Possibly. I don't believe he was happy working on the project. He could have come into conflict with someone with a different agenda."

"Or he could have destroyed his work himself."

Tara's lip twisted. "I don't think he destroyed all of it." She told him about the scrapes on the USB ports.

"Where would he have hidden it?"

"At home, with former colleagues, with friends or relatives. We should start with them."

"Sounds good. But we also have to address the last possibility: Magnusson is alive."

Tara wrapped her arms around her knees. "Then two possibilities branch from there: he disappeared of his own accord, or someone has taken him."

THE FIRST RULE IN TRACKING IS TO KNOW ONE'S ENEMY.

A tangled skein of property records led Adrienne to Tara's cabin. She'd purchased the property through an attorney, and it had taken some digging to correlate this with the attorney who had handled Juliane's estate. Backtracking through public records with the name had given her a location.

Adrienne left her motorcycle not far from the road. She was forced to pick her way down the overgrown path on foot. Bleached tassels of grasses poked up through a thick layer of snow. Chunks of gravel and ice crackled underfoot as Adrienne walked down what once might have been a driveway, but had been allowed to return to the earth.

In spite of herself, Adrienne approved. As a nomadic sort, she was accustomed to sleeping under the stars . . . Adrienne had not willingly lived under a roof since she was a child. It was too confining. She could appreciate the next best thing . . . isolation in the middle of nowhere.

The cabin was perched in a small clearing. More than twenty years old, the wood siding had faded to brittle silver, and the tin roof glinted in the meager porch light that had been left on. Adrienne waited at the edge of the tree line, watching the cabin. She circled the property and peered into the windows, holding her breath to keep it from fogging the glass.

No movement in the house. Not that she'd expected any. The bed in the only bedroom hadn't been slept in. Adrienne knew Juliane's daughter had gone to chase the scientist. With effort, Adrienne held her desire to rush into the house in check. For all she knew, Tara might have left someone here, behind her.

Adrienne paused at the edge of the property, pressed her bare fingers to the frosty earth. This place was strongly Tara's; she could feel her residue in its sluggish, wintry pulse. For a geomancer, such earth was nearly as good as access to her prey's flesh for magickal purposes. She scraped aside a patch of snow and reached into her jacket pocket for an empty bottle. She unscrewed the cap and filled the bottle with slivers of frozen earth. The bottle felt icy against her ribs when she tucked it back into her jacket, as if a shard of ice had been embedded between her ribs.

She gathered a handful of small sticks from the perimeter of the property. This was Tara's land, and the roots of the trees extended below the small cabin. The trees absorbed sun and shade, and a good deal of the daily hum of Tara's psyche and habits. They would make excellent divinatory fodder.

Traditionally, runes were cast with stones. In the Viking system, stones were marked with one of twenty-one runes and selected at random to interpret the underlying meaning of a question. Adrienne had found using materials from a subject's location was often more effective than using a static set of tools.

She paused in a small clearing, holding the bundle of sticks in her hand. She centered herself, breathed her intent to them with frigid breath steaming through the sticks. "Tell me what I need to know about Tara."

She opened her hands and scattered them throughout the clearing. To the untrained eye, they landed in a disorganized mess of pick-up sticks lying among stones and desiccated grass clumps poking up through snow. Adrienne's eye roved over them, searching for a configuration of sticks corresponding to the runes carved into her memory.

Her eye skimmed to the northernmost part of the clearing. North was the cardinal direction of earth, of stability, of material things. Her attention caught on a pair of sticks crossed in an X shape, crowned with a stick broken to form a *V*. The formation reminded her of the rune Othila. Othila was a rune of separation, of inheritance. Judging by the remoteness of the property, Tara had thoroughly separated herself from the rest of the physical world. This could be good for Adrienne. It was unlikely a woman in exile would have made much of an effort to maintain her professional contacts or physical resources.

Oriented to true north, the rune was reversed. This suggested Tara had become bound by her exile, trapped or unwilling to move to new patterns. The rune also suggested inheritance. In this case, Adrienne suspected the inheritance aspect of the rune dealt more with the line of succession established by the Pythia, and Tara's rejection of it.

Adrienne stuffed down a flash of rage and turned her attention back to the makeshift runes.

The cardinal direction east represented the mind and intellectual faculties. It was the direction of messages. Adrienne probed the sticks for a weakness she could exploit. She found a trio of sticks forming an angular, reversed *F*. The rune Ansuz spoke of signals and messages. Tara had accepted Sophia's summons. But Ansuz was also sacred to the Norse god, Loki. Loki was a notorious trickster. Adrienne suspected Tara had not been told the whole truth, that there was some element of deception to the message. Tara did not, by her reading, have a true grasp of the situation.

South was the direction of passion, fire, strength. In this quarter, Adrienne found a single stick perfectly aligned with true north. Isa, the rune of ice and winter. This part of Tara's life was at a standstill, frozen. Adrienne smiled. Tara was as weak as she'd expected.

West was the realm of emotions. Two sticks crossed lopsidedly, leaning to the left, in a fair imitation of the rune Nauthiz. Nauthiz represented constraint and sorrow. In this orientation, it was reversed from its traditional vantage point, suggesting a deep shadow had fallen over her quarry, as Adrienne's shadow fell over the rune now.

Adrienne stretched her cramped muscles and strode to the front door. She bent to examine the lock: a strong one, new. The bright brass of it gleamed in stark contrast to the weathered door.

Small obstacle, that.

Adrienne fished a set of lockpicks from her boot and made short work of it. The door swung open, and Adrienne slid her hand along the interior of the wall for a light switch. Her brow wrinkled, though. The place was still warm . . . Why was the heat on, if no one was home?

A growl emanated from the darkness, and Adrienne's hand stilled on the wall.

She smiled, flipped the switch.

In the center of the floor stood a gray tomcat. He'd been awakened from a sound slumber, by the looks of his rumpled fur and the fact that only the fur on his back and his tail were fluffed up properly.

Adrienne shut the door behind her. "Are you the watchdog?"

The cat hissed and bolted for the back bedroom. Adrienne didn't bother to chase him. Instead she wandered to the kitchen counter. At the edge of the beat-up refrigerator, the cat's water and food dishes were full. Someone had been here. Feeding instructions had been left for some-one—perhaps Sophia?—in a sharp-edged scrawl.

Adrienne ran her fingers over the ink. This was her enemy's writing. It was terse, composed of no unnecessary ornamentation or flourishes. Juliane's daughter was not a frivolous woman.

Juliane, herself, had had a touch of whimsy about her. As a child, Adrienne remembered seeing Juliane in the circle of priestesses, or watching how she would some-times build houses from her Tarot cards to delight the children. Her dark hair hung over her shoulders, wound with tangles of jasmine. Adrienne had watched how the Pythia had favored her, how she had braided the other woman's hair and spoke with Juliane in hushed tones beyond the limits of Adrienne's hearing.

And the Pythia had favored Juliane's daughter. Tara had shown little interest in her mother's work. The few times Adrienne had seen her, the older girl had her nose stuck in a book, or else was distracted by counting stars or pebbles. She'd been shy and awkward. Bookish. Not a leader.

Adrienne's mouth thinned to a hard line. The girl had no appreciation for what her mother could have taught her. At least Tara *had* a mother to teach her.

Adrienne's parents had abandoned her quite young, beyond the reach of her memory. She had been shuffled from the house of one of Delphi's Daughters to the next. The Pythia had said this was to develop her talents, but Adrienne knew the truth: no one wanted to be bothered with her for any length of time. Adrienne had a knack for getting into trouble: she was always the one to disappear during hide-and-seek for hours at a time, to set her bedroom curtains on fire with a magnifying glass. She'd been the girl who refused to wear shoes, whose clothes were always filthy with mud.

But she'd grown into her talents—as they had feared. Adrienne had heard it whispered that the Daughters of Delphi had only taken her in to keep her from becoming something monstrous.

Adrienne smiled. They knew she was the most powerful of Delphi's Daughters. The formal arts of geomancy: pendulums, casting stones, dowsing—those she had been taught by Delphi's Daughters. But she'd learned other things, largely through her own experimentation. How to scatter handfuls of earth that would indicate the direction of any quarry she chose. How to read ley lines, the spirit roads departed souls wandered. The Earth hummed to her, spoke to her, became the mother she'd never known.

The title of Pythia was her birthright.

Why give it to another, to one who had never shown the slightest interest in it? Why surrender it to Juliane's distracted daughter? Especially now, when the Pythia sensed a great and terrible technology on the horizon, one that could be used for war as easily as it could be used to instill peace.

Adrienne's hands balled into fists. She could sense it, hear it whispered when she pressed her ear to the earth: something wasn't right. Someone was interfering with the balance of earth, cleaving it in ways it shouldn't. All of Delphi's Daughters could hear it, in their own ways, whether it was in their scrying bowls or hinted in their astrology charts. Something terrible was coming. The Pythia was too old to see it clearly. And Tara was too weak and broken to stop it.

But Adrienne would. Whatever it took.

Adrienne paced through the living room. Her fingers plucked up strands of Tara's hair from the couch, sifting through the short pieces of striped cat hair. She paused at Tara's old work boots near the door, held the soles of those shoes up to her own. Tara possessed a slighter build, smaller feet.

The bedroom smelled like cedar. Adrienne felt something take a swipe at her ankles when she walked by the bed. The cat. Adrienne ignored it and crossed to the closet. Tara's clothes were not what she would have expected from a former government agent. Only jeans and loose shirts hung in neat rows. No dresses, blouses, or anything to suggest femininity. Adrienne reached for one of the shirts, a light blue chambray. She shrugged out of her jacket and T-shirt, buttoned Tara's shirt over her chest. The shirt was a bit tight on her, but it was like trying on the quarry's skin. Adrienne rubbed her fingers over the worn cloth, twiddling with the buttons as she searched the closet.

Adrienne leaned forward, sniffed. Below the cedar, she smelled gun oil. An empty case for a Ruger SP-101 lay open on the floor of the closet. The foam inside the case was dented, but the revolver was missing. Adrienne guessed the gun had been stored there for a very long time.

Her eyes slid to the dresser. She rummaged through the drawers. She found little of interest: jeans, old jewelry boxes, sweaters covered in cat hair.

On the top perched a framed photo of a young Tara with her mother. It was the only photo of Tara Adrienne had seen in the house.

Royal succession for the Pythia's favor. With a swipe, Adrienne knocked it over. The glass cracked on the surface of the dresser.

She felt a small stab of regret. She wanted to leave no trace of having been here, of having worn Tara's skin or flipped through the pages of her books. She was reminded of the furious creature underneath the bed. Perhaps this transgression would be blamed on the cat.

Adrienne turned out the light and stretched out on Tara's bed. The springs squeaked as she shifted. She was too accustomed to sleeping outdoors, and the bed felt like a ridiculous luxury. The pillows smelled of her quarry's sweat and tears.

She lay, staring up at the ceiling, with her hands behind her head. She looked forward to experiencing those smells in person, when she'd chased her quarry down and killed it.

Chapter Five

Harry Li left shortly after the moon set, leaving Tara with her notes, photographs, and the only tangible artifact of Magnusson's disappearance: his watch. The room seemed a little less . . . alive . . . with him gone.

She held the cool metal of the watch in her hand. Judging by Harry's reaction, he didn't feel the same odd, sticky aura about it that she did. It seemed somehow vacant, as if something was missing. It felt too light, and it rattled when she shook it.

She dug in her cosmetic bag. Its contents were spare: lipstick, mascara, a bit of plum-colored eye shadow. They'd gone a bit stale and gloppy; she wondered why she'd brought these things with her. She knew the answer: because it was expected of her, and it was part of the mask she'd always worn while working a case. Habit.

She dug a pair of nail clippers from the bottom of the

bag, folded out the metal file, and began to crack the case of the watch. It took some doing, but she managed to open it without scratching the case.

What she saw inside surprised her . . . or rather, it was what she didn't see. She expected to see the usual mass of gears, maybe a circuit chip. There was only one thing inside: a mass of tiny copper wires, finer than hair, spiraled in on themselves in an infinity loop, bordered by a backing of green circuit board. The rest was smooth and empty. Time had disappeared from the watch, even as it was running out for Magnusson.

Tara closed the case up, contemplative. There were too many things that seemed missing at the scene. The inordinately small amount of rubble and now the guts of Magnusson's watch. To say nothing of Magnusson himself.

She reached for her cards, spreading her mother's scarf out on the bedspread. She pulled out the Magician card, lay the watch below it to focus the reading, and cleared her mind to focus on the investigation. She meditated on the Magician, on his stance and his inscrutable, secretive smile. What was he hiding? What had he conjured from the elements before him, what forces had he summoned from the darkness?

She shuffled the cards, feeling the familiar flex and flip of them in her hands. Amazing how easily she was falling back into this life, and that worried her.

"Where do we stand now?" She drew one card, placed it on the far left of the scarf. A picture of a man hanging upside down by his ankle looked back at her. He was dangling from a wire drawn taut between two trees. His hands were held behind his back as he hung over a misty chasm. It was impossible to tell if his hands were bound behind his back, or if it was simply an attitude of contemplation.

The Hanged Man. It represented suspension, sacrifice, limbo. Tara wasn't surprised. The investigation had been blatantly stonewalled, and it felt like more than sheer territoriality.

She wrote down in her notebook the date and *Magician*. Below, to the left of the page, she wrote *Hanged Man*. Beside that, she wrote the first word that came to mind: *stagnation*.

"Where do we want to go?" She shuffled the cards again, until her shuffle felt smooth and even, and picked another card, laying it in the center of the scarf.

The Six of Wands depicted a man on horseback, holding a flowering staff with a laurel crown attached to it. Surrounding him were people holding up other wands bursting with flowers. The sky was blue behind them, and the overall attitude was one of victory, of a conquering hero returned to his homeland.

Tara frowned. The card also represented mobilization, promotion, public acclaim, and the acknowledgement of others. Why would she want the acknowledgement of others?

Her eyes slid back to her makeup case, and she recalled slipping and letting Harry see one of her scars. Perhaps she cared more than she wanted to admit about what other people thought.

But perhaps this card didn't relate so much to her. She

recalled Harry's situation of being in political exile. Perhaps he sought a way out, might see this case as an opportunity to move out of the shadows. She looked back at the Hanged Man. That may also speak of Harry, his state of career limbo.

In her journal, she noted this, but she also wrote *Whose victory?*

She framed her third question in her mind, and voiced it aloud. "What's the path to get there?"

She pulled a card from the deck that seemed to draw her eye, placing it to the far right. The Star again. The smiling maiden poured water from ewer to ewer under a night sky. She'd pulled this when she'd read the cards back at the cabin. When she drew cards more than once, it usually indicated she was overlooking something important.

She flipped back through her journal for her initial impressions of the card, recalling what she'd used to focus her first reading: the picture of Magnusson and his daughter. Her mind skipped through its familiar nonlinear thinking, like a butterfly over a field, and she let it light on Magnusson's daughter, Cassie. She let her thoughts roam over the hills and valleys of her impressions, not guiding them, waiting for a flash of intuition to light her way, a flash that would quicken her pulse with knowledge.

She grabbed some of the papers Harry had left, scanning them for more information about Magnusson's daughter. She found a notation about her birthplace: Ithaca, New York . . . and her full name: Cassiopeia Marie Magnusson. Just the kind of name a physicist would saddle a child with.

Her mind seized that. Cassiopeia. The maiden in the card was looking up at the stars. It could be the constellation Cassiopeia.

Magnusson's daughter might just be the key Tara was searching for.

HARRY KNEW HE WAS BEING WATCHED.

From the time he'd left Tara's room, his skin had crawled. He scanned the darkness of the motel parking lot, unholstering his gun. Pools of the buzzing sulfur lights picked out the shapes of cars: his, the night clerk's beat-up Datsun, a Winnebago belonging to the retired couple watching game shows loudly downstairs, and a station wagon driven by two harried parents dragging their kids kicking and screaming to the Grand Canyon, as evidenced by the maps and toys littering the seats.

Concealing the gun behind the empty pizza box he'd intended to take to the Dumpster, he stepped down the metal stairs, wincing at the loud echoes his steps made. Below the perforated metal steps, he glimpsed movement, a figure receding around the corner of the motel. It disappeared beyond the edge of the blacktop parking lot hidden by the side of the Winnebago, and did not emerge.

An eavesdropper? Surveillance? Harry's eyes narrowed.

Harry followed, crossing around the front bumper of the camper. His sneakers made no sound on the asphalt, and he listened. He could hear the pings made by the Winnebago's engine as it cooled down, the high-pitched whine of the parking lot lights overhead, his heart hammering in his throat.

He swung out around the edge of the Winnebago, flipping the pizza box under his right arm to reveal and brace the gun.

"Agent Li." Richard Corvus stood, hands in his pockets, watching him with amusement. Streetlight outlined him in saffron, reflecting off his glasses. The effect made his eyes entirely unreadable.

Harry sighed, holstering his gun. "Hello, sir."

Corvus sniffed at the pizza box. "That stuff'll kill you."

Harry shrugged. "I can think of many worse ways to go than by way of double cheese and pepperoni." He cast the box, Frisbee-style, into the nearby Dumpster. It landed with a hollow slap that made Corvus twitch. "What brings you here?"

"Checking on your progress. I might have asked you the same." Corvus gave him an arch glance.

Li responded stoically. "Comparing notes." He didn't like Corvus's insinuation. It seemed both possessive and invasive.

"What have you found?" Corvus cocked his head. Li was reminded of a bird, a balding crow in his black coat.

Li swallowed. "We didn't get much from DOD. Major Gabriel is busily mopping up the crime scene, and we can't drag out of them what Magnusson is working on. Judging by his research, I'm guessing it has to do with particle physics, but we'll keep looking.

"DOD hasn't released any trace evidence to us. I've put in a request for copies through official channels. Magnusson's office is clean." Li withheld the information about the photos and the watch. Deep down in his gut, he never trusted Corvus, though he still had to play the game. But Harry would keep some pieces to himself.

"Any signs of foul play?"

"None yet, but that's not ruled out." Li stubbornly wanted to keep that door open.

"I suggest that you rule it out as soon as you can," Corvus said mildly, but his statement chilled Li.

"We'll rule out all dead ends as soon as possible."

Corvus looked at him sharply over his glasses. "You didn't come to see me when you were finished today."

"Dr. Sheridan's suit containment was compromised. We were busy taking care of that. I intended to call." Li forced himself to shut his mouth before he dug himself in any deeper.

"Dr. Sheridan has the habit of attracting catastrophe."

Li couldn't help himself. "Then why did you ask her to consult on this case?"

Corvus's mouth tightened. "That was not my call," he snapped.

Someone from above had told him to investigate, and who to use. "But you've worked with her before."

"Yes. We were assigned together in Special Projects years ago." Corvus took off his glasses and wiped them meticulously on his sleeve. "An unfortunate incident derailed her career, which had seemed quite promising. If not for that incident, you would likely be reporting to her now. She was, by all assessment, a brilliant profiler."

"What happened?"

Corvus smiled. Li could see he had the irritating habit of keeping tantalizing nuggets of information, parsing them out only when necessary. "You've read about the serial killer who called himself the Gardener?"

"That was the guy, five years ago, who was cutting girls up and burying them alive in Missouri. Amos Dalton. He planted flowers over the sites where he buried them." Li dredged his memory for the newspaper headlines. "He was killed in a raid, never went to trial."

"Yes, that's the one. Dr. Sheridan was working as a profiler at the time, trying to find him. She had an unfortunate encounter with Mr. Dalton."

Li blinked. His thoughts traced back to the scar he'd glimpsed on Tara's shoulder.

"Dr. Sheridan managed to escape," Corvus continued. "However, it had been a harrowing experience. She resigned immediately and we expect she's sustained permanent psychological damage from her contact with Mr. Dalton."

Li's eyes widened.

"As a result, I would advise you to keep Dr. Sheridan out of the way as much as possible. We may be required to humor her presence on this case, but I would prefer she not place herself—or anyone else—in harm's way again. Are we clear?"

"Crystal, sir."

"Good. Have your report on my desk in the morning."

"Of course."

"Good night, Agent Li."

Harry watched Corvus walk away across the parking lot, turn left on the sidewalk, and disappear.

What Corvus had told him explained a great deal. And yet, he knew Corvus never offered information without motive. Underneath that brittle façade, Corvus clearly sought to keep Tara out of the investigation . . . and perhaps by extension, this would mean Harry's own work would be limited.

Harry couldn't imagine what it would have been like, even in Corvus's stripped-down description, to be the prisoner of the Gardener. Harry remembered the articles, the file photos of the blood-soaked boxes Amos Dalton had built. The claustrophobia she'd confessed to today seemed such a minor side effect.

His eyes drifted up to the second floor of the motel, where Tara's room light had gone out. He admired her for being able to go to sleep in the dark, years after.

EVEN WITH THE LIGHTS OUT, IT WAS TOO BRIGHT TO SLEEP. Too accustomed to the total pitch black of night at the cabin, Tara found the light from the parking lot leaking around the cheap drapes to be too distracting. When she closed her eyes, the swish of traffic on the highway and the buzz of the parking lot lights kept her awake. In a nearby room, someone was watching television with the volume cranked up just loud enough to hear the laugh track, but not loud enough to make out the dialogue. Someone on the floor above her was taking a shower after a noisy bout of lovemaking, and the water sluiced down the pipes in metallic rattles.

She stared at the ceiling, sweat glistening on her brow. Her head thumped under the force of the pulse in her temples. When she moved to sit up, her stomach lurched, and her hand pressed against the pillow, soaked with sweat.

Tara stumbled out of bed to the bathroom, fumbled with the light switch. Blinding fluorescent light washed over her vision, and she sank to the floor. Vomiting into the toilet, she distantly wondered if the motel's other occupants could hear her as clearly as she'd heard them.

She leaned back, face pressed against the mercifully cool tile of the wall that smelled like Pine-Sol. She tried to steady her breathing, pulling her hair away from her scaldingly hot face. The nausea attacked her again, until she hit dry heaves and crawled to the bathtub. She opened the cold water faucet over her head and let the water course down over the back of her neck. She lifted her head. With shaking hands, she scooped water from the flow and splashed it on her face.

Radiation poisoning. She knew the symptoms usually presented themselves within the first twelve hours. There wasn't any way of knowing how bad it was . . . but given that the symptoms had taken several hours to emerge, and she wasn't showing any sign of burns, she hoped this would be a mild case.

Unsteadily, she climbed to her feet. In the glare of the mirror, her pale face shone like the moon, dark circles like bruises under her eyes. Clutching the edge of the counter-top, she considered her options.

She thought, briefly, about calling Harry. Tara shook her head. No. He would do the right thing: take her to the emergency room, bring her things, and then leave. She would not give him a reason to exclude her from the case. There was little to be done for a case of radiation poisoning. The only good a trip to the ER would do for her would be prescription antiemetics and anesthetics . . . and being trapped under observation would not help Lowell Magnusson. She could feel, in her bones, that the case was too important to abandon. She was resolved to finish it.

She found the last fragments of ice in the ice bucket in the bedroom, popped an ice chip in her mouth. The chill spread from her tongue to the rest of her body. She dragged the ugly comforter off the bed, wrapped it around her shoulders, and sank to the bathroom floor.

Tara fell asleep in the brilliant glare of the bathroom light, the sounds of the television from upstairs echoing against the tile.

Instead of bright light, cool tile, and the smell of Pine-Sol, Tara dreamed of darkness, of the chill of dirt at her back. She could feel her breath condensing hot against her face, the thinness of the air in her lungs, and the weight of earth creaking over her. She tasted warm, coppery blood, felt it slick on her fingers as she tried to move. Fertilizer stung the wounds lacing her body and her fingertips, where she'd torn her nails off clawing into the dark. She could smell the harsh tang of the chemicals, taste them in the back of her throat. Her face was wet with tears and mud.

Buried. The fear drained into her, paralyzed her. Her breath came fast and shallow, and she felt the dizziness from lack of oxygen setting in. She couldn't move, couldn't see, couldn't breathe. All she could do was whimper in the back of her throat.

Could this truly be her fate? Suffocating to death in the ground? Her cards had never predicted this. But she felt help- less against the terrible weight pressing against her, unable to distinguish up from down.

A voice whispered in her ear, a woman's voice. "Fight."

She forced her breath to slow. She was hallucinating from lack of oxygen. Not a good sign.

"Fight."

The voice emanated from her right and behind her . . . Per- haps that was the way up. She struggled to turn over, feeling dirt trickling into her mouth. She spat it out. Tara dug her fingers into the earth, feeling her fingernails peel. Splinters of wood dug beneath them, and she cried out.

"Fight."

She pushed against that terrible weight with the palms of her hands.

"Fight."

She had no other choice but to push against the terrible darkness.

Chapter Six

"How did you sleep?"

"All right." Tara sipped her water from a paper cup, alternating swallows between Rolaids tablets. Li noticed dark circles shadowed her doe eyes, blue as a bottle of overturned ink. "You?"

"As well as could be expected." He watched her out of the corner of his eye for a reaction as he drove. "I got a late-night visit from Corvus."

She hesitated, mid-sip, and the thick fringe of her eyelashes fluttered. "What did he want?"

"He warned me to wrap things up quickly. He also insinuated you weren't reliable."

"I suppose Corvus would think that," she said mildly, but he watched the muscle in her jaw tighten.

"What is it with the two of you?" He was being bullish, direct. "Did you two have a thing going on, or something?"

She blinked, looked at him in shock. "A thing? With Corvus?" Horror washed over her pretty features. She wasn't conventionally beautiful, but there was something deeply attractive about her. She swished water around in her mouth, as if trying to wipe out a bad taste. "Gah. Absolutely not."

Harry relaxed his grip on the wheel, though he hadn't realized he'd been tense. Now that it was blurted out in the open, it sounded absurd. He couldn't picture cold-fish Corvus as being a love struck inamorata. Tara . . . He could picture Tara with her hair fanned over a pillow, drinking tea and reading the Sunday paper in bed with a lover. But not Corvus.

"He's quite interested in keeping you out of the way."

Tara wrapped her hands around the cup, and it was some time before she answered. "Look, he made a pass at me once, a long time ago. I turned him down. We were partners for a year after that, but it was more . . . competitive. At that time, Special Projects was a new division. He and I were both ambitious, and we clashed. Often. I eventually left Special Projects. He got what he wanted, and I . . ." She smiled, without warmth. "I got out."

Uncomfortable silence settled in the car. Harry didn't want to force her to talk about why she left. "And why did you come back now?"

Tara shrugged. "An old friend asked me to. She felt Magnusson's disappearance was important."

The neighborhood they drove through, Magnusson's neighborhood, was heavy with the silence of early morning. This was an older section of the north edge of town, made up of a mélange of houses from various eras, most of them mid-twentieth century. Newspapers lay at the edges of driveways; garbage cans at the curb were yet to be picked up. A few isolated lights had come on in the kitchens and bathrooms, windows fogging with shower steam. There was no evidence of young families with children, no toys in the sparse yards or cars decorated with teenagers' decals or ornaments in rearview mirrors. Tall fences and strategic use of shrubbery and trees to block the views suggested this was a place where people pretty much left their neighbors alone.

Harry pulled into a crushed-gravel driveway shaded with pine trees taking a broad curve away from the road. "You must have some powerful friends."

"They surprise me with their nosiness, every so often."

She wasn't going to give him any more than that, and Harry let it drop. He parked the car behind a small bungalow screened from the street by overgrown pine and cherry trees. The cherry trees were just beginning to bud, bringing a suggestion of life into the colorless landscape. The small yard had been xeriscaped with gravel, boulders, and native sage plants. Brown skeletons of coneflower and columbine rattled near the porch, heavy with beams and pillars in need of painting. Mail peeked out of the black mailbox. Harry snatched the letters, leafing through them. Bills, a couple of journals, a lingerie catalog.

Tara had climbed to the porch and peeked in the window. "Looks like someone's been here before us. It's been tossed."

Harry tried the door. Locked. But it was a simple knob

lock, no dead bolt. He fished in his wallet for a credit card, slipped it between the tongue of the lock and the hole in the doorjamb, and jiggled it back and forth until he felt the card slide behind the tongue and pull it back. Drawing his gun, he pushed the door open. Tara mirrored him on the other side of the door. Harry hadn't realized she'd been carrying.

He pushed the door open into the house. "Hello?"

No answer. A potted plant lay broken in pieces just inside the door, splaying its striped spidery tentacles all over the terra-cotta, as if it were trying to gather itself together. A sign of a struggle. He smelled urine. This was not going to be good.

He heard a sudden burst of motion—a thundering gallop, the rattle of chain—and he braced his stance to draw down on a shadowy assailant barreling down the hallway toward him. Like the Grim Reaper itself, it lunged in a blur of jingling darkness. Harry was knocked to the wooden board with an echoing slam, pulling his gun away and over his head . . .

. . . as a chocolate Labrador retriever bounded out of the house as if its ass were on fire, charged into the yard, and squatted on the gravel to take a leak.

"Poor thing." Tara's voice washed soothingly over Harry, until he realized it wasn't him she was clucking over. He rolled over to see her scratching the ears of the dog in the yard, who seemed to be holding five gallons of streaming water in its bladder. "You really had to go, didn't you? When was the last time you were let out?" The dog whimpered back at her, finished its business, and slobbered on her cheek.

"You okay, Harry?" she called over her shoulder at him, an afterthought.

"I'm fine," he grumbled as he climbed to his feet, swallowing the surge of adrenaline that had nearly caused him to shoot the animal. "Who's the guard dog?"

Tara read the brass tags on its collar. "This is Maggie."

"Maggie evidently had to pee."

Maggie bounded up the porch steps and jumped on Harry. In spite of himself, Li rubbed her ears, and she made awful faces of enjoyment, tongue lolling. He let the dog lead them into the house, tail low and wagging, nails clicking on the hardwood floors. She looked sheepishly at them when she walked past the broken potted plant, and tucked her tail between her legs when they passed the puddle on the floor of the kitchen. Chastised, she rolled her baleful brown eyes up at Harry and Tara.

"It's okay," Tara murmured at the dog. Maggie leaned against her, forcing her head under Tara's hand. She patted the dog's sides. This dog hadn't missed many meals, a nice layer of fat encasing her ribs.

Advancing down the hall, Li did a quick check of the rooms. Nothing else seemed out of place. The living room held a tattered sofa, a CD collection, and an HDTV that made him salivate with envy. The coffee table was stacked with newspapers dated two days ago. The floor was strewn with dog toys, most of them pretty well destroyed. Li's shoe brushed the remains of what might once have been a stuffed turtle, now wet with dog spit and leaking stuffing. When he stepped on it, it emitted a halfhearted squeak.

The bathroom smelled vaguely of bachelor mildew, with a lonely toothbrush perched in a chrome holder. Magnusson's bedroom was what Li would have expected: unmade bed, physics books stacked on the unmatched side tables. He peered under the bed and spied a stack of magazines he didn't want to touch. He would have expected a man like Magnusson would've been more tech-savvy with his porn. Most people got theirs from the internet; Magnusson was apparently old-school and liked paper princesses.

"It looks like no one's been here yet." He felt a stab of triumph at that.

Maggie trundled in, with Tara in tow. She sat down with a huff beside the bed, her tail slapping against the floor like a metronome. Was it too much to hope that the dog had scared them off? Maggie grinned up at him, drooling. Ferocious beast.

Tara's eyes burned dark, considering. "They either have, and left things alone, or they're watching to see who comes looking."

She left the room, whistled for the dog. From the kitchen, he could hear running water and noisy slurps as Tara watered the dog. He heard her puttering around the kitchen, riffling through the drawers and cabinets. The crackling of a paper bag and the unmistakable rattle of kibble in a metal bowl made him smile. For all Tara's cool reticence, she did seem to have some sympathy after all.

Magnusson's office interested him the most. The original casement windows let in wan, late winter sunshine, striping a desk made from a door balanced on top of two file cabinets. Magnusson's slippers lay, cast aside, beneath the desk. Papers and books teetered nearby on a battered bookshelf. His heart dropped when he saw the power and USB cables snaking across the desk, connected to nothing. A laptop computer had been used here at one time, but it was gone now. He stabbed the power button on the laser printer, but it spat out no forgotten queued printer jobs.

They had not been the first to arrive. He felt a twinge of disappointment at that. The tight net cast by Gabriel over Magnusson's workplace may have reached even this far.

TARA FOUND MAGGIE'S EMPTY WATER BOWL AND FILLED IT from the kitchen tap. Enraptured, the dog leaned against her thigh and attacked the water with mighty slurps that splashed liquid on the tile floor.

Only a lonely coffee mug rested in the bottom of the sink. Tara opened the fridge, studded with magnets emblazoned with pizza delivery numbers. Refrigerators were often the best places to get a sense of a person, and Magnusson's fridge was no exception. The fridge light illuminated a few bottles of microbrew beer, energy drinks, ketchup, a loaf of bread, and a takeout container. Magnusson lived the life of a distracted intellectual, for certain. There was no sign of a woman's touch in the fridge, either.

She shut the fridge door. The sight of food made her stomach turn. Though she didn't feel nearly as weak and sickly as she had last night, she didn't want to tempt fate. She felt too unsteady on her feet, and didn't want to risk barfing on the evidence.

As she popped another Rolaids tablet, her gaze roved the counters. An expensive espresso machine perched next to the sink. Magnusson was a gadget man, a man who would indulge a luxury or two. Or else, he was a man who was extremely hard to buy for during holidays.

She pawed through his cabinets, finding several kinds of whole-grain cereal, a half-used jar of peanut butter, plenty of multivitamins, and prescription bottles half full of Xanax and Ambien. The original refill dates were pretty recent. Magnusson was perhaps dealing with more stress than usual. She turned the Xanax bottle over in her hand. If Magnusson had left town willingly, he would have brought his meds with him.

Maggie shoved her nose into Tara's thigh, blinking up at her with all the sadness only dogs can muster. Magnusson wouldn't have left the dog behind, either. The amount of toys in the living room and the layer of pudge encasing the dog suggested Magnusson wasn't a neglectful dog parent.

"You hungry, girl?"

Maggie whimpered.

Tara rummaged around the lower cabinets and found a fifty-pound bag of dog kibble. She dragged it out and unrolled it. Though the cartoon hound on the bag cheerfully announced the bag contained organic diet dog food for overweight dogs, it didn't seem to have had much effect on Maggie. She upended the bag, trickling kibble into the stainless steel bowl on the floor. Maggie shoved her nose into the stream of food, crunching noisily.

Something shifted inside the bag. Frowning, Tara

turned it back up, tore it open to look inside. A piece of clear plastic poked into view like a prize in a Cracker Jack box. She reached in after it, and fished out a small laptop computer encased in a plastic zipper bag. Jackpot.

She took it back to Magnusson's office and placed it on the desk before Harry.

"Where did you find that?" Harry's eyebrows crawled up his forehead, and he grinned.

"In the dog food. Magnusson evidently wanted whoever would feed the dog to find it."

"And no one doing a cursory search would have seen it." Li opened the greasy zipper bag to retrieve the computer. He punched the power button, drumming his fingers as it booted up. The screen blinked on, demanding a password.

"Shit."

Tara scanned the office, turning on her heel to fully absorb it. This place was where Magnusson had done his real work.

For the first time, Tara could feel the force of Magnusson's personality. Where much of the rest of the house was strictly utilitarian, as evidenced by the mismatched dishes and lack of interest in décor, this was his nest, feathered in books, paper, and bits of debris that spoke of who he was. A worn rug muffled her steps underfoot, stained with coffee. Maggie's dog bed was tucked in the corner, strewn with soggy rawhides. As Maggie didn't seem the type of dog to be far from her master, it implied Magnusson spent more time here than he did in his bedroom. Magnets cut in the shapes of cartoon aliens studded the file cabinets, holding notes of mathematical formulae. A chipped coffee cup on his desk proclaimed he was *#1 Dad* and held an assortment of very expensive fountain pens and mechanical pencils. No wonder he'd eschewed the cheap, government-issue ones from work. A half-evaporated energy drink sat open on the desk beside a paperweight carved to resemble a happy Tiki god. A telescope perched before the window was aimed somewhere over the tree line. Tara wondered what Magnusson thought at night when the moon and stars crossed its glass eye. She wondered if Cassiopeia was visible this time of year.

Tara paused to examine a poster of the Earth at night tacked up onto the rough plaster wall. Taken from a satellite, it showed the bright illumination of cities and power sources, leaving the rest of the planet to its soft, sleepy darkness. Dark and light, the chiaroscuro was exquisite, the energy and black seeming to seethe together as a living thing, full and empty at the same time.

Her fingers traced over the titles of Magnusson's books: *Black Holes: The Armpits of the Universe*, *A Unified Theory of Quantum Physics*, *Field Theory Equations*, *The Tao Te Ching*. She picked the last one up and flipped through the pages. The philosophy of dark and light, again. Cryptic notes were scribbled in the margins, some legible, some not. She paused at a dog-eared page and a trio of passages Magnusson had underlined:

Spokes are tied together to form a wheel. Yet, it is in the hollowness that the usefulness of the wheel depends.

Clay is sculpted to make a vessel, but it is in the hollowness that the usefulness of the vessel depends.

Just as we take advantage of what exists in the physical world, that which can be touched, we should recognize the usefulness of nothingness.

Beside these, Magnusson had scribbled *How to detect that emptiness, that immeasurable and fluid darkness?*

She thought back to the articles she'd skimmed in Magnusson's file, about his research interests in dark matter and energy, in the vast portion of the universe that was unseen. Her eyes flickered back up to the poster. If he was right, then only a small proportion of matter—light matter—would be visible, like the city lights. The rest of the universe, like the Earth, would be in darkness.

Had Magnusson come too close to this darkness?

A car engine roared and died in the driveway. Hearing the clomp of boots and a key in the lock, her head snapped around. Harry rose from the desk, unholstered his gun. Maggie bolted toward the door at a dead run, collar jingling and claws scraping on the hardwood.

Maybe she was a better guard dog than they thought. Tara followed Maggie and Harry to the entry.

A young woman pulled her keys out of the lock. Her jaw-length hair was dyed jet black, with blue highlights. She wore a long black coat two sizes too big for her that smelled like patchouli. Her waffle-soled black combat boots flopped unlaced, snapping against the floor as she walked into the foyer. Kohl-rimmed eyes were fixed on Maggie, who bounded up to her and pressed her paws to the girl's shoulders. The girl giggled, wrapping her arms around the dog.

"Cassie?" Tara asked. Though she looked nothing like

the file picture of the clean-cut girl beaming beside her father, the resemblance was unmistakable: the same startling blue eyes, the thin frame.

"Who're you?" The girl stepped back, eying Tara and Li with suspicion.

"I'm Tara. This is Harry. We've come to find your father."

"Do you work with him?"

"No. We're not with the military. We're with the Department of Justice."

Cassie took a deep breath, and her lower lip shook. "He—"

She took a step back and tripped over the dog as a gunshot rang out. The leaded glass of the kitchen window shattered, and Tara lunged forward. The girl, the dog, and Tara fell together in a tangled pile as the plaster foyer wall blistered open above them.

HARRY DUCKED AND SPRINTED TO THE FRONT DOOR, swinging out onto the porch. Maggie surged ahead of him, barking and snarling. He followed, trying to keep his footing in the gravel as the dog launched through a stand of pine trees to the fence at the property line. His breath burned in his throat, scalding his hammering heart. Maggie flung herself at the fence with such force the posts rattled.

He reached up for the dog-eared edges of the fence and swung up as another shot splintered into the cedar fence, close enough to shake dew from the pine trees. He swung his leg over and dropped to the ground in the neighbor's cactus garden. Swearing under his breath, he crouched behind a decorative boulder, scanning the scene over his gun for movement, some sign of the shooter. Trapped behind the fence, Maggie howled as ferociously as chained Cerberus.

There. Movement flickered around the corner of the house: a man stuffing something under his coat. Gravel crunched as he fled. Harry ran after him, ordering him to stop. As they tore through yards, lights came on, dogs barked, and suburbia woke with a start and a snort.

The shooter sped down a driveway, toward the street. Harry got a good look at him for the first time: he was utterly nondescript, with brown hair, tan skin, muscular build, dark coat and shoes. He'd blend in anywhere, except for the barrel of the rifle peeking out the edge of his coat. As soon as his feet hit the street, Harry heard the rev of an engine.

He's going to get away, he thought desperately as a tan SUV rounded the corner and picked up speed. The shooter leaned out into the street as the SUV slammed on the brakes.

Harry ran so hard he thought his lungs would burst, his legs jackhammering against the pavement. The shooter popped open the door and scrambled in. Before the door shut, the getaway car squealed away, leaving Harry in the empty street, panting, with neighbors peering out their windows. Harry recited the license plate number to himself, burning it into his memory, "DCD-1397 . . . DCD-1397 . . ."

"Hey, buddy. You miss your car pool?" a man in the

next yard asked him, newspaper tucked under his arm, as he locked his front door.

Breathless, Harry gestured at the sound of the garbage truck two streets over. "Missed putting the trash out."

"They change it every holiday . . . It's one day later after each holiday." The man nodded to himself and got into his car. "It's hard to remember, with all those damn federal holidays."

Harry ran back to Magnusson's house. He could hear Maggie tearing up the fence, and hurried around the back driveway to check on Tara and Cassie. He hoped they'd hit the deck soon enough. While the thought of the girl getting hit terrified him, imagining Tara being struck trying to save her froze his chest.

It was then he noticed Magnusson's garbage can was out. If today was trash day, he must have put it out two days earlier.

Magnusson had known he'd be gone.

The thought lanced through his mind as he ran back up the driveway, raced up the porch steps, into the foyer, where his breath caught and blistered in his throat.

There was blood. It stained the white plaster of the foyer in a misty, high-velocity blood spatter pattern. Tara and Cassie crouched in a ball on the floor, below the line of the fire.

"We're getting out of here."

Tara turned as Harry spoke, blood smearing from her jacket on the white plaster. All color had drained from her face. Maggie whimpered and jumped up on her, paws scratching on the wall. Under Tara's arms, Harry could see Cassie's dark coat and a frightened eye. Tara dragged her back from the broken kitchen window, protected by the wall studs in the foyer.

Harry raced for Magnusson's office, crouching below the level of the windows. Though the shooter had gone, he had no reassurance there weren't more, and he was certain the house was still being surveilled. He snatched the laptop from the desk, jammed it under his arm as if it were a football.

Harry sprinted outside for the car. Heedless of the landscaping, he drove it on the gravel, right up to the edge of the porch. He rolled out of the passenger's side, gun drawn, popping open the backseat door. He scanned the yard, the neighbor's fence, the street, as Tara and Cassie stumbled out of the front door. Tara had flung her coat over the girl, and they piled into the backseat. Maggie, whimpering, clambered in after them.

Harry looked back in the rearview mirror at the women and the dog. Maggie was vigorously licking Cassie's face, slapping Harry's arm with her tail. Tara kept her hand on the girl's head, keeping close to the floorboards.

Harry threw the car in gear and rattled back out of the driveway in reverse. The tires squealed when they hit the street, passed the garbage truck, and tore out of the cul-de-sac into the gray winter morning.

Chapter Seven

THERE WERE always places to find dirty jobs, if one knew where to look. Black hat work didn't bother Adrienne much. As a geomancer, she didn't mind getting her hands dirty—literally or figuratively.

Adrienne stood in the back of a dive bar, arms folded, watching the room. Her boots had stuck to the floor, littered with peanut shells. The bar displayed a selection of liquors illuminated by a television above the bar showing a basketball game. Perched on bar stools, playing pool, drinking in the shadows at booths, were buyers and sellers of services. Judging by the ramrod postures and buzzed haircuts, many of these men were current or ex-military in civilian dress. A few biker types in leathers and long hair mixed in, and there were no other women. Some of the faces were familiar, those of former employers. Adrienne came here when she was looking for work, and never stayed long.

She knew Tara was searching for the missing physicist, Magnusson. Odds were, if she was looking for him, more shadowy types were, as well. Adrienne knew she stood a better chance of finding Tara if she allied herself with someone looking for the same thing. Geomancy had taught her all lines of power, most ley lines, ultimately intersected . . . if one knew where to listen. And unknown to most humans, this place that the black hats gathered was an intersection point for these lines.

Adrienne reached into her pocket for a milk quartz pebble tumbled into the shape of a perfect marble. Tracing its labyrinthine occlusions with her eyes, she breathed her intent into it. *Find me someone who can lead me to Tara Sheridan.*

She knelt and set the marble on the floor. Giving it a nudge, she watched the marble roll a few feet from her. It wobbled and began to spiral, fanning outward as it wove behind the pool table, between feet, around chair legs. It spiraled more quickly, gaining speed as it traced its way through the peanut shells and cigarette butts. Finally, it came to rest against a polished black boot.

Adrienne straightened and strode toward the owner of the boots.

"You have a job for me." It was a statement. Black hats never asked for jobs.

Gabriel drained his drink and set it down on the scarred table. He gestured to the empty seat opposite him. "Have a seat."

Adrienne slid into the booth, placing both her hands on the table. She knew Gabriel from previous jobs. He liked to see people's hands; it put him at ease. She waited for instructions.

Gabriel lit a cigar, gave it a couple of puffs before he began with his terms. "I've got a problem. I need you to track someone for me. The daughter of a scientist. She's being protected by a couple of rogue operators. They also have some data I want."

Gabriel shoved a grainy, folded-up photograph across the table. Many employers brought photos to black hat interviews. Some black hats were squeamish and superstitious, and would reject a target on sight, without explanation. Some wouldn't work on assignments involving women or children. Adrienne knew one black hat who, for whatever reason, wouldn't take out anyone who owned cats. Better to know at the interview than out in the field. "These are the operators." A grainy surveillance photograph of some type showed what Adrienne assumed to be a military installation, bounded by a chain-link fence. The photograph captured a man and a woman standing outside the car. Adrienne didn't know the crisp-suited Asian man, but she recognized Tara. Her quarry was looking off in the distance, a distracted expression on her face.

"This is the primary target." He flipped down a photo of a young woman clipped from a college newspaper. She was standing in a crowd, holding a sign protesting global warming.

Adrienne smiled, but it did nothing to warm her cold eyes. "What are the terms?"

"Loose. First priority is the data. Having the girl taken alive is negotiable. I prefer the rogue operators to be rendered inactive. Time's of the essence on this contract."

"Rendered inactive" was bureaucratic double-speak for "dead." And that was how Adrienne preferred it.

"Terms accepted," she told him.

"OSCAR?"

Sophia's key slid from the lock of Tara's cabin. The tabby usually came running to her, winding between her ankles before she even had a chance to take her coat off. Sophia clomped the snow off her boots on the rug inside the door.

"Oscar?"

No cat. Alarm twitched through her. Tara would never forgive her if she'd let harm come to Oscar. It had been two days since she'd been here, and the tomcat had seemed perfectly hale and hearty. He'd coughed up a hairball in front of the refrigerator, but Sophia had thought it was normal—she'd never met a cat who couldn't throw up at will. She glanced at his dishes. Still full.

She peered underneath the couch, arthritic knees creaking. She opened the closet doors, peeked behind the fridge, and finally found a tight, furry gray ball under the bed. The ball didn't respond when she spoke to it.

"Oscar." She reached under the bed. *Please don't let him be dead . . .* Her lips worked around a prayer as her fingers grazed his ribs. He was still breathing. One amber eye peered up over his spine, and Oscar mewed.

"Come here, baby."

Oscar slowly crawled out, ears flattened, into Sophia's arms. He worked his way under her open coat and jammed his head into her armpit. Sophia stroked him and cooed at him. He was acting like a cat who'd just been to the vet: frightened. She ran her fingers over his ribs, tummy, spine, and legs, finding no sore spots.

"What happened to you?" She stood slowly, holding the cat now permanently attached to her ribs. Her gaze swung around the room.

Something had happened that had terrified him. She saw the glitter of glass on the dresser. Gingerly, she plucked up the remains of a photo frame with a picture of Juliane and Tara inside.

Someone had been here. Of that much, she was certain.

She stared down at the broken glass on the surface, and her attention settled on a large shard. She blew out her breath, allowed her gaze to soften in the glare of sunshine on the glass. She breathed into the light, willing an image to surface.

"Show me," she whispered. She didn't have the dramatic talents of pyromancy the Pythia had, but she was not without her intuitive tools. Scrying was a more subtle art, but no less effective. "Show me who was here."

The sunlight in the glass wavered, then resolved into a misty outline. An outline of a woman dressed in black with eyes as opaque as agate marbles.

Sophia sucked in her breath. "Adrienne."

The image of Adrienne opened her hands. Sophia could see they were covered in blood and dirt. She was reminded of Adrienne as a little girl, when she had cut her hands on thorns pulling up Sophia's roses.

Sophia recoiled from the image. She had to warn Tara.

Cradling Oscar, she crossed to the kitchen and punched Tara's cell phone number into the phone on the wall. No answer. The phone rang until Sophia hung up.

She had to tell the Pythia. The Pythia could reach her.

With the furry lump under her arm, Sophia headed for the door.

"You're coming with me, Oscar."

The cat tensed, and one ear poked out.

"Don't worry. The Pythia likes cats."

The cat looked at her with a dubious eye, and ducked back behind her coat.

"WHERE ARE WE?"

Tara awoke with a jerk, blinking in the molten light. Afternoon sun slanted in the car windows, warm on her face. Maggie lay with her head on her chest, looking up at her with worried brown eyes. Maggie had bad breath.

Her arm ached, thumping in time to her pulse. Her fingers felt swollen and rubbery as she flexed them. Looking down, she could see her blouse had been torn open to her shoulder, and her arm had stopped staining the make-shift bandage of Harry's tie with red. A small wound, but it still made her queasy. Maybe the radiation poisoning was still affecting her. Or perhaps it was the memory of older, more serious injuries that made her unable to stomach the sight of her own blood.

Tara remembered trying not to look at her bloody

sleeve in the house, trying to focus on Cassie. She remembered the fear piercing her chest, her quickening breath, and the smell of blood, far too close. Her mind lapsed into panic mode, remembering; it had simply shut down once she was sure Cassie was safe, that Harry was back and had it under control.

She'd lost her edge.

Thank God Harry had been there, or the gunman would have invaded the house and Cassie might have been killed.

"North to Colorado. We're going someplace safe." Harry's eyes scanned the rugged landscape before them: violet mountains, dense pine trees laced in frost, and stale, thawed, and refrozen patterns of snow clotting the needles.

Beside her, Cassie had wrapped her arms across herself, hands gripping her elbows, her fists white-knuckled. "You're going to turn me over to them, aren't you?"

"To who?" Harry's eyes flickered back at her in the rearview mirror. "Why do you think they're after you?"

"The people my father worked for. The ones he was trying to leave."

"No. This is someplace that belongs to a friend. Somewhere off the grid."

Tara struggled to sit up under a hundred pounds of wriggling dog. "Are you sure we aren't being followed?"

"We had a tail for the first half hour. He's gone, now."

Cassie rolled her eyes. "Yeah. I have yet to recover from the car sickness." Her grip on her elbows tightened. "So, where the hell's my father?" Her tone was harsh, but Tara could see the fear in her eyes.

"We don't know." Tara answered her truthfully. "There was an explosion where he worked. There's some evidence to indicate he was at the scene, but we aren't sure if he was caught in it." She paused to rummage in her bag with her good hand and brought out the watch. "Do you recognize this?"

Cassie clutched the piece of metal, running her fingers over its face. "Oh my God. That's his watch." Her face crumpled, and Tara thought she was going to dissolve. Tara reached forward to stroke her arm through the coat, and the girl didn't pull away from the comfort of her touch. Maggie wriggled around to lay her head in Cassie's lap.

"Who asked you to go to your father's house?" Tara asked, wondering why DOD hadn't better prepared her. Someone should have notified her, but the girl seemed to know nothing of her father's disappearance. The alternative explanation was that she'd fallen into a trap set up specifically for her. Tara could see why DOD would want Tara for questioning: in Magnuson's absence, maybe the girl would have information.

"Um . . . no one. My father left me a message, said he was going out of town for a while. For work, he said. He wanted me to come get Maggie as soon as I finished with exams." She rubbed at her eyes with a knuckle. "It's a long drive from Minnesota. After I got on the road, my roommate called my cell, told me that some guy from the military wanted to talk to me. I didn't call back . . . I wanted to talk to my dad, first."

"Do you remember the name? Was it Major Gabriel?"

"Yeah. I think."

"Do you know what your father was working on?" Harry asked.

Cassie stared at her pale hands combing through Maggie's fur. She was silent for a long time, and Tara could see she was weighing whether to trust them or not. Tara waited patiently. She saw Cassie's gaze flicker to Harry's bloodstained tie wrapped around Tara's arm, back to Maggie lying with her butt in Tara's lap. Tara didn't push. She waited, letting the girl work out things on her own time.

"He was working on detecting dark energy," she finally said.

"What's that?"

"Only a small percentage of the universe is made up of what we'd call conventional, visible matter and energy. Actually, only about thirty percent of the universe is made up of that." Tara could see Cassie falling back into more ease as she spoke. She was her father's daughter, and this was clearly her area of study; Tara and Harry were just undergrads to instruct. "Dark matter and dark energy are the stuff that physicists expect most of the universe is made up of. They can't be detected through electromagnetic energy, or any other means other than gravity's effect on them.

"Dark energy and dark matter are very sparse, very loosely distributed. No one's had much luck detecting either one, even some guys up in Minnesota who are trying to see if any would randomly hit some super-cooled germanium and silicone they've set up deep in an old mine. It's a theory, but it's the best one we've got. And I don't claim to understand anything near what my father was doing. I'm just a grad student. He's been working with this stuff for decades."

Tara rubbed her arm, winced. "So . . . what brought your father from Cornell to Los Alamos?"

"Particle accelerators can theoretically cause mini black holes and those might be able to draw some dark energy into their fields, just long enough for detection to take place. Cornell has a particle accelerator, but it's not powerful enough to generate that kind of effect, nor would they be really inclined to let my dad poke holes in space to see what would happen."

"I can see where that wouldn't be popular." Tara tried to imagine the damage to the annual alumni relations fundraising campaign that would be wrought by sucking freshmen into black holes. At the very least, it would probably put a dent in enrollment.

"Yeah. So the Department of Energy offered to let my dad experiment with the accelerator at Los Alamos. As I understand it, they were interested in the idea of dark energy to power some big stuff . . . aircraft carriers, subs. Dad was okay with that, and it seemed like it was going well . . . for the first couple of months, anyway.

"After he got there, he got really quiet. I got the impression they wanted to use his research for other purposes. Dad never said what they wanted, but he wasn't happy about it."

Harry's cell phone began to ring, the ringtone Blue Öyster Cult's "(Don't Fear) The Reaper." He fished it out of his pocket.

"Who's that?" Tara already knew the answer, but she wanted to know if Harry would be straight with her. Harry's ringtone evoked a Tarot card image in her mind's eye: Death. A gaunt, black-robed figure surrounded by white roses foretold the finish of one life and the beginning of a new one. She wished she could pull out the notebook and cards from her purse to explore the sudden intuitive correlation.

"Corvus." He gave a sheepish half smile. "As if it wasn't obvious by the ringtone."

"Are you going to answer it?"

He hesitated before clicking it on and pressing it to his ear. "Li."

Tara could hear the indistinguishable murmur of a transmitted voice. The squawk did not sound happy. "Yeah. We ran into some trouble. A sniper was set up on the house. Tara got grazed. Magnusson's daughter is fine. I'm taking them to a safe house."

More murmurs. Tara could imagine his questions.

"I got the sniper's plate. DCD-1397." Harry made a face. "Sir, you're breaking up. I'll report back to you ASAP." He snapped the phone shut, powered it off.

"Does Corvus know where we're going?" she asked. It was clear Harry didn't want to tell him. There was a seed of distrust between the two men, and Tara wanted to see how deep it had taken root.

Harry shook his head. "No. The fewer people who know, the better."

He turned off the curving two-lane highway onto a dirt road without a marker. Dust rose in a cloud behind the car as he guided it into a thick maze of pine trees. The switchback trail was narrow enough for only one car to pass, and Tara tried not to think about what would happen if any traffic came in the opposite direction. It seemed Harry followed a trail deep into unknown territory. Tara had no map, no knowledge of how far they were from the nearest town.

She hoped she could trust Harry. She hoped he was truly taking them someplace safe, as he promised, and there would be no men with rifles waiting for them at the end of the winding road to nowhere.

CORVUS LEANED BACK IN HIS CHAIR. THE CELL PHONE DIS-play played green light over his face as it powered down. He rubbed it carefully with an antibacterial wipe before he stowed it in his pocket. There was precious little light in this place, and each glimmer drew attention. His temporary office gleamed with metal and glass, a one-way window providing a view of workers milling in a data processing room, but there were no windows to the outside. Beyond the false window, the blue screens of computer displays glowed, compiling and sifting massive amounts of data, searching for some forgotten note or algorithm that would unlock the keys to Magnusson's research.

All they'd found so far had been garbage. The only deciphered strings of data were references to old *Star Trek* episodes. The joke was on them. So far.

"Well?" Gabriel asked him. He scraped muck from the bottom of his boot onto the bottom corner of Corvus's desk. Corvus tried not to show it bothered him, but couldn't quite control the twitch under his left eye.

"Li and Sheridan have Magnusson's daughter. She's unharmed."

Gabriel frowned, ran his hands over his buzzed short hair, and laced his fingers behind his head. The buzz cut showed the unevenness of his skull; Gabriel had clearly been in more than a few fights. "Those snipers you sent had shitty aim. Where are they now?"

"I've got enough of a cell phone signal to triangulate their current position. It'll take some time, but we should be able to narrow down the general area." Corvus stared with distaste at the crumbles of mud on the carpet and leaned back imperceptibly as Gabriel placed his grimy coffee mug on the desk. He more than suspected Gabriel did this shit just to piss him off.

"Do that." Gabriel rested the top of his boot on the edge of the desk. "And when you're done, I'll send a more properly equipped welcome party than the one you put together. I hired someone special."

Gabriel gestured through the glass beyond the door. The door opened under the gloved hand of a tall woman with hair the color of straw and eyes pale as agates. Corvus winced at the dust covering her leather coat, and his nose wrinkled. She smelled like winter and dirt and more than a bit of gunpowder.

"Corvus, meet Adrienne."

Adrienne inclined her head. "Gentlemen." She folded her hands primly behind her back and stood with one boot leaving dirt on his carpet. She had the lanky grace of a ballet dancer. "I'm pleased to be working with you."

Corvus eyed her suspiciously. "She's not military." The stance was too casual, and she moved too fluidly.

Gabriel snorted. "Of course not. I use untraceable people for dirty work. Freelancers."

Adrienne smiled icily. "I prefer the term 'outside consultant.'"

"And you charge consultants' rates." Gabriel grinned. "I'll be billing her to your department, Corvus. Look for a line item called 'Miscellaneous project tools.'"

Corvus frowned. "What can she do that our people can't?"

"I'm a tracker, Mr. Corvus." Adrienne's voice could frost metal.

Gabriel nodded. "I've worked with her before on cleanup details. Remember that independent film team that was caught in the avalanche in the Rockies last winter?"

"Those guys filming the documentary about old missile silos?"

"The very ones. Adrienne was the one we hired to find them."

"None of them were found alive. That's not a very impressive bullet point on a resume."

"Exactly." Gabriel leaned back in his chair, smiled as Corvus absorbed the meaning of the statement. He swiveled his chair to the young woman. "Adrienne, our tech department will fill you in on the subjects. You can deploy when ready."

Her pale gray eyes narrowed in anticipation. "Right away." She stepped briskly from the room, and Corvus thought she seemed a bit too eager to be under way.

Corvus cocked his head at her receding shadow. "Are you sure that—?"

"She'll get it done. She shows a lot of enthusiasm. I like enthusiasm."

"That's not what I meant. Do we have to . . ." Corvus struggled with the word. "Do we have to eliminate Li and Sheridan?"

Gabriel snorted. "You don't get the luxury of a conscience, Corvus. Not after the things I know you've done."

Corvus felt the blood drain from his face. "I don't know what you're talking about."

Gabriel picked up his coffee cup, took a swig out of it. "I did some checking up on you, Corvus. I know you're an ambitious man. Ambitious enough to make sacrifices."

"That's true of anyone in my position." Corvus steepled his fingers in front of him, pressing the tips together to keep them from shaking.

Gabriel leaned over the desk, letting coffee drip on the polished surface. Corvus's attention was fixed on the droplets.

"But you made sacrifices of people around you. Of Dr. Sheridan."

Corvus felt a twitch beginning around his left eye. He kept his face blank. "I don't know what you mean."

"You knew the Gardener had her. And you didn't act. You left her there, because it served your purposes." Gabriel smiled. "That's cold, Corvus, even for someone like me."

Corvus narrowed his eyes. "This, from a man sending snipers and assassins to shoot a twenty-three-year-old girl."

"My way is quick. It's painless. And it has to be done, for the sake of national security. It's not lying buried in a box, bleeding out, for . . . how long was it? Hours? A day?"

Corvus shut his eyes and rubbed the bridge of his nose. He tried not to imagine, but the thought of Tara entombed in a pine box, in the dark, still haunted him. The image often surfaced in his dreams, and he awoke often to the scratching of fingernails on wood.

He'd seen the pictures: the broken glass, the blood ground into the wood, the bloody footprints leading into the darkness. He kept the complete file in his desk drawer, as if he someday might act on his knowledge. He never did. The file was never too far from his hands. Or his conscience.

"If that girl lets loose her father's secrets, we could have an unaccounted-for WMD that could fall into terrorist hands. There's no comparison to that and your little scheming ambitions, Corvus."

Gabriel pushed away from the desk and stood.

"Don't take it personally, Corvus," he said jovially. "I always make sure to get something on anyone I'm working with. Keeps them loyal. Your skeletons just had more meat on their bones than most."

Corvus's knuckles whitened on the desk. "How did you get this information?"

Gabriel shrugged. "Those files you keep in your desk. I followed up on your cell phone records the night Dr. Sheridan disappeared. And . . . I have your house wired. You talk in your sleep."

He left the room, leaving Corvus in darkness with his guilt.

"I can't reach Tara."

Sophia paced the length of the Pythia's living room. A city skyline spread below the glass wall to the south, showing buildings clustered beside a river. Noon traffic clogged the streets, though they were too far up to hear the honking of horns. The gray of the day had seeped into the room, into the Pythia's oriental lamps and plush carpets, into the luxurious oil paintings of women eating apples and the deep ebony woods of furniture. Only the fire in the massive fireplace seemed to keep the chill at bay. The Pythia, draped in a scarlet caftan adorned with gold fringe, sat before the fire on a cushion. She meditatively stared into the flames, eyes round as coals.

The Pythia shrugged. "I haven't been able to reach her for years."

Sophia pressed her lips together. She didn't know if it was due to the waning of the Pythia's power, or whether it was a result of Tara's stubbornness. It didn't much matter. It was not as if Sophia could ask.

"What do you see, Pythia?" she asked instead.

"Precious little," the Pythia admitted, clasping her hands around her knees. "I see that Tara is safe. For now. And you? What do you see?"

Sophia stared at her reflection in the floor-to-ceiling window. It seemed she looked older, the worry mark on her forehead deeper, every time she saw her reflection. She focused on remaining still, on looking softly at her eyes. Her reflection pulled her in, and she allowed herself to see through it . . . through her image, through the city landscape, and even through the gray sky. Past all of it. The image of herself in the city burned away to a fine gray mist. In that misty expanse, she saw a cold darkness, spangled with snow. A crow walked along the edge of a desolate road, its tracks quickly washed over with dark and ice.

Sophia swallowed, and her hand fluttered to her throat. She'd not seen that image since Juliane had died. Like many oracles, her visions were not always literal, but required interpretation of the symbols that came bubbling up. This one was crisp and unmistakable.

"I see death," she said.

The Pythia stared into her flames. The fire intensified and licked outward, toward its mistress. Sophia had no talent for pyromancy; oracles usually only had one talent, sometimes two. It was impossible to know what the Pythia saw, if she did not say. If she saw anything at all.

The Pythia nodded sadly, and it seemed the years piled on to her, all at once. The lines around her eyes deepened, and the silver streaks in her hair seemed more abundant than they had a moment before.

"We must warn Tara," Sophia insisted. "There must be a way to tell her."

"There is. But she won't like it."

Chapter Eight

Light had begun to drain from the trees when Harry turned the ignition off. He'd parked the car at the end of a winding trail in the mountains. It was probably as far as he could have driven; the snow had deepened the further into the mountains he drove. Without snow chains, the tires had little traction and the road had become treacherous. More than once, Tara had felt the tires lock and slide beneath them on the way up.

A porch light glowed from a small, aluminum-sided trailer, casting shadows among the stripped trees and pine. Smoke curled from a metal chimney, with wood neatly stacked outside, partially covered by a tarp. A beat-up pickup truck was nestled under the shelter of a pine tree. Bending under the weight of the snow, the tree had sloughed off a small avalanche on the hood. Behind the trailer, Tara could see a makeshift shed constructed of corrugated steel. The carcasses of deer hung from the ceiling, draining onto pink patches of snow.

Cassie reached for her hand when they got out of the car. Apparently, the girl had decided to trust Tara, considering she'd taken a bullet for the girl.

"It'll be okay," Tara told her. "Harry knows what he's doing." But doubt rattled around her mind, and she did not feel the confidence of her words. For all she knew, Li could be leading them into a trap.

The trailer door opened, and a man in a flannel jacket stepped out onto the makeshift porch. He was a bit crooked with age, clean-shaven ebony face craggy and weathered as a piece of knotty wood. In his left hand, he held a flashlight. In his right, he held a shotgun. Tara reached inside her jacket and wrapped her fingers around the grips of her gun.

"Hey, old man." Harry walked around the front of the car.

"Harry! What the hell are you doing here?" The man's face split open in a smile. At that smile, bright as a lantern, Tara felt her sense of alarm drain away. She let her fingers slip from the gun.

"What else? Trying to stay out of trouble."

"If I know you, you're not succeeding."

The two men clapped each other on the back, and the older man ruffled Harry's hair as if he were a teenager.

"Tara, Cassie. This is Martin."

Maggie bounded up to him, looked up at him with adoring eyes. Martin rubbed the dog's ears. "And who's this?"

Cassie found her voice. "This is Maggie." She'd followed the dog, wound her fingers in her collar. It was clear she was clinging to the dog, her only piece of security in this mess.

Martin's eyes twinkled. "Lovely ladies, please come in from the chill." He opened the door and ushered them inside. "You, too, Maggie."

The trailer was warm, lit in an orange glow from a potbellied stove in the corner. Rust-colored shag carpeting covered the small living room floor, where a worn plaid couch dominated. A barrel-shaded, fringed lamp from the 1970s cast a pool of yellow light over cascades of spider plants and stacks of books tucked neatly along the walls. A radio played big band music at low volume, and Tara smelled bread baking.

Cassie's stomach growled audibly. She blushed, wrapping her arms around her belly to silence it.

Martin jacked a shell out of the shotgun's chamber and leaned the shotgun beside the door. He moved to the tiny galley kitchen and peeked in a Crock-Pot. "Have a seat! Dinner's almost ready."

Cassie and Tara sat down on the couch. Tara felt the day's exhaustion settling into her. The radiation sickness seemed to be wearing off, but a tiredness that made her bones and teeth ache was left in its place.

"C'mere." Harry beckoned for her to follow him. With effort, she dragged herself to her feet and followed him down the short hall of the trailer to a tiny bathroom. Harry clicked on the light, revealing a small, clean space with a plastic shower curtain decorated with fish and nonskid turquoise flower decals strewn across the base of the shower. The Formica counter with gold flecks was clear of clutter. Harry opened the medicine cabinet and rummaged about.

"Let me see that arm."

She protested. "It's fine."

"You don't get to eat until I take a look."

Reluctantly, she pulled off her ruined coat and dropped it on the shower floor. Tara extended her arm toward Harry. She looked away, knowing what he saw: Jack Frost patterns of scars disappearing under his makeshift bandage.

Harry, to his credit, didn't comment on the old wounds. He gently unwrapped the tie, peeling it from the clotted fresh injury, turning her arm over to look. Tara stifled a hiss. The bullet had sliced through the upper part of her biceps. It ached, but it had run clean through.

"I'm sorry about passing out in the car." She bit her lip, embarrassed. It wasn't a big wound, but it had triggered a series of fears that caused her to shut down, like a machine with a rock caught in its gears. She seemed to be apologizing a lot lately, and she wasn't good at it.

"Quit apologizing. You lost a lot of blood." Harry swabbed the area with cotton soaked in hydrogen peroxide, and she tried not to react.

"Does it need stitches?"

"A few."

"Great," she groaned, leaning against the countertop.

"I can take you back into town to get it done."

She shook her head, trying to shake the disinfectant

smell of hospitals free of her mind's eye. "The hospital will have to report any gunshot wounds, and that'll lead whoever is after Cassie to our doorstep. We can't let her be found. Besides," she shrugged, "I'm not winning any beauty pageants. As long as it doesn't get infected, it'll be okay."

"It needs to be sewn up, or it will," he persisted.

"We can't take that risk."

"I can do it, or you can let Martin do it. But I warn you, Martin's got early-stage Parkinson's."

Damn, he was stubborn. She looked into his serious brown eyes. "You can do it." She would trust him.

He nodded. "Okay." His quick assent made her think he had done this before.

As Harry investigated the medicine chest again for more supplies, she blurted out, "Look, I'm afraid I'm not being much use to you on this case." She let her hair fall over her face, hiding behind it.

Harry gently brushed her hair back from her face. His gaze was intense. "Stop it. You saved that girl's life and found Magnusson's laptop. I don't care if you're squeamish or claustrophobic."

She ducked her head, didn't answer.

"Hey. Look at me." He turned her chin toward him with two fingers, forcing her to look at him. "We're good, okay?"

She nodded, swallowing. She refused to admit to herself that some forgotten part of her thrilled at that small touch, his gentle concern. She buried that part deep in her chest.

Harry had located a needle, thread, a bottle of iso-propyl alcohol, and a paper cup. He deftly threaded the needle and placed it in the cup. After pouring the alcohol in, he dug around in a counter drawer, grinning when he found a tube of Orajel. He dabbed the tooth desensitizer on the edges of the wound

Tara looked away as he fished the needle and thread out of the alcohol bath.

"Ready?"

She nodded, closing her eyes as the needle slipped into her skin, dragging the shock of pain and memory with it. She concentrated on her shallow breathing rattling quick in the back of her throat. Sweat broke out on her brow, and she tried to concentrate on not passing out, locking her knees.

"Sit down." Harry let go of the needle, picked her up, and set her on the counter as carefully as if she were a broken doll. He turned back to his work, picking up the needle that bounced against her elbow.

It seemed interminable. She propped her head in her hand, bracing it with her elbow against her knee.

"Trust me," he muttered, irony dripping through his tone. "I'm from the government."

In spite of herself, she laughed.

As the night wore on, Tara slipped away. She slipped away from Li trying to crack the password on Magnusson's computer, sitting cross-legged on the floor, hunched over it with a furrow deep in his brow. She slipped away from Cassie and Martin, sitting beside each other on the couch, soaking up the remnants of their venison stew with warm, baked bread. Maggie stretched over their feet, the dog's belly warmly distended with stew. Cassie and Martin held a quiet discussion about music, and the light conversation seemed to draw a curtain of normalcy over the exhausted girl.

Tara slipped into the bathroom and showered the dried blood from her body. The hot water made her lightheaded and she sat on the plastic floor of the shower, among the turquoise flower decals. She let the water sluice over her scarred skin, over the old wounds and the new stitches Harry had set in her arm.

Such a small wound, this, in comparison to all the others, thousands of stitches making their white tracks over her skin. But this new one had jolted her awake, terrified her. Deep down, she yearned to run, yearned to flee back to her safe nest in the forest, to hide under her blanket with Oscar's purr under her chin. This morning's shooting had elicited a deep sense of panic she could feel vibrating in her bones, chasing away that soft, numb lassitude she'd wrapped herself in with the sharp, real edge of pain.

Perhaps this fear was a sign she was still alive, she thought. Perhaps her instinct to protect Cassie, her claustrophobia in the radiation suit, how her stomach twisted at the smell of her own blood . . . perhaps these were signs she was waking up to life once again. Perhaps the knight in effigy she'd seen in the Four of Swords card had cracked, letting some painful light into her prison.

She shook her head, slinging water against the shower curtain. Her mind fixed on the tiny thrill of Harry's gentle, unquestioning hands on her as he sewed her wound. Despite the sting and nausea of the procedure, some small part of her craved that touch . . .

She shied away from the thought. Harry was a practical man, the Knight of Pentacles. He didn't know the full extent of her physical and mental injuries . . . No grounded, sane man could want a broken woman. And if he knew her methods, if he knew that her way of profiling was not a strict science of probabilities and statistics, he would surely think her mad. The magic of synchronicity, the shadows of coincidence, didn't exist in his bright world. Her world and his were like Magnusson's dark and light energy: one visible, open, and the other hidden. At the root, they were polar opposites. Tara had concealed her talents with the cards for years, from everyone she'd worked with, even before she'd gotten hurt. Especially Corvus.

She scrubbed her hair, willing thoughts of Harry to be rinsed from her mind. Besides, he was one of Corvus's men, no matter how hard he seemed to try to shake off Corvus's leash. As such, he could not be entirely trusted.

Corvus. Her wet brow wrinkled at the thought of seeing him again. After all this time, he still elicited a gut sense of distrust, an unreasoning reaction. But it remained. And Tara, if nothing else, had learned to believe her feelings.

Tara pulled herself from the bottom of the shower, bracing herself on the wall against a wave of dizziness, and reached for a towel and clothes. Martin had generously given her some of his clothes: a blue flannel shirt, a T-shirt, thick socks, a pair of jeans, and a belt.

"I apologize for not having more feminine clothes at hand, Miss Tara," Martin had said over her protestations at his generosity. "But the lady of the house is a bluebird. She lives in a little nest in the branches of that tree." He pointed through the living room window to a lush pine tree. When he pointed, Tara saw his hand shake slightly. "And I'm afraid she's an unrepentant nudist."

Tara had laughed. She'd found herself taking an immediate liking to Martin, to the old man's concern for their basic needs: food, clothing, shelter. He asked no questions and asked for nothing in return.

"Thank you for your hospitality," she'd said. "Having strangers on your doorstep in the middle of the night is—"

"Is no trouble at all," he finished, waving away her concerns. "Harry is like a son to me. His friends are my family, too."

"How long have you known Harry?"

Martin's eyes crinkled. "I've known Harry since he was a tadpole. His mother was killed in a car accident. No father around. Very sad."

Tara had glanced down the hall at the intense man perched over the computer, his lips working silently over combinations of passwords, lost in his own world. She tried to imagine what he would have been like as a child.

"Harry came to live with me when he was nine. Of course, at that time, we lived in Chicago. He used to play street hockey with the neighbor boy, Tom, who lived across the street . . . Harry's been like a son to me."

Tara had looked at Harry, a bubble of sympathy swelling in her throat. Though Tara had lost her mother as an adult, Harry had barely known his. But it was clear he'd made Martin proud.

She dressed quickly in Martin's clothes. They were too big for her, but she managed to cinch the waist of the pants tightly with the belt. Conscious of the steam pulsing against her skin, she cracked the tiny sliding window open an inch. The cold air against her face braced her, seemed to cleanse her lungs of doubt, fused her breath with clarity.

Back to work.

She wiped her wet footprints from the floor, checked to make sure the door was locked. Unzipping her purse, she took out her cards and little notebook, thankful she hadn't left them with her luggage at the motel. Experience had taught her to keep them close at hand while working a case.

Sitting cross-legged on the linoleum, she spread out her mother's scarf. She wouldn't ordinarily do a reading on a bathroom floor, but she'd done readings in stranger places. Serious questions called for serious measures, and as long as she treated the space and the cards respectfully, she'd always gotten good results. Closing her eyes, she focused on the investigation and shuffled the cards.

Where do we go from here? She exhaled, breathing the question to the universe. In her mind's eye, she imagined it leaving through the open window into the darkness.

She drew nine cards, laying them facedown on the scarf in three rows of three cards, starting from the top: left, center, right, and repeating twice more. This was a spread she'd used in the past to shed light on decisions. Though the decisions to be made in this investigation were wide-open, this felt like the best spread to use. Tara always used the layout that first flashed before her mind's eye, even if she made one up on the spot.

The topmost row represented past influences on her question. She flipped the cards over, one by one.

The first image showed a skeleton robed in black riding a white horse, surrounded by white roses, trampling corpses in its wake: Death. This card rarely indicated a physical death, but was a card of endings and transformations. Involuntarily, her mind replayed the "(Don't Fear) The Reaper" ringtone from Harry's cell phone, and she thought of Corvus. This figure from a past cycle had reappeared in her life, in a powerful way.

Tara had never thought of Corvus as being an agent of change. But the image of Death's horse walking over the pale corpses resonated with her. Corvus would walk over anyone to achieve his ends. Whatever his influence on her past, he clearly had influence on the current situation. Tara made a note of this card and its position in her notebook, and moved to the second card.

The Page of Swords, reversed. A lithe figure held a sword raised, watchfully surveying a bleak landscape. Traditionally, the Page represented spying and covert actions. Reversed, it suggested a nasty surprise and deviousness. As the card was upside down, the Page's sword was pointing down at Tara. She imagined the rifle that must have been concealed beneath the shooter's coat as he fled Magnusson's house. Her eyes roved over the Page's face. In Tara's deck, the pages were all depicted as women. Pages were missing from the modern playing card deck.

Insignificant to modern games. But Tara sensed feminine power strongly from this card, and it confused her. The only conclusion she could draw was that the card signified more than one concept in the reading, that perhaps there was another player in the game: a woman. A dangerous woman.

She turned over the last card in the past events row. The King of Wands, reversed, showed an armored man holding a flaming staff, charging forward on a black horse. Only his eyes were visible under the helmet. She thought of the difficulty in reading Gabriel's body language when she met him yesterday, owing to the obscuration of the radiation suit. Reversed, the King of Wands signaled a severe, aggressive, or overbearing man. It warned of danger, a dispute with a powerful man.

Tara took in the whole row: Death on the white horse paralleled the King of Wands on his black mount. They were mirror images, and there were no coincidences in the Tarot. Between them lay the shooter, the Page. Pages were always messengers, and acted at the behest of other powers. Deep in her chest, she recognized their proximity, knew all three were in league with one another.

In her notebook, she jotted down the layout, with the note *Corvus + shooter + Gabriel.*

She turned her attention to the second row, representing the present situation, flipping the card below the Death card over. The Two of Cups depicted a man and a woman holding a chalice, gazing into each other's eyes. A winged lion spirit rose from the chalice with the symbol of the caduceus, the traditional physician's symbol of healing.

The card signified the balance of opposites, a partnership or friendship, possibly the early stages of a relationship.

She thought about Li. So far, it had proved a workable, if rocky, partnership. The card spoke of trust, reliance. Her eyes flickered up to the nearby Death card. This Two of Cups felt shadowed by Corvus's presence. She had been Corvus's partner, once upon a time.

Still, she made the conscious decision to trust Harry. Perhaps their divergent perspectives would prove to be an asset. She deliberately chose to ignore the skip her heartbeat had made when she first saw the card. Anything more than a professional relationship was out of the question. Though Harry was an attractive man, she knew, deep down, she had nothing to offer him.

The card beside it, still in the present, was the Hermit. Tara's feeling of trust from the Two of Cups carried over to the Hermit. She let her mind rove over the landscape of the card: an old man, standing before sunset-drenched mountains, holding a staff and a lantern that captured a star. It represented solitude, reflection. She thought of Martin on the steps of his trailer, holding his flashlight and his shotgun. This card was placed beside the partnership card she associated with Harry. Not surprising.

The third card in the present, the Nine of Swords, depicted a sleepless woman, sitting up in bed and holding her head in her hands, weeping. Above her hung the threat of nine sharp swords. This was the card of nightmares, representing anxiety, the despair of inner doubts. The card spoke of illusory fears.

Tara thought of her own sleeplessness, the disturbing

dreams of darkness and enclosed places that came to her in slivers in the night. These nightmares were based in reality, her mind stubbornly insisted. Still, some part of her wished they could be sent away as easily as an illusion.

The last row of three cards represented the future, what could come to pass if events were allowed to unfold without interference. Tara knew no future foretold by the Tarot was immutable or ever set in stone. Rather, it was a possibility that could be embraced, or, with enough determination, deflected. But until resolved, similar situations would often arise, again and again.

She turned over the Moon, the card of illusion. It showed a serene moon goddess in a dark sky, flanked by two pillars representing two separate paths, a black pillar and a white one. A wolf howled at the full moon, and a crayfish emerged from the sea to behold it.

The Moon suggested intuition, dreams, illusion, fluctuation; the need to discern that which is hidden. It whispered of secrets, hidden knowledge. Tara sensed the investigation was moving toward a precarious time, and frowned.

The next card showed a man driving a chariot pulled by a black horse and a white horse. The fierce horses pulled in opposite directions. Her attention turned back to the Death and King of Wands cards, which made a triangle with this card and mirrored the horses. The Chariot was a card of conflict, struggle, forward movement. She felt Corvus and Gabriel would be relentless in their pursuit.

She turned over the last card, revealing the Nine of Wands. The card pictured wounded, despairing soldiers leaning on their staffs. The card encouraged determination, perseverance in the face of larger forces. Tara rested her chin on her hand. This was the correct attitude to assume in this situation, she was convinced.

She scribbled notes in her book, eying the overall spread. Harry, Cassie, and Tara would not be able to remain here; she could feel the struggle would move relentlessly forward. They would have to find a better way to protect Cassie.

Troubled, she sought more clarification. Thinking on how to protect the girl, she pulled one more card from the deck.

The Seven of Swords depicted a man stealthily making off with five swords slung over his shoulder, leaving two behind stuck in the earth. The man's expression was surreptitious as he fled into the darkness. The card suggested the need for guile, evasion, and deception. The swords left behind caught Cassie's attention . . . What could they mean? What had been left behind? Her thoughts immediately jumped to Magnusson's computer. What had he left behind for Cassie, locked in the secrecy of his passwords?

A knock rang on the door. Tara jumped, reflexively covering her cards with her hands.

"Hey, you okay in there?" Harry's voice, sounding very close through the thin metal.

"I'll be right out," she called, gathering up her cards and tucking them into her bag.

They'd given her much to reflect on. She didn't think Harry would like those ideas, at all . . . to say nothing of where they'd come from.

Chapter **Nine**

I DIDN'T SAY thank you." Cassie pulled the covers of Martin's bed up under her chin. Dressed in Martin's too-big flannels, with the makeup washed from her face, Cassie looked very much like a small child. "Thanks."

"You're welcome." Tara crawled in the other side of the bed, clicked out the bedside light. She could hear Martin snoring on the living room couch. He'd insisted Harry take the second futon in the small second bedroom, declaring he slept better on the couch. When Harry had protested the overwhelming hospitality, Martin had threatened to cut off the home-baked bread.

A dog collar jingled as Maggie launched herself into bed, snooted, and circled. Dog paws poked ribs, and a cold nose sniffed over exposed faces.

"Oof." Tara rolled over to keep her injured arm out of the way.

"Maggie, lie down." Cassie ordered. The dog settled down at the foot of the bed across the women's feet, giving an audible sigh.

Silence stretched out, like an unraveling string. Cassie was first to seize it at the frayed ends. "Do you think my dad's alive?" Her voice was very small, as if voicing a doubt could make the unthinkable come to pass.

Tara looked up at the shadowed ceiling, her hands folded over her stomach. Her intuition was silent, not nudging her one way or the other. "Honestly, I don't know. But I can promise you that Harry and I will do our best to find him. We'll do whatever it takes, okay?"

"I can't lose my dad. I just *can't*." Cassie let out a shaking breath. "He's all I have."

Tara turned over in bed to look at her. The girl's fingers gnawed at the edge of the blankets.

"I know that it's almost unfathomable . . . to imagine that the one constant in your life could disappear. But you're going to get through this."

"You don't know what it's like," Cassie whispered. "It's like he was there, and now he's not. It's like there's a hole in space."

"I *do* know. I lost my mother last year."

"I'm sorry. I didn't . . ."

Tara frowned. "It was a shock to me, too, having her missing all of a sudden. One day she was there, all was normal. The next, she wasn't, and everything had gone to hell."

"What happened?"

"Cancer. I didn't know about it . . . She didn't tell me.

I was wrapped up in some of my own problems. I think I'd expected that she'd always be there, that she'd always come to my rescue . . ." Tara's voice trailed off. "It makes me angry to think it could have been different."

"How?"

"She . . . didn't continue medical treatment. She abandoned it. I think she didn't tell me because I would have tried to force her into it. Instead, she just let it eat away at her." Tara's vision blurred, and the darkness became softer. "She told an old friend of hers, but she didn't tell me." Tara's mouth tightened. She hadn't forgiven Sophia and the Pythia for standing by and doing nothing, and she probably never would.

"You still sound angry at your mom."

Tara paused, startled. "Yes. I guess I am. She always expected me to fight, to survive . . . but when it was her turn, she just . . . she just laid down and died." She scubbed her soft flannel sleeve over her eyes, changed the subject of the conversation. "But my mother is not your father. Your father is a fighter."

"I'm afraid . . . I'm afraid my dad is in far over his head. I mean . . . he's a professor. What the hell is he doing out here, taking orders from men with guns?" Cassie's tone burned bright with anger. Perhaps Tara's admission of her own fury gave the girl permission to voice what bubbled through her thoughts. "How could he leave me alone like this?"

"He didn't leave you alone. He left you with clues," Tara insisted. "He knew you'd come, and he left his laptop in a place where only you would find it."

"But I don't know the password," Cassie moaned. "It's about as useless as a big, light-up brick!" Her fingers picked at the satin binding of the blanket. "I'm supposed to have a photographic memory," she muttered. "I can remember what I had for breakfast three years ago on this day, and what's been in every load of laundry I've ever done. I can even remember all the names of the dolls I had when I was three. But what good is all that . . . data . . . if I can't find the answer to something this important?"

"It'll come to you," Tara said with certainty. "He wouldn't have left you a puzzle you couldn't figure your way out of." The Moon card suggested hidden knowledge, but she had faith in Cassie's ability to triumph over those. Tara had associated Cassie with the Star card in her mind, and all the success and hope it encompassed.

"Hnh. You're much more confident in him than I am."

"Tell me about him." Tara rolled onto her back and stared at the fuzzy ceiling, thinking about the Magician Tarot card, bringing matter from spirit in his own secret alchemy. "I've got a profile of him in my head, but it feels thin."

Cassie was silent for a moment. "What do you want to know?"

"Anything that jumps to mind. What kind of sense of humor does he have? What does he do in his free time? Does he wrap his spaghetti around his fork, or does he cut it?"

She could see Cassie smiling in the dark. "He cuts his spaghetti. He thinks rolling it is an impractical affectation."

"Cuts to the chase, does he?"

"Yup. He also licks the filling out of Oreos and puts the chocolate wafers back in the bag for later."

"Impatient . . . achievement-oriented . . . and likes to give others surprises?"

"You could say that." Cassie's grin faded. "You know, I always wanted him to be proud of me. I don't think I ever really grew out of that. You know how some kids go through a rebellious phase?"

Tara resisted the urge to comment on the blue-streaked hair. "Sure. I went through a phase where I shocked my hippie mom by telling her I was going to grow up and become a cop."

"Yeah. Like that. Only I never did that."

"You never rebelled? No sneaking out of your bedroom window to chase boys or smoking on the back porch at three AM, freezing your ass off in the dead of winter?"

"Nope. Never did it. I guess I really . . . I really craved Dad's approval when I was younger. Got straight As. Got good scholarships. Went to grad school in his field." She flipped her hair between her fingers, voiced Tara's thought. "He hasn't seen the hair yet. Or know about the art-school boyfriend." Cassie's voice softened. "I think I never did grow out of wanting his approval."

Tara reached over and squeezed the girl's hand.

"I'd give anything for it now."

"I know." A parent's blessing could be a powerful talisman, invisible until the caster was gone. Its power was never really felt until then, when you had to pick up the pieces to carry on the spell.

• • • •

"Fight."

Tara could smell blood and earth, copper and clay. She could hear her breath moving in this small space, surrounding her. She didn't know which she'd run out of first: air or blood. She shivered from shock, cold, her clothes sticking to the slash wounds crisscrossing her body. The darkness overwhelmed her. If she screamed, no one would hear.

She struggled to remove her belt, ripping off the buckle. She awkwardly tied it in a tourniquet around the fast-seeping wound in her thigh, gripped the buckle in her slick, sticky hands.

Tara dug the sharp edge of it into the wood above her, working it back and forth, hearing it splinter, feeling dirt trickle into her face.

She would not lay down and die here, would not surrender to the darkness. Her mother had raised her to be a fighter, and she was going to fight until she saw daylight.

Tara woke with a jerk, hands clawing the air, breath shallow in her throat. She lurched upright, wanting to seize the feeling of being awake. Her arm burned. She could see the black tracks of the stitches in the dark, seeming to twist against her pale skin, reminding her of what it was like to feel precious fluid seeping through her skin. At her feet, Maggie stirred. Beside her, Cassie slept peacefully, fingers wound tightly in the pillow.

It was too close in here. The ceiling felt only a finger's breadth from her nose, and the walls were near enough to touch. The covers were too thick, suffocating, and she threw them off.

She slipped out of bed and felt around for her clothes. Tara climbed into the old jeans, buttoned a flannel shirt over Martin's T-shirt. Grasping her shoes and her ripped coat, she tiptoed through the half-open bedroom door and down the hall.

Martin snored softly on the plaid couch, his hands folded over his chest. He'd kicked the blanket off his bare feet to feel the warmth in the fading embers of the potbellied stove.

She carefully disengaged the safety chain, opened the door, and stepped out onto the little porch.

Her breath steamed in the darkness. Stars spilled out above her in a sweep of light, marking the Milky Way's path across the sky. The road to heaven, she thought, craning her neck to follow it from horizon to horizon.

Tara crept down the porch steps, careful not to make a sound, and wrapped her arms around her elbows. She always associated the open sky with freedom, and smiled. Her mind's eye traced the familiar constellations: Canis Major, the dog, lifting his head to bark at the moon hidden below the horizon; Auriga, the charioteer, ascended high in the sky; Gemini, the twins, nearly setting out of sight.

These pictures in the sky reminded her of the cards she'd drawn earlier in the evening: the Moon, bayed at by the dog; the Chariot; and the Two of Cups. Her subconscious was nagging her to reveal the hidden information quickly, before . . .

Her brow wrinkled, and she fixed on a moving star, across the chest of Auriga. It was too fast to be a satellite, and no distinctly colored left and right lights, as she'd expect on a plane. A forward light flashed in front of a steady taillight.

The screen door squeaked behind her.

"What is it?" Harry padded down the steps, yawning. His hair was mussed from sleep in spikes, and he wore the sleeping bag draped over his shoulders.

Tara pointed up at the sky, and he squinted after her hand. Sleep cleared from his eyes as he focused on the distant light. Another one emerged, traveling at right angles to it.

"Helicopters, flying in a search grid," he muttered grimly.

"I take it that's not the Forest Service looking for lost hikers."

"No. It's not." His mouth was pressed in a grim slash. "They're looking for us."

Tara's heart dropped, and she sat down on the porch steps. "How long until they find us?"

"They can't see much at night. They're just looking for lights, now." Harry sat down beside her. "A couple of days, maybe. Depends on if they're just looking from the air or on the ground, too."

"Won't they know your . . . Martin is here?"

Harry shook his head. "I doubt it. Pops—Martin—lives pretty well off the grid. He's got his own natural gas and water wells. I'm not sure the electricity is legal, but I don't want to know." He smiled sheepishly.

"Sounds much different from growing up in Chicago."

"It is. Pops always hated the noise, the traffic. He saved up his whole life for this, for the peace and quiet." Harry smiled. "We used to come out this way summers, on vacation. He fell in love with it. So did I."

"I understand, I think." Tara stared up at the stars. "I have a little place tucked away in the woods, too. In Tennessee. That's where I was until I was called in on this case."

"Pondering the thoughts of Walden?"

"Sometimes. It's a good place for forgetting."

"An oubliette."

Tara paused, thinking on what Sophia had said, of the Four of Swords, the knight lying in effigy in a church. Was it a dungeon or a haven? She wrapped her arms tighter around herself, shivered. "Yes," she admitted. "It's a good place to forget myself."

"You're cold." Harry opened the edge of the sleeping bag, like a wing. "C'mon. I won't bite. Hell, Martin would throw me out for displaying bad manners if I did."

Tentatively, Tara scooted over and let Harry drape the edge of the sleeping bag over her shoulders. Harry's shoulder was warm, and she tucked her cold fingers between her knees.

"Thanks."

"You're welcome."

"We're going to have to figure out how to hide Cassie, at least until we figure out what's on that computer and can hopefully use it as leverage."

"Yeah." Harry rubbed the bridge of his nose with his fingers. "Magnusson has some impressive security on that laptop. I've been trying to brute-force my way through it, but the password's too strong. I would need a data forensics lab to bypass the hardware to even try to get at it. Even then, there's some risk to the data. God knows what booby traps he's got programmed in there."

"Magnusson wanted Cassie to find it. That means that, somehow, she knows the password. We just have to get to it."

"Got any profiler magic that can do that?"

Tara shrugged. "I could put her under hypnosis."

Harry looked sidelong at her. Skepticism was written all over his face. "Really? You can do that?"

"I am still licensed to practice psychology in two states."

"I mean . . . does that really work?"

"It can't hurt, Harry. If she agrees to it, there's no harm to be done. She's got that information in there somewhere."

Harry shook his head. "Honestly, I have no idea how you do what it is you do . . . how you pull evidence out of thin air . . . the watch, the computer, saving Cassie's life."

Tara drew away a bit. "I can't really explain it." She *wouldn't* explain it. Harry's cynicism ran too deep.

"Try me."

She looked into his face, at the earnest expression in his almond eyes. She wanted to trust him, but he didn't belong in her irrational world.

"It's not a scientific process. It's not about assembling profiles based on statistical likelihoods . . . at least, it's not that way for me. Are you familiar with synchronicity?"

Harry frowned. "That's from Jung. The idea of totally unrelated events having meaningful coincidences."

"Yes. Jung believed there was an undercurrent . . .

a collective unconscious . . . of archetypes and symbols underpinning human experience. Sometimes, symbols bubble up in the mind that we correlate to our own lives in ways we ascribe meaning to. I give my mind permission to follow those symbols, to make intuitive connections over small things other people might overlook."

"So . . . it's about observation?"

"Partially. The underlying idea is that everything and everyone are connected in unseen ways. Sure, the observer has to be alert for those happenings and symbols, but there's also an element of imagination involved to make the connections, the associations between disparate things."

Harry was silent for a moment, digesting. Tara had to give him credit for trying. This was the closest she'd come to explaining her methods to anyone she'd worked with. Deep down, she wanted him to understand, and wanted him to respect her. That desire for approval startled her. Out here, in the remote cold, under the stars, under the weight of exhaustion . . . anything seemed possible.

She tried again. "We're used to thinking of the mind as a machine that works linearly, as a train that moves forward along a single track: from point A, to B, to C . . . and also in reverse, from C, to B, to A. But the mind can jump tracks, if you let it, move forward from A to M and parallel to 3.

"One of Jung's favorite quotes on synchronicity came from Lewis Carroll's *Through the Looking-Glass*. The White Queen tells Alice, 'It's a poor sort of memory that only works backwards.'"

"So you're following thoughts down whichever rabbit holes strike you?" he asked.

"Pretty much," she admitted sheepishly. "I warned you it wasn't a scientific process."

"You get good results. I'm a bottom-line kind of guy. I don't know that I agree with your line of thinking, but it's hard to argue with the results, however you get them."

Tara lapsed into silence, changed the subject. "Have you spoken to Corvus?"

Harry shook his head. "No, and I won't. There's too much potential for eavesdropping."

Tara framed her thought carefully before she spoke it aloud. "I don't think Corvus is being entirely forthcoming."

His eyes narrowed. "What do you mean?"

"I think he's tied to Gabriel. I don't know who's pulling whose strings . . . but those two are on the same side."

"That's a pretty serious assumption." Harry's jaw hardened. "Are you prepared to back it up?"

She spread her hands under the sleeping bag, a gesture of resignation. "No. I can't prove it. But I'm certain of it."

"Corvus has an impeccable record. He's untouchable." Harry ran his hands over his spiky, sleep-tousled hair. She could hear the resistance in his voice. He didn't believe her. Not yet. "Why would he stick his neck out, and for what?"

She wrapped her arms around her knees, feeling a stab of worry for Harry. "I know, and I can't explain. Just be careful of him."

"I'm always careful of Corvus. He's the master of the poison pen, transferring staff to the hinterlands of hell." He gave a lopsided half smile. It was charming, and something in Tara's chest thrilled to see it. "I quake in fear of his furious penmanship."

"That's not what I meant." She shook her head. "Corvus can be very dangerous."

"Hey." Harry caught her chin, turning her face back to him. "I know you've got your reasons for distrusting the Division. I think you're allowing your feelings to color your view."

"That's what I do," she said softly. "Most of the time."

His touch was light as if he were handling glass, giving her every opportunity to turn away, to escape. His hand slipped over her jaw, behind her neck. But she stayed, rooted in place, feeling the warmth of his fingers slowly winding in her hair. Her heart hammered as he gently pulled her face toward his and brushed his lips against hers.

She drank the kiss in, feeling the warmth creeping through her body. She could feel it sinking into her body from his chest, his arm lightly curving around her shoulders and wrapping her in the sleeping bag that smelled like cedar and wood smoke.

A yip and a scrape from the door of the trailer made her jump. Harry drew back, rolled his eyes at the door.

"Maggie."

A pathetic *grrrmmmmrr* issued from the other side of the wall.

He disentangled himself from the sleeping bag, offered her a hand to her feet. He opened the door and the dog bounded out, collar jingling, sniffing for the perfect doggie place to squat.

Tara glanced at Harry, feeling suddenly shy and more than a little awkward. Harry stood before her, looking at his bare feet, hands in his pockets. Watching him stand before her in his T-shirt and jeans, Tara had the sudden urge to wrap her arms around him, listen to his heart beat in his chest. She suspected that sound would drive away any nightmares. But she kept her hands tangled in the sleeping bag, frozen.

He leaned over, smiled a beautiful white smile that shone in the dark, and kissed her on the forehead.

"Sweet dreams."

She wished that Harry had the power to make those words true.

Above, in darkness, Adrienne watched, with her eyes closed.

The *thump-thump-thump* of the helicopter blades drowned out all sound, except for the voices transmitted by the pilot back to base through the electronic headsets. The green and red lights on the instrument panels were the only illumination. Cold wind ripped through the seams of the helicopter, making frost on the inside of the glass the copilot kept scraping away. The pitch and yaw of the helicopter as it turned rattled a pen on the floor of the compartment back and forth. Every few minutes, it would roll back against Adrienne's boots. The MH-6, nicknamed the Little Bird, was designed to be a light observation helicopter, the kind used in urban police departments to track speeders in short bursts. It wasn't built for comfort on long, tedious missions.

In the back of the helo, Adrienne tuned those distractions out. She listened only to the sound of her own breath and focused on the tension of the chain suspending the crystal pendulum from a ring on her middle finger. In the darkness, the quartz crystal shone like a star. The helicopter's unsettling turns and changes in altitude made using the pendulum difficult; Adrienne found it hard to separate that motion from the subtle tug of the crystal, seeking her target. Geomancers used elements of earth to accomplish their divinations, and the pendulum was one of her favorite tools. She'd spoken to stones and crystals since she was a little girl. They weren't like people. Stones always told the truth. She could trust the shifts in their subtle energy, rely upon what they told her without question or guessing at ulterior motives.

But this far from the ground, the crystal's power was shaky; like a magnet pulled too far from metal, its pull was weak and thready. Adrienne listened to it, through the ring and the chain and the veins in the crystal, searching for any sign that would lead her to her quarry.

Under her hand, the crystal twitched for a moment. Adrienne concentrated on the pull, her breath fogging the plastic visor of her helmet.

"West," she told the pilot through the microphone. Echoing in her helmet, her voice seemed tinny and mechanical.

The pilot looked back at her. Adrienne knew he couldn't fully see what she was doing in the back of the cockpit, but he'd been ordered to do what she told him to.

"We haven't completed the A6 part of the grid . . ." the

copilot began. The night vision display before him cast green shadows on his helmet.

"West," she told him, her staticky voice crackling like the frost on the windshield. "We go west."

"Yes, ma'am."

The pilot leaned to the left, and the Little Bird flew away into the blackness.

Chapter **Ten**

"Take slow, regular breaths. In . . . out . . . in . . . out . . ."
Tara sat on the bed beside Cassie, her back against
the wall. The bedroom was dim, the blinds drawn against
the bright morning sun. The girl seemed small, lost inside
Martin's too-big clothes, stretched out under the yellow
chenille bedspread with the warm sunlight streaming in.
She lay with her hands tightly folded on her stomach, not
seeming to be sure what to do with them. Tara could see
her resisting the effort to pick at her chipped blue nail polish. Though Cassie had agreed to try hypnosis to see if her
father's password was rattling around somewhere in her
head, there was no guarantee it would work. Tara was
excited to imagine what might be lodged in Cassie's photographic memory. All the data was in the girl's head, she
was convinced. They just needed a road map to get there.
A good subject had to be hypnotically suggestible . . . She

had to be willing not to work against Tara's verbal directions.

"I want you to roll your eyes upward, as far as you comfortably can, toward the wall." This was the quickest, most shorthand test Tara could administer to gauge suggestibility, the Hypnotic Induction Profile. The less of the iris and cornea that could be seen, the better.

Cassie complied, rolling her eyes back so only a small sliver of her blue eyes showed beneath her lashes.

"Very good. You can relax now, and close your eyes."

"You're not going to make me do the chicken dance, are you? They do that at the county fair," Cassie murmured.

"I can't make you do anything. Your mad dancing skills are safe. All we're going to do is look back through some of your memories and see if there's anything that jumps out at you. It will feel like daydreaming, and you'll be aware of everything you and I say."

"Okay." Cassie settled in, stopped fidgeting. "As long as there will be no dancing."

"No dancing, I promise. I'll be right here with you, the whole time. There's nothing to be afraid of."

Tara glanced at the closed door. Shadows moved beneath it and the floor creaked as someone walked down the narrow hallway. She'd told Martin and Harry not to make Cassie self-conscious by watching the process, but it seemed as if curiosity was getting the better of them. Voices carried in the trailer; she knew the door didn't block any significant sound from the living area, but she wanted to give Cassie the illusion of privacy. And Tara wanted to work without Harry's skeptical eyes on them. Never mind the distraction . . . Tara was glad Cassie's eyes were closed and she didn't see the blush that crawled over Tara's cheeks at the thought.

"Close your eyes and continue to follow your breath." Tara looked down in her lap at the notebook. The blank page intimidated her, and she swallowed. Much time had passed since she'd put anyone under hypnosis. She used to do it quite often for crime victims and witnesses, to enhance the recall of details, but that seemed a lifetime ago.

"Slow, regular breaths. In . . . out . . . in . . . out . . . Good."

Cassie's breathing became less self-conscious, evened out to a soft roll. Tara guided her through a simple relaxation exercise, alternately tensing and relaxing the muscles from her feet all the way to her head. As Tara continued to speak, Cassie's breathing shallowed, flattened, and barely seemed to move her chest. From the living room, Tara heard a snatch of a snore. Martin had been eavesdropping. She smiled. She wasn't as rusty as she'd thought.

"Imagine you and I are walking down a well-lit staircase, down into the vault of your memory. With each step, you become more relaxed, softer, more at ease. Ten . . . imagine your thoughts softening. Nine . . . slow, deep breaths. Eight . . . letting go of worry. Seven . . . letting go of doubt. Six . . . breathing out any fear. Five . . . feeling deeply relaxed and open.

"Four.

"Three.

"Two.

"One." Tara could see, behind the girl's eyelids, her eyes twitching. Good. She was in a light hypnotic trance. "We're standing at the bottom level of the staircase, in a room lined with shelves upon shelves of books, reaching to the ceiling, extending down limitless hallways. Sunshine shines in through tall windows, illuminating every volume.

"This is where all your memories are kept. Nothing is ever lost, no detail too small to be recorded. Everything is here. All your memories are catalogued in perfect order. All you need to do is to think of a subject that interests you, and all your memory about that subject will be at your fingertips. You are in complete control of your mind, and have perfect access to your memory.

"Now, think of your father. Develop a fully dimensional image of him in your mind: the way he walks, talks, smells, and looks. Can you see him?"

"Yes." Cassie's voice was fuzzy and distant.

"Very good. Now, let him guide us through your memory, to the book on the shelf containing information on secrets he may have told you or whereabouts of hidden knowledge. When you're ready, follow him to the bookshelves, and tell me what you see and read."

"He's asking me to follow him. He's holding that dumb coffee mug I got him when I was ten."

"The one that says *#1 Dad*?" Tara remembered seeing it in his office.

"Yes. He's drinking some tea that smells like shit. Earl Gray, I think."

"Go ahead and follow him. I'm right behind you."

"I'm walking down a corridor, books everywhere . . . Christ, there's even my old coloring books   Wait He's pointing to one from a top shelf."

"Good. Reach up for the book and take it down."

"I have it."

"Tell me what it's like. What color is it? Is it heavy or light?"

"It's blue, paperback, very light."

"Open it and tell me what's inside."

Tara was very still, waiting. Some hypnotized subjects had a hard time reading in their visualizations. She thought Cassie, being an intellectual, could handle it. But she still leaned slightly forward on the bed to watch the girl's eyes move from left to right under her eyelids.

"It's his grocery lists. Coffee, beans, ketchup . . . how can he live on stuff like this?" Cassie's nose wrinkled slightly in her trance. "Ugh. What the hell does he do with parsnips?"

"Go ahead and put it back on the shelf. Ask him to show you another book."

"Okay." Cassie fell silent for a moment. "He's pointing to another book."

"Describe it."

"This one's heavy. It's navy blue, and the binding's shot . . . I remember this book. He gave it to me when I was a kid and he took me stargazing."

Tara remembered the first photo she'd seen of Magnusson, posing with his daughter before the radio telescope in Hawaii. "Tell me about that."

"He took me along on all his conference trips. We'd sleep all day, and he would go to the observatories at night. I'd read, play outside, peer through the telescopes. Sometimes, I'd fall asleep and wake up in the back of the car on the way home."

"When did he give you this book?"

"It came from a used bookshop in Hawaii. It was illustrated, showed all the constellations and the legends behind them. We sat outside and Dad showed me the constellations in the sky and, by flashlight, in the book."

Tara thought of the Star Tarot card, how often it had shown up in her readings. She felt they were getting close. "Your father named you after a constellation?"

"Yes, after Cassiopeia. The beautiful queen, seated on her throne. I will never be as beautiful as the picture in the book. When I was a little girl, I imagined she was my mother, watching from the sky."

"What did he tell you about Cassiopeia?"

"He said Cassiopeia was very proud of her beautiful daughter. He pointed up at the stars and told me that all I ever needed to know was in Cassiopeia's heart. It sounded really lame at the time, and I told him that. But it was really kind of sweet."

Tara paused, intuition humming, pen poised above the paper. She reached behind her, noiselessly reaching into her bag slung over the headboard for her Tarot cards. She flipped through the deck, searching for the image Cassie had painted in her mind, the image of the seated queen.

A-ha. The Empress. The Tarot card showed a beautiful woman seated on a throne, holding a scepter, and looking serenely out on the world. Her loose robes draped over the curve of her pregnant belly, symbolizing motherhood and fertility. At her breast dangled a pendant, and Tara looked very closely to make it out. It was in the shape of a star. She tucked the cards back into her purse, and her thoughts buzzed with excitement. She was very close to the answer; she felt it.

"Please thank your memory of your father for the assistance, Cassie. You've done very well." She thought she saw a tear forming in Cassie's eye.

"Wait. There's someone else here," Cassie said.

Tara's brow wrinkled. She tucked the card into the bottom of the deck. "Tell me."

"It's not someone I know."

"Describe the person." This wasn't part of the script. She wondered where Cassie's mind was taking them.

"She's short, shorter than me. Black hair, black eyes. She's wearing a long dress, but no shoes."

"What's she doing?"

"She's just standing, watching us. She's smiling."

Dread washed over Tara. "Ask her . . ." She steadied her voice. "Ask her what her name is."

Cassie paused. "She says her name is Pythia."

Tara leaned protectively over Cassie, touched the girl's wrist. Her skin was fever-hot. There was no way Cassie could know about the Pythia. Was there? Was the Pythia powerful enough to project herself into the girl's trance? Tara kept her voice low and even. "It's time to come back now."

"Not yet." The girl's voice changed in timbre, lowering, and an accent flickered through her words. "We're not finished here."

Tara recoiled. She knew that voice. "Pythia."

Cassie's lips curved upward. But it wasn't her smile. It was the voluptuous smile of the Pythia. "I've been wanting to talk with you."

"I've got nothing to say to you. Let go of Cassie."

"Then listen instead." The Pythia's voice was harsh. "There's someone coming for you."

"There are a lot of people after us. That's not news."

"Not just men after the girl. One of us. After you."

Tara's brows drew together. "Who? Why?"

"Adrienne. She wants what you have."

Tara shook her head, not understanding. "Why the hell would she want anything of mine? And who sent her?"

"Not I. But you've been warned. You must fight."

Cassie's eyelids fluttered, and her chest rose and fell in a sluggish rhythm.

"Pythia?"

No answer. The Pythia was gone.

Tara brought Cassie out of the trance, stepping up the mental staircase to full awareness. Cassie opened her eyes, stretched.

"That wasn't nearly what I thought it would be."

"How so? I promised you, no chicken dancing," Tara said lightly. She didn't know if the girl had any memory of the Pythia's voice. And she didn't want to scare her.

"It was like you said, like daydreaming . . ." Her voice trailed off, and Tara could see she was thinking of her father.

Tara patted her sleeve. "Take some time to wake slowly, and come out when you're ready."

Tara left the bedroom in darkness. She closed the door behind her and nearly ran into Harry in the tiny hall.

"Did you get anything?" he asked, arms crossed over his chest. Behind him, Martin sawed logs on the plaid couch, his hands folded softly on his chest. The sound would have been enough to blot out the voices from the bedroom. She hoped. She didn't want to explain the Pythia to Harry. Not now. Not ever.

"I'm not sure yet." Her eyes roved the stacks and stacks of books lining the walls. "Does your dad have any books on astronomy?"

MARTIN'S PERSONAL LIBRARY COVERED AN ASTONISHINGLY broad array of subjects, from mammals to music to mechanical engineering. Tara and Harry dug through the stacks behind the couch, while Martin searched in boxes tucked in a closet. The books were organized in no discernible order other than Martin's lines of imagination: *An Apprentice's Guide to Metalworking* lay beside *Battle Strategies of World War II*, interspersed with well-worn vinyl LPs.

"What the heck?" Harry picked up a book and held it up for his father to see. It was titled *The Ambience of Sensual Massage*, depicting a hirsute man with 1970s sideburns and mustache in a romantic clinch with a woman with waist-length hair and a flower tucked behind her ear.

Martin popped his head around the corner, narrowing his eyes. "You snooping, or are you asking to borrow it?"

Harry dropped it like a hot potato.

Martin's muffled voice emanated from back in the closet. "I *thought* so."

Tara smothered a grin and pulled aside a stack of paperback spy novels to find a blue book titled promisingly enough: *The Stargazer's Catalog*. She flipped through, scanning for Cassiopeia.

"Found it." The constellation sprawled across the page in a loose *W* pattern. Superimposed on the stars was a picture of a seated queen on a throne. With her finger, Tara traced the constellation to the star in the queen's chest, labeled *Segin*. The next page listed its ascension and declination, the coordinates of how the star moved through the night sky.

Harry powered up the laptop, and Cassie wandered into the living room. "What's going on?"

"We're wildly chasing the geese of Tara's imagination," said Harry.

Cassie stepped over *The Ambience of Sensual Massage*, paused, and picked it up. Her nose wrinkled as she opened it to a dog-eared page. "Feathers. Interesting."

Martin cruised through the living room, plucked the book from her hands. "You're not old enough for that."

"I'm old enough to drink, drive, vote . . . What's the deal with a little smut?"

"And you'll never be old enough to do all that at the same time, young lady. And it is not smut. It's . . ."

Harry looked up, the picture of attentiveness.

"It's for therapeutic purposes," Martin finished.

"Therapeutic purposes," Harry repeated.

Martin swatted the back of Harry's head. "If you were luckier in getting your own therapy, young man, you'd have less time to worry about mine."

Harry pinched the bridge of his nose. "Okay. About that password . . ."

Tara brought the book, looked at the star in Cassiopeia's chest. "Try *Segin*."

Keys clattered as Harry tried the password. "No luck."

"Capital *S*, small *e-g-i-n* . . . one hour, fifty-four minutes, twenty-three point sixty-eight seconds." She added the ascension to the star name.

"No."

"Segin . . . Here, let me show you in the book." Tara pointed to the star's ascension in the book: 01^h 54^m 23.68^s. "And here, the declination . . ." $+63°$, $40'$ $12.5''$.

Harry typed, paused. He looked up at her, a smile spreading over his face. "We're in!"

Tara, Cassie, and Martin crowded behind Harry, peering at the screen. Harry opened Magnusson's recent documents, and they scrolled before him in a flurry of diagrams and notations. It was a foreign language to Tara, but she could see Cassie studying them intently for a long time, tapping her bottom lip with a chipped thumbnail.

"Holy shit," she whispered. "Go back."

Harry scrolled back to a list of equations, and her eyes scanned over them.

"What is it?"

Cassie chewed her bottom lip. "I think . . . I think my dad may have proven the presence of dark energy . . . and opened a black hole to do it."

Chapter Eleven

"Back the truck up. Explain this to me again."

Cassie rolled her eyes, flipped out a fresh sheet of paper, and drew on it with a pencil. She sketched an atomic nucleus and a small solar system of electrons around it. She'd spent the last few hours staring at her father's laptop and trying to translate to the non-physicists. "The particle accelerator takes a heavy atom stripped of electrons"—she erased the electrons—"and collides the nuclei together at high speeds using magnetic force. Stripping the electrons results in a positive atomic charge. Since a positive charge is magnetically attracted to a negative charge, the collider uses that magnetic attraction to move the nuclei at high speeds.

"The collider my father used is a variant of the storage ring collider." She drew an infinity loop and indicated the intersection of the track. "Particles are accelerated in opposite directions and collide at the intersection, here."

"Then what?" Harry asked.

"Then, if superstring theory is accurate, these collisions could result in mini black holes."

"So . . . what's keeping these black holes from devouring the planet? We didn't see any while we were at the lab. Space and time seemed relatively safe."

"Theoretically, these black holes would only exist for a brief period of time before they would annihilate themselves in radiation caused by the collison of matter and antimatter. But they might exist for just long enough to attract particles of dark energy to them, enough to measure and collect them."

"And dark energy is supposed to be all around us?"

"Well, it accounts for about seventy-two percent of the stuff in the universe. It just isn't particularly common in our neck of the woods. The particles in our solar system are rare, and far between."

"What does it do, exactly?"

"Dark energy is the force that keeps the universe pushing outward. It's the driving force of the Big Bang. It creates negative pressure, expansion. Think of it as gravitational repulsion."

"So . . . it's explosive?"

"In a manner of speaking. There's the idea that dark energy has quintessence—the density of the energy increases over time, and creates a sort of phantom energy. Dark energy is usually not terribly dense. But as the density decreases, it could cause an amplification of the Big Bang, a Big Rip, which could eventually tear the universe apart."

Tara blinked. "Your dad was ripping the universe?"

"No. At least, I don't think so. What his notes show is that he was using the particle accelerator at Los Alamos to create these mini black holes to analyze dark energy. He had visions of storing these particles in a kind of cell or battery for energy usage . . . and DOD seems to have told him it was interested in powering aircraft carriers and subs through this type of technique." Cassie bit her lip. "It looks like they wanted this for another purpose: to use the cells to harness that gravitational repulsion, to weaponize the expansive power of dark energy. It's pretty explosive stuff, theoretically."

"Do you think he tried to sabotage his own research?" Harry asked directly.

Cassie spread her hands. "Maybe. If he cranked the collider up far enough, if he allowed the mini black holes to exist for longer than they should . . . if he overloaded the dark energy storage cells he'd built . . . it could have happened."

"That might explain the lack of debris at the explosion site," said Tara. "There were walls, ceiling missing . . . but not enough rubble to account for them."

"Tell me about the cells. What do they look like, and how do they work?" Harry slurped his coffee, and Tara could almost see the gears in his brain whirring, trying to keep up.

Cassie drew the infinity loop again on the paper. "As near as I can determine, it's based on the shape of the infinity-loop collider. The dark energy particles race in the same direction around the track until the energy is released, by making a contact or connection with the circuit." She drew a slash in the infinity loop. "I don't know how big or small they are. They could be as big as a water tower, or as small as a microchip. It depends on how many particles are stored."

Martin had been silent so far, running his thumbs over the lip of his coffee mug. "So your father basically unzipped the underbelly of the cosmos, took the invisible force out of it that keeps the universe going, and stuffed it in a can that explodes when it's opened."

Cassie nodded. "Exactly."

Harry leaned back in his kitchen chair. "Shit."

Cassie agreed. "Shit."

Tears glistened in the girl's eyes. Tara leaned forward and rubbed her shoulder, while Martin reached to grab her hand. Harry pushed away from the table and left the kitchen.

"Look, the military is trying very hard to find him. That means they think he's still alive," said Tara. She believed that much to be true.

Cassie sniffled. "But do *you* think he's still alive? I mean, a black hole could have eaten my father! It sounds like something out of a bad sci-fi movie."

"I don't know, but we're going to find out."

Martin patted Cassie's hand. "No parent would leave his child without answers. You're going to have them."

Harry stuck his head back into the room, holding Martin's powder-blue corded phone. He'd been checking his cell messages remotely, reluctant to turn on his cell phone in the event cell towers could triangulate their position. He gestured for Tara, who slipped out from behind the table to join him.

"Another message from Corvus?" she asked. He'd gotten several. The calls had progressed from requests for status updates to threats. She thought he'd been ignoring those, but wasn't certain.

"No," he answered, pressing the receiver against her ear. "Listen."

Tara cupped the phone, hearing a familiar voice:

"Agent Li, this is Barbara DiRosa. I want to talk to you about Lowell Magnusson . . . I've found some information you may find useful, and I don't . . . I don't want to send it up the chain of command. Please call me right away."

She left a number, and an electronic voice proclaimed this to be the end of the message. Tara handed the phone back to Harry. "What are you going to do?"

Harry blew out his breath. "I'm going to have to talk to her."

"It could be a trap, to try and find out our position."

"Quite possibly. But what if it's not?"

The question hung, suspended. Tara reached out, tentatively, and put her hand on his sleeve. He slid his warm hand over hers.

"We'll just have to hope no one's watching."

HARRY BLOCKED THE CALL, TRANSFERRED NUMBERS TWICE through two different operators, but wasn't confident at all that the call to DiRosa wasn't traceable. Tara sat beside him on Martin's couch, listening through the volume cranked up on Martin's 1980s receiver. Frankly, he was amazed Martin even had phone service out here.

"Hello."

"Dr. DiRosa? This is Agent Li. You said you had some information for me."

"Yes . . . I wanted to talk to you about Magnusson."

Harry paused, waiting for her to fill in the silence. She seemed to take her time answering. Not a good sign. He glanced at his watch. It took at least thirty seconds to establish a good trace, and she'd already taken up ten.

"I've been able to retrieve some of Magnusson's corre-spondence from our e-mail server backups, and I think you might want to see them." DiRosa blew out a nervous breath. Harry couldn't tell if she was anxious to be talking to him, or ill at ease to be participating in a phone tap.

"It seems Magnusson had some conflicts with the chain of command here . . . and it seems there were some threats, in both directions. I'd like to meet with you to give you the infor-mation. I'm concerned that the info is going to be destroyed."

"When and where?"

"Tomorrow . . . at Bandelier National Monument? At the first scenic overlook . . . Five-thirty?"

"Why not today?" he challenged. Harry knew he couldn't get there from here so soon, but he didn't want to give any eavesdroppers additional clues to their location.

"I think . . . I'm being watched. I can get away from work tomorrow."

"All right." Harry hung up, staring at the sweep hand on his watch. Not quite thirty seconds. Still, he didn't feel safe.

Tara was watching him under that thick fringe of eye-lashes, watching him sweat. "You're going?"

"Yeah." He could nearly hear the jaws of a trap scraping shut, but there was no choice. He scrubbed his hands through his hair, thinking. In the kitchen, he could hear Cassie and Pops talking over the clink of dishes in the sink. He needed to form a strategy with Tara, but didn't want to have to censor what he thought for fear of Cassie overhearing.

"C'mon," he said, standing and offering Tara a hand. "Let's go for a walk."

She took his hand and shrugged into her coat. Harry stuck his head in the kitchen.

"We're going out for a little while. Be back soon."

Pops gave him a knowing look, a smirk Harry wanted to wipe off his face. Pops dried his hands and stabbed a thumb in the direction of his library of practical and esoteric information. "You can still borrow my book, if you want."

Cassie chortled.

Harry resisted the urge to tell the old man exactly what he could do with his book. He snatched his coat and headed out the door behind Tara, letting the screen door bang behind him. Maggie nosed through the door and followed.

The day was crisp and cold, snow still clinging to the shady spots under the trees. Harry had been so focused on cracking the computer that he'd forgotten to look outside. He saw no planes overhead, not even contrails. That could either be a sign they'd stopped looking in this area, or that their location was already known.

Maggie vigorously sniffed the ground, inhaling ferociously enough to get snow up her nose. She snorted and took off into the brush, tail wagging. In her dog's imagination, surely a rabbit had become a great and fearsome beast in need of a good chasing.

Tara stuffed her hands in her pockets. "Your dad has quite the sense of humor."

"My dad . . . sticks his nose in a lot of things. Pay him no mind."

She nodded, following him down the porch steps into the woods. Underfoot, where snow had melted, the exposed patches of pine needles were soft and rotting. The branches that still held their needles cast fringed shadows over her face. She was an enigma to Harry . . . She spoke little, seeming to strive to blend into the environment and soak it up. Harry never knew what was really on her mind, behind that face as blank as a porcelain doll's. But he found her impossible to ignore. Try as she might to fade into the background, Harry always saw her in his peripheral vision.

"We're going to have to move Cassie," he said. "And I am all out of secret hollows in the woods."

Tara was quiet for some time as they walked. She seemed to be chewing on something, and her words were reluctant when she spoke. "I know someone who can take her."

"You trust this person?" He didn't know how to read the reluctance in her voice.

"For this one thing . . . yes, I do."

"That's not a resounding endorsement."

"She was an old friend of my mother's. If anyone can keep Cassie hidden, Sophia can."

Harry nodded, kicked at a broken branch. If she trusted this Sophia, that would be good enough for him. She'd trusted Harry to take them to Martin. "If you can get in touch with her, we'll take off in the morning. You take Cassie to Sophia, and I'll head south to meet with DiRosa. Martin has a truck. It's old, doesn't have heat, but it'll get you where you need to go."

"And then?"

"And then, we'll meet back up at Los Alamos."

"This assumes, of course, that DiRosa isn't the bait in a trap."

"We don't have much choice." Harry kicked at the stick. "Better one of us than both of us walking into it."

"Harry." She put a hand on his chest, and he hoped she couldn't feel its quickening under his coat. "You don't have to be chivalrous and fall on your sword."

He put his hand over hers before she could draw it away. "Nothing chivalrous about it. I'm being practical here. Somebody has to protect Cassie and Magnusson's laptop. We don't want to think about what would happen if they got into the wrong hands."

She nodded, and a curtain of hair fell over her face. "Just be careful, Harry. And please remember what I said about Corvus."

"Hey." He brushed the hair back behind her ear. That motion revealed the beginning of a scar curling behind her jaw and disappearing into the collar of her coat. Instinctively, she shied away. "I'm not forgetting."

He supposed he could understand that, her shyness about those marks that disappeared into her clothes. He couldn't imagine the trauma behind them. But he wished he could make her understand they made no difference at all to him, that whatever suspicion she held surrounding the Division need not extend to him.

On a gut level, he could understand her dislike of Corvus. And there was clearly some bad history there. But Harry had no evidence to show that he should not trust Corvus, that the man was anything other than what he seemed. Corvus might be a perfect jackass, but he was still Harry's superior jackass.

But he wished he could somehow wipe it all away, that unknown thing that kept her awake at night, that thing that caused her to look away from him with sad, downcast eyes. Harry wanted her to see what he saw: the powerful, insightful mystery, that beauty wrapped in scars of thorns. He was drawn to her like metal to a magnet, to the way she challenged him, forced him to think . . . and yet was unconditionally behind him.

He wanted her. Impulsively, he reached out for her, kissed her. Her cheeks were cold against his palms, and he felt her eyelashes fluttering against his skin in surprise. He felt her melt against him, fingers wrapped in the collar of his coat, yielding to the kiss that scalded him with its intensity. His fingers brushed over the scar on her neck, sliding to the warmth of her collar. He trailed a kiss behind her jaw, feeling her pulse thud against his lips, and wrapped his arms around her. He could feel his heart beating against the cage of his ribs, and he wanted, more than anything, to feel her bare skin against his hands.

She gasped and he drew back, with effort. Her cheeks were flushed with cold and desire. "Harry, I . . ." Tears glittered in her eyes. "I'm more broken than you think. I've been cut up, dissected, head to toe." She seemed to force herself to say the words, to be honest with him.

"It doesn't matter to me."

"How could it not?" she said, and her tone was hopeless. "How could it not matter to you?"

"It just doesn't. What matters is what you feel. What I feel. The rest is immaterial."

She sniffed, ran her gloved finger under her dripping nose.

Still caging her in his arms, he told her, "You come to me when you're ready. I'll wait."

BARBARA DIROSA CLICKED HER CELL PHONE OFF AND STOWED it in her purse. She walked briskly down the busy midday street, the wind tearing at the edges of her coat. Her shoes clicked along the pavement, and she clutched her briefcase tightly. In sharp contrast to the time she'd spent lately in radiation suits, her taste in civilian clothes was impeccable and expensive: wool pencil skirt, silk blouse, custom-tailored jacket. When she was in civilian attire, she eschewed the anonymous shapelessness of the white plastic suits she was forced to wear day after day.

Her heart hammered in fear, and she kept glancing behind her to make sure she wasn't followed. She just had to hold on until tomorrow. She could stall Gabriel until then, keep Magnusson's correspondence safe until she could turn it over to Li.

Blinking, she stared up at the blue sky. It was impossible to believe Magnusson was gone, dead or otherwise. She'd fallen hard for her mentor months ago. And she was beginning to believe he was starting to return her attentions. He'd seemed so apart from the rest of the research team, walking distractedly along another plane of theory. She longed to bring him back down to earth, for there to be something more.

And it seemed to be flowering. He let her feed him. DiRosa had dragged Magnusson to half the restaurants in town after work. Over filet or dim sum, he was still guarded. He rarely spoke about his personal life. Most of it seemed to center around his dog. Their conversations were overwhelmingly work-related, though Magnusson seemed to tentatively probe the edge of sensitive subjects:

"What brought you here?" His slender fingers sketched the world outside the window of the bistro they once sat in. "How did they bring you in all of this?"

DiRosa paused, twirling her linguine around her fork. "Honestly?"

"Honestly." His blue eyes seemed hungry for the answer.

She shrugged. "Nobody else could afford me."

That didn't seem to be the answer he was looking for. He pushed his ravioli around in silence.

"How about you?" she asked. "Why are you here? To be honest, you don't really fit in."

"Any more than Prada does among the jarheads?" He was teasing her now. He always called her Prada.

"Hey, we established that I'm here for the money. What's your excuse?"

Magnusson's eyes seemed hungry. "I'm here for the machines, Prada."

DiRosa glanced at him coyly over the moist rim of her wineglass. "Boys and their toys."

He sighed, pushed away his plate. "It's what the other boys will do with the toys that bothers me."

"Why does it bother you? What they're going to do with our research is too far above our pay grade to worry about," she chided him.

"I guess I'm naïve, but I'd like to know what they're going to do with it. Make sure they're not going to start World War Three. That kind of thing." His hand was balled in a fist around his napkin.

DiRosa rested her sharp chin in her hand. "You are being naïve. But it's kind of endearing."

"Prada, I suspect that they're gonna weaponize it."

She paused. The possibility had been so much a part of her reality for so long that she was shocked Magnusson hadn't seriously considered it. He was more naïve than she thought. "And . . . ? Look, our government has always had the shiniest, most expensive toys. Some of them go boom. Loudly. It's better we develop them before someone else does, right?"

Magnusson took a swig of his wine. "Right." He didn't sound convinced.

She frowned at him. "We're here not just to serve our own interests. Part of the deal is that we also serve . . . and national security is part of that."

"Right, Prada."

She leaned forward. "Why are you all right with building a power source for engines of war, but actual weaponry is wrong? Where do you cross that line?"

"I don't want to be Oppenheimer quoting the Bhagavad Gita." He swished his wine around in his glass. 'Now I am become Death, the destroyer of Worlds,' and all that."

"You're not Oppenheimer."

He snorted. "I want to build things. Not destroy them. We've got an amazing opportunity to build technology that could end the energy shortage around the world . . . This could create a tremendous positive impact on human history."

"And we will. But there's a price to pay for that." He never sounded convinced that they were on the side of the angels. She'd had to kick him in the shins in meetings for asking too many questions. And she worried what he had found out. Damn the man for being saddled with such a limited, simplistic ethical range.

DiRosa wiped at her watering eyes with her glove as she walked down the street. For a smart man, Magnusson could be really stupid when it came to politics.

"Dr. DiRosa."

She turned, nearly tripping over her expensive Italian shoes.

Major Gabriel was striding toward her, hands in the pockets of his military coat. His face, as always, was carefully neutral. Had he been following her?

"Shouldn't you be at work?"

"Had some errands to run, sir." The fewer details she gave, the better. She could feel her ears turning red. She was a terrible liar. And Gabriel had a more . . . evolved sense of situational ethics than she did.

"Come walk with me." He grasped her elbow, and DiRosa knew that she had no choice but to go with him as he pulled her down the street with an iron grip. She furtively glanced around her, wondering if she could make a break for it in her impractical shoes. She wondered if anyone would come to her aid if she screamed.

"Have I ever told you the story how I got into this business, Dr. DiRosa?" Gabriel asked, his tone conversational.

She swallowed. "No, sir."

"In-house, we call it the Clean-Up Crew. We're good at cleaning up other peoples' messes. I put in for the transfer after I saw what happens when well-intentioned people don't have a view of the big picture."

"What do you mean?"

"I used to be with Criminal Investigation Command, investigating a breach of intelligence at the Centers for Disease Control. There was a guy there who didn't think that the lab should be studying a strain of a hemorrhagic virus that could infect humans. Felt that the hazards were too great, and he felt the need to share his concerns with the press. He talked to the papers off the record.

"But the damage was done. The leak inspired a group of would-be terrorist lunatics who wanted to create some snazzy new bioweapons. They cobbled together enough intel to intercept the delivery of the virus samples."

DiRosa's brow wrinkled. "I never heard of that."

"Of course you didn't. We caught them before they crossed the state line, contained the samples. Well, we contained most of them. Two of them disappeared."

"Why are you telling me this?"

"Because I want you to understand why we have to contain leaks."

Gabriel walked her to a car parked on the side of the street, where Richard Corvus sat behind the wheel. Corvus nodded to him, the satisfied look of an owl whose shadow was falling over a mouse.

Chapter Twelve

Tara stared at the shadows of tree branches on the ceiling. Beside her, Cassie lay curled up in a tight ball, asleep. Maggie lay perpendicular to her, as long as she could stretch out, shoving Tara to the edge of the bed. In the living room, Martin snored softly on the couch. All was quiet, but her thoughts raced.

Adrienne was after her. She hadn't told Harry . . . How could she tell him that a member of a secret society of women was harboring enough of a grudge to try and chase Tara down? He'd send the men with the white coats after her for certain.

She'd called Sophia this afternoon, when Harry and Martin and Cassie had been outside with Maggie. Sophia had picked up on the first ring. Unnerving, that habit of hers.

"Adrienne has been at your house," Sophia told her.

Tara swallowed. "Is Oscar okay?" If that bitch had hurt Oscar, she'd tear her throat out.

"He's fine. He's with me. He's eaten two chicken sandwiches from the drive-through and is taking a nap."

"What the hell does she want from me?" Tara dimly remembered her as a tall, grubby girl who rarely spoke. They'd probably exchanged a half dozen words that she remembered.

"She thinks you're competition for the title of Pythia."

"Whoa. Back the truck up." Tara shook her head. "What?"

"She knows Juliane was the Pythia's chosen successor. Juliane's gone."

Tara's jaw hardened. "I want nothing to do with Delphi's Daughters. Period."

"I know that. But Adrienne sees things differently. She sees you as competition."

"Well, the Pythia needs to jerk a knot in her tail."

"It's not that simple. The Pythia has . . . faded." Sophia's voice broke. Tara couldn't imagine what it cost her to admit it. Sophia had always been unquestioningly loyal to the Pythia. "She's not what you remember her to be. Her power has greatly diminished."

"What are you telling me? That the Pythia has no control over Adrienne?"

She hesitated slightly. "Yes."

"Shit." Tara rubbed the bridge of her nose. "Look, I've got a bigger problem. I need a favor, but you've got to tell me if you're going to be able to help me." Tara was out of options; she had no choice but to ask.

"Anything." There was no hesitation.

"I need you to hide someone for me. A girl. And you have to tell me honestly whether or not you can do it."

Sophia had listened quietly to Tara's request for sanctuary for Cassie and the laptop.

"Of course," she said. "Meet me tomorrow." She'd specified a meeting site several hours away, and Tara had scribbled the information down in a hurry.

"Sophia," Tara said. "You might want to bring . . . reinforcements. There's a strong likelihood I'll be followed. And not by Adrienne."

Sophia laughed her bell-like laugh. "Dear child, we will see that she's safe. Don't worry about us." Her voice lowered in seriousness. "Worry about your current situation."

Cassie had been reluctant to be handed off to another caretaker. Tara had told her, "It's the only choice. Sophia can keep you safe."

"Where will I be going?" The girl's eyes were large with anxiety.

"I asked her not to tell me, for your own good." Tara tried not to think of the worst case scenario, what could happen if Cassie and her location were revealed. "But you will always be able to contact me. And . . ." she added desperately, "Sophia is a wonderful cook. She makes a miraculous strudel."

Cassie's ears perked up at the mention of the word *strudel*. "I suppose a strudel maker can't be that bad."

Tara looked wistfully out the window, emotions churning. She hoped Cassie couldn't sense her ambivalence about the situation. "No. She can't be."

Now, Tara lay staring up at the ceiling, hoping she'd made the right call. The only other option would be for Tara to go on the run with Cassie, herself . . . but her chances of discovery were higher with Adrienne in the mix. And, truth be told, she was reluctant to leave Harry alone in this mess. She sensed he was more alone than he knew, that Corvus would not be the backup he hoped for. It was as if she could see a trap closing around him, and was powerless to retrieve him from its jaws.

She sighed, turning over to watch the constellations tangle in the tree branches. Her emotions were getting in the way, and she was feeling too protective of him. She blushed, thinking of this afternoon's kiss that made her lightheaded enough to cling to him. Emotions long buried, something hot and wanton, bubbled up within her, and they conflicted with her fears.

As gentle and determined as Harry seemed, she still doubted his ability to withstand the force of her fears, her fears about her body, and her fears about what he would think about how she worked. Her fingers brushed her lips, pausing to remember his kisses. Ah, to fall into that warmth, even for a moment . . . It was as if he'd kissed her awake. But he knew not what he'd awoken.

She listened to Cassie's breathing, even and regular. Tara reached under the bed for her purse, leaned over to pull out her cards. By the dim glow from a tiny nightlight, she shuffled them, her heart a conflicted knot of fear and desire. She imagined Harry asleep in the next room, was struck by the greater fear of him falling into Corvus and Gabriel's trap, of never seeing him again, of never knowing what it would be like to feel her hands and breath on his skin.

She drew the card that she, on some level, knew she had no choice but to draw: the Lovers. In a sunlit field of lilies, two lovers gazed into each other's eyes. It was a card of testing, of deciding whether to be ruled by one's heart or one's head.

She blew out her breath. She was decided.

She slipped the card under her bag, pulled back the blankets, slid out of bed. Her heart hammered as her toes clutched at the shag carpet, as she stepped into the hallway to Harry's door, silent as a wraith.

She opened the door, tiptoed inside. She could see the waxing moonlight outlining his shoulder, the curve of his arm under an unzipped sleeping bag, the zipper glinting in the light. She closed the door, leaning against it with her hands behind her back. Surely he could hear her heart thundering loud enough to wake him?

It seemed she stood there for hours, watching the moon track over the planes of his face, his shoulder, running through his hair. She was jealous of the moon, the way it caressed his body, how it felt the rise and fall of his chest.

She approached the bed, crawled in behind Harry, and wrapped her arms around his chest. She felt his chest expand as he inhaled, the quickening of his pulse beneath her hands. Tentatively, she pressed her lips to the back of his neck, felt his sharp intake of breath as she did so. His hands laced in her fingers, and she molded her body to his, feeling his delicious warmth down the length of her body.

"You came," he sighed.

He turned over, pulling her into his arms, and kissed her deeply. The kiss drove the breath from her and ignited long-dormant desire. Her hands slipped under his shirt, feeling the hard muscles of his abdomen tensing as he moved. She seized the chance to pull his shirt over his head and splay her fingers against the heat of his chest.

Harry buried his lips in her neck, trailing the neckline of the old flannel shirt, covering the scar crossing her collarbone. The fingers of one hand slipped up the small of her back, delicately exploring the fine white ridges crossing her flesh, while his other hand moved up to cup her breast.

Tara wanted to cry out, to let him know how his touch affected her, but she bit her lip to keep from waking Cassie and Martin. His thumb circled her sharp nipple, while his mouth covered hers, stealing a soft groan from her and pressing her into the pillows and blankets. He plucked open the buttons of her shirt and laid her chest bare to the dim light.

Her breath caught, fearing his judgment. But none came. Instead, a slow shower of kisses began at her collar, crossed over her ribs in the white feathery pattern of the scars. She wound her fingers in his hair, feeling his lips insistent on the scars, which seemed more sensitive than ever before. He turned his attention to her breasts, seizing a nipple in his mouth. Arching her back, she silently scraped her fingernails through his hair.

He didn't judge her. He worshipped her with his mouth and hands, delicately skimming her flesh with the lightest of touches with his fingers and the firmest gestures of his mouth. His hands teased the sweatpants below her hips, kissing the hip bone exposed to the pale light. He pulled the rest of her clothes away, his attention riveted to her body, his hands sliding up the lightning-white scars on her legs, over the swell of her hips. In this light, they were not nearly as awful as she believed them to be in the day.

"Beautiful," he murmured against her ear. "Like the Snow Queen."

He gasped in her ear when she reached to stroke him through his pants before she unbuttoned them. She craved his hardness inside her, grasping his firm buttocks to guide him.

But Harry wasn't having any of her impatience. "Not yet."

He kneaded her muscles with his hands, sliding his touch over her stomach, over her hip, and parted her legs. Tara inhaled sharply as he buried his fingers in her warm wetness, teasing, exploring, withdrawing to work her clitoris until she wrapped her legs around him. She clutched his shoulder, pressed against him. She was certain she'd come if he so much as breathed on her.

"Not yet," he whispered.

He teased her flesh with his mouth, down her breasts, over her navel. He parted her thighs, tenderly kissing the soft flesh inside, cupped her buttocks in his hands . . . and stroked her with his tongue so relentlessly Tara buried her fingers in the sleeping bag and her face in the pillow. When orgasm overtook her, she clenched her teeth to keep from crying out, trembling in a current of desire that left her gasping for breath.

Harry slid on top of her, his warm skin heightening the tremors that spasmed through her. Gathering her in his arms, he slowly worked his way inside her.

It had been years since she had made love, but Harry was incredibly gentle. Though she could feel the taut desire in his body, he restrained himself, sliding into her inch by inch. Winding his fingers in hers, he began to thrust, slowly, evenly . . . Tara could feel his restraint, his fear of hurting her.

"You won't hurt me," she whispered. Tara took his buttocks in her hands and moved against him. Breasts pressed against his chest, hips moving below him, Harry lost all concentration, thrusting into her . . .

Tara arched her back as the second orgasm flooded over her. She wrapped Harry's body with her legs and arms, clinging to him as he embraced her with one arm and clutched the headboard with the other. At last she felt him buck inside her, felt the explosive exhalation of breath on her shoulder as he came.

He raised himself on his elbows, looking searchingly into her face. "Are you okay?"

"I am . . . much better than okay." She grinned back at him.

He tucked her hair behind her ears, kissed her. Harry rolled over, spooning her against his chest. She felt safe, protected. And that was a very rare feeling for Tara.

When she drifted off to sleep in Harry's arms, the moon had set and plunged the room into darkness. Her sleep was entirely without dreams.

• • • •

Harry woke early, before the sun rose. Tara had left, slipping back into the bed she shared with Cassie. He'd been reluctant to untangle himself from her arms and the sleeping bag, wanting to bask in her warmth for as long as possible. He wanted to stay here, to put aside the next phase of the search for Magnusson, the misstep that could land him in harm's way. These last hours had been glorious, and a twinge of fear twitched in his chest at the thought of losing what he'd just gained, this sense of serene wholeness.

But there was no stopping time.

Finally, he left the bed and trudged toward the kitchen to make coffee. Maggie lumbered along in his wake, her claws clicking on the linoleum.

On the couch, Martin awoke to the steam and hiss of the coffeepot. He turned over and fixed Harry with a bemused glance. "You never used to make coffee."

"It's definitely an acquired taste." Harry grimaced as he took a sip. "And your taste in coffee takes more acquiring than most."

Martin harrumphed. "That's the good stuff. I ordered it from Australia. It's made from fruit bat guano. The bats eat the cocoa beans, and then they collect the guano . . ."

Harry stared into the cup. "You'd better be pulling my leg." He looked at the label. It was, indeed, from Australia.

"Maybe." The old man crossed his arms. "Maybe not. You got something against fruit bats?"

Harry set down his cup. "Look, Pops, I appreciate everything you've done for us. I realize I put you in a bad situation . . ."

"You're family, Harry. Anything I can do for you, you know I will."

"There might be some people coming to look for us. You might want to take a vacation."

Martin stubbornly waved his suggestion away. "This *is* my vacation. I've got it all under control. It's you I worry about."

"Everything's gonna be fine with me, Pops."

The old man looked under his tangled eyebrows at Harry. "Maybe there's hope for you, yet."

"What's that supposed to mean?"

"Tara. She's a good woman. She's different from you, and that's good for you."

Harry rubbed his eyebrow. Shit. Had the old man heard them last night? "Is that what your book says?"

"That's what your Pops says." Martin picked up a coffee mug. "Differences can create conflict, if you let them. Or they can be complementary, and you can use them to compensate for each other's strengths and weaknesses. It's the law of the universe . . . the harmonious attraction of opposites. Yin and yang . . . dark and light . . . peanut butter and jelly . . ."

"Pops, I appreciate the thought, but it's way too early for the cosmic ruminations . . ."

Martin wagged a finger under Harry's nose, slurping his bat guano coffee. "You think your Pops doesn't know what he's talking about. But I'll have you know, back in the day, I was quite the lady's man. Do you remember your friend Tom's mom from across the street?" The old man's face split into a craggy grin. "Well, let me tell you about Mrs. Cloverfeld and the hot tub . . ."

"Urk." Harry fled the kitchen, trying to scrub the mental picture of Martin and Mrs. Cloverfeld from his mind. Passing the bathroom, he heard the hiss of the shower and Cassie's off-key rendition of the latest emo hit from the radio.

He cracked open the door of the back bedroom to wake Tara. The gray morning light picked out an expression of soft contentment on her face as she slept, one arm crooked under the pillow. Her breath was deep and even, and he wondered what she dreamed.

Harry knelt beside the bed to drink her in, this early morning peace, the rise and fall of her pale shoulder, the buttons on her shirt in the wrong buttonholes. He smiled, remembering their lovemaking, wishing for more time with the Snow Queen, to thaw more of that ice she'd buried herself in.

He reached forward to caress her cheek to wake her, when his knee bumped something on the floor. Tara's purse. He shoved it away, paused when he spied something underneath it. A piece of paper.

No . . . something else.

He picked it up. It was an elaborately decorated card depicting two people in a passionate embrace, titled *The Lovers.* He recognized the image from when he'd been shuffled to the occult crimes unit several years ago, busting a phony psychic bilking retirees out of their savings. It was from a deck of Tarot cards, the kind used by fortune-tellers to scare their victims into forking over more cash.

The edges were well-worn. It had been in Tara's hands

often . . . and it dawned on him that perhaps this was the key to her intuition, that she made countless critical decisions based on what a deck of cards told her to do. That she had decided to come to him last night, based on what a random card had told her.

He looked up to see her looking down at him, her smile dissolving when she saw him holding the card.

He tried to keep his tone even, failed. "What's this?"

TARA OPENED HER EYES TO SEE HARRY, AND SHE SMILED. BUT the expression drained from her face, her heart crumpling as she saw what he held in his hand, at the hard set of his jaw. She could see the hurt, the anger in him, and she instinctively recoiled from it. How could she have been so careless?

"Harry, I . . ." She forced herself to reach out and touch his sleeve. "This isn't what you think."

He seemed to want to believe her, but doubt clouded his eyes. He didn't move to take her hand. "Then what is it?"

She wanted to have this conversation with him, someday, but she wasn't ready now, didn't have anything that made sense rehearsed. She blew out a nervous breath and waded into the churning water. "It's the way I organize and focus my thoughts. I pull a card at random, and reflect on how I feel about the symbols on it."

"And then, what? You do what it tells you to?"

"No. I do what I feel is—" She broke off, hearing the unmistakable staccato slice of helicopter blades overhead. Maggie galloped into the room, ran across the bed, and crammed her nose through the blinds. Her barks obliterated anything else Tara might have said.

Harry swore and leaped to his feet. He charged to the window, peering through the blinds over the dog's head. A tan UH-1N helicopter stirred the soft branches of pine trees, turned left, and wheeled away in the sky, searching for a place to land. The Huey could hold up to fifteen people. It was primarily a personnel mover in domestic operations, and that meant Gabriel's men were coming for them, in force.

"We've got to get out of here, now."

Tara rolled out of bed and scooped up her purse and her shoes. Harry charged into the hallway, pounding on the bathroom door for Cassie to get dressed. The Lovers card lay on the floor, forgotten. Vision blurring, she picked it up and stuffed it into her purse before she bolted from the room.

Cassie was dripping wet in her coat, clutching her father's laptop, trying to get her shoes on. Harry was arguing with Martin. "We have to go. You're coming with us."

The old man stubbornly shook his head. "I'm not going anywhere. You kids get moving."

Harry stabbed his finger out the window. "We've been found . . . and we're not leaving you behind, Pops."

"I'm not going." Martin parked his backside in his recliner. "That's the end of it."

"They're going to come, ask questions . . . We don't know what they're going to do." Harry's voice was desperate. Tara wasn't entirely certain he wouldn't pick the old man up and throw him in the trunk.

Martin rocked back and forth. "Let 'em come. I'll tell 'em some of my best stories. Time's a wastin', kiddo."

Harry growled in frustration, but gave the stubborn old man a hug. Tara saw the old man's eyes glisten. "I'll tell you how it went when you get back."

"I'll hold you to that."

Tara buckled on her holster, peeked out the door. No aircraft or people in sight, though the forest was too dense to be certain. Sunlight glittered on snow melting from the trees, the bits of ice rattling through the canopy casting false shadows of light and movement.

Harry tossed her a set of keys. They had to be the keys to Martin's truck; the key ring was decorated with the hood ornament of an old Cadillac.

Tara looked at Harry, and a lump filled her throat.

"Be safe," was all he said. His eyes were dark with pain, and she ached for being the cause of it.

"You, too." She raised her hand to touch his arm—

He was already at the door, weapon unholstered, eyes scanning the clearing. Ever the chivalrous knight, she thought bitterly, as he slammed open the screen door and strode into the still day. She flinched at the sound of the door hitting the side of the trailer, harsh as a gunshot. Harry crossed to his car and unlocked it. He stood behind the door, gun raised, and motioned for the women to follow under the cover he provided.

"Cassie," she whispered, and the girl was at her elbow, holding on to Maggie's collar with one hand, backpack in the other. Maggie's ears were lifted, listening. Tara, Cassie, and Maggie clattered down the porch steps to the side of the trailer, where Martin's beat-up old Chevy pickup sat. Tara popped Cassie's door first, and crossed to the driver's side with her gun in her grip.

The key stuck in the cold ignition. It had been a long time since the truck had been started. She cranked the engine over, and the sound of it roared through the silence like a growling bear. She flipped the wipers on, dusting snow from the windshield.

She glimpsed Harry through the glass. He nodded at her, started his car, and disappeared down the switchback dirt road. The frost kept down the dust, and there was no evidence he'd ever been there.

She followed, but as fast as the truck bounced over the unpaved dirt, she could not catch sight of him again.

CHAPTER **THIRTEEN**

HARRY TRIED to put as much distance between himself and Martin's nest as he could. Once he'd seen the old man's truck rattle down the driveway, he gunned the engine, allowing the trees to enfold his view in the rear-view mirror. He hoped that whoever was watching them would see him first, take the bait, and leave the old man, Cassie, and Tara alone.

His heart was leaden, seeming to slow his progress and drag his thoughts back to what he'd left behind. It was heavy for Martin, fearing what interrogation he might face at the hands of the men who'd tried to kill Cassie. Martin was a formidable foe with the shotgun, but these men were beyond the solitary poachers and teenage burglars Martin was accustomed to dealing with. His knuckles were pale on the steering wheel, praying they wouldn't hurt the old man. Martin was harmless, and there was nothing he could tell them. Even Martin didn't know where they were going.

His heart was heavy for Cassie. He was beginning to believe, more and more, that her father was dead. He wouldn't admit it to her, wouldn't admit it to anyone but himself, but there was no evidence yet suggesting he'd survived. He'd left messages for his daughter, riddles for her to solve, but there was no concrete proof he hadn't died in the destruction of the particle accelerator—whether it was an accident, act of sabotage, or murder—and been devoured by one of his black holes. If Magnusson had been eaten by one of his own monsters, the probabilities of keeping Cassie safe for any prolonged length of time dwindled. He'd asked Tara not to tell him where she was taking Cassie. Where Harry was going, that knowledge might become a distinct liability.

Sun splintered through the branches of spiky trees, and Harry's tires finally hit paved road. It would be many hours before he would be back in New Mexico to meet DiRosa at Bandelier National Monument. He looked east and west on the two-lane highway. No cars.

He blew out his breath. He wasn't being followed so far. He hoped that boded well for Cassie and Tara.

Tara. His heart was heavy for her, too . . . and confused. To go from the peace and certainty he'd felt last night to the mixed feelings of doubt and uncertainty he'd confronted her with this morning . . . It was like swallowing concrete mix and trying to digest it before it solidified. He feared that last night had been a random draw of a card, that she had been leading him and this investigation based on signs and portents dictated by a deck of cards.

It made him angry to think it. What wrong turns might they have made? What other decisions might have been reached, if he hadn't accepted her intuitive flashes and gut feelings as truth?

Corvus had warned him about this. Corvus had warned him she'd retained some "permanent psychological damage." What delusions, what rituals of comfort, had she picked up along the way? Or . . . what if this was the way she had always worked?

He tried to partition out his feelings about how she made decisions in her personal and private lives, but failed. Harry had wanted her to feel something for him and come to him on her own . . . not because she had been compelled to, by him, or by anyone—or anything—else. That stung.

He clicked on the stereo, allowing the bass rhythm of death metal to wash over him, to pound the dash and jangle the change in the console. It was a good day for death metal. He stomped the gas pedal, and his unzipped duffel bag rolled from the passenger seat to the floor. *The Ambience of Sensual Massage* slid out onto the floor mat.

Harry had to smile in spite of himself. Pops and his sense of humor.

If it had been any other time, he would have taken some time to cool off, to talk with Tara about it. But that was now impossible . . . The case demanded his full attention. He knew the likelihood was high that someone other than DiRosa would be there to meet him at the park, that he would be detained, questioned . . . Under military jurisdiction, he had no idea what would happen. But there was a small possibility the information she offered was real, that it might lead to Magnusson, and he had to take that chance.

He glanced at the rearview mirror, saw a helicopter on the horizon. All of them—Harry, Tara, Cassie, and Martin—would be lucky to get out of this mess at all, much less have heart-to-heart chats over hot chocolate.

Still, he wished he hadn't left it like that with Tara. It felt sharp and unfinished, and it might have to remain that way. Forever.

MARTIN HAD BEEN EXPECTING A KNOCK. MAYBE SOME SIRENS, or even a phone call from the local sheriff checking to make sure he hadn't been taken hostage.

He had not been expecting a dozen men with submachine guns to surround him when he was taking his trash out to the burn barrel.

Martin walked out to the rubbish barrel in his fishing boots and Carhartt coveralls, holding his trash in one hand and his shotgun in the other. He'd been thinking about Harry. The boy hadn't given him details on what he was planning, but it sounded as if he was drowning in some pretty serious business. Whatever it was, he hoped Harry had the sense to rely on Tara's judgment. Harry could be bullheaded, obstinate, and unbelievably obtuse . . .

He heard the unmistakable *click-click-click*s of a dozen gun safeties being released, was told, "Freeze! Get down on the ground!" by one of the men dressed in camo fatigues and ski masks. Martin found himself looking down the barrel of an MP-5 and wishing he'd dressed for the occasion.

Martin laid down the shotgun, then the rubbish, and stretched out on the cold ground. Immediately, men swarmed over him, patting him down for more weapons. He heard their boots clomping on the porch, inside his home. His cap slid over his ear, and he could hear the men above him grumbling about all his pockets . . . They found two fishing lures from last spring in his jacket, a can opener in his shirt, and nail clippers in his pants.

When they sat him up, a stocky man squatted over him. "What's your name?"

Martin smiled broadly up at him. "I'm Martin Davis. Who're you?"

The man ignored him. "We're looking for Harry Li, Tara Sheridan, and Cassie Magnusson."

Martin put on his best senile act and looked to the side. "Oh, I'm afraid you've given me a dreadful fright. Let's see . . ." He tapped his hands on his chin, making sure to allow them to shake. "Visitors."

"Have you seen any of these people?" the man demanded, shoving a faxed page of photographs in the man's face.

Martin leaned forward, squinting. "I'm afraid I don't have my glasses." Inwardly, he rolled his eyes. Despite his black suit and serious expression, Harry's outdated file photo made him look barely old enough to drive. Tara was a smokin' hot fox, smiling enigmatically at the camera. Older picture, but very, very nice. She reminded him of Mrs. Cloverfeld. A picture of Cassie, apparently taken from the masthead of her school newspaper, showed her with pink hair and the glitter of a nose ring.

A tall woman in motorcycle leathers paced around the perimeter of the conversation, watching them with eyes narrowed. She wasn't military; Martin couldn't figure out what she was. Except that she was trouble. "They've been here," she insisted. "Beat it out of him."

"Find the man's glasses," the questioner snapped to one of the soldiers beside him. "Glasses first, then beating."

"I think they're on the coffee table," Martin replied helpfully. He knew damn well they were in the cutlery drawer in the kitchen, next to the scissors.

It took the men nearly a half hour to toss the place and find his glasses. The woman threw up her hands and walked away. A breathless soldier ran back and handed the worn velour case to the officer in charge. By this time, Martin's ass was frozen numb. He wiped his glasses carefully, perched them on his nose, and looked again at the photos.

"They were just here." He knew they knew that. "I think. I don't know about the flamingo-haired girl. It might have been her."

"How long ago?"

"Oh . . ." Martin felt for his watch. He wasn't wearing one. "After breakfast." He smiled brightly. "We had toast."

The officer in charge rolled his eyes under his ski mask. "Get up." He reached down to grab the old man's arm. "Obstructing justice is a serious charge, old man. These people are fugitives."

Martin's eyes fluttered. He flopped limp as a rag doll, clutched his chest. He gasped, spittle flecking the officer's camo shoulder. "Oh! My chest . . . I need to sit down."

He grabbed his heart as the officer lowered him to the ground, and rocked back and forth. "Ohhhhhhh . . ." He moaned in apparent agony.

"Medic!" the officer snapped.

Another soldier knelt before him, tried to pry his arms from his chest. "Where does it hurt, sir?"

"Ohhh . . . my chest! My arm!" Martin's face twitched, and he screwed his eyes shut enough to prevent the medic from prying them open. His pulse raced and the medic looked up, alarmed.

"We need an ambulance, sir."

"Shit. Sergeant, are you telling me that we just gave that old man a heart attack?"

"Possibly, sir."

"Call it . . ."

While Martin writhed on the ground, he smiled inwardly to himself. He was a better actor than Harry gave him credit for. Now, just to keep his pulse racing, he'd have to think more on *The Ambience of Sensual Massage,* at least until he got to the hospital. He doubted many interrogations went down in hospitals, and he had enough ailments to keep the hospital staff busy for days . . .

THE OLD MAN WAS A WASTE OF TIME.

Adrienne pawed through the clutter in the trailer. The place reeked of her quarry. She smelled Tara on the flannels in the hamper, a towel in the bathroom, on the bedspread in the bedroom, in the fading musk on the bed in the back room.

Adrienne rooted around in the kitchen sink. She cast aside a worn sponge, a clutch of spoons, and cracked coffee cups. At last she plucked a dirty fork from the pile of dishes. She grinned. The bright sunlight gleamed down on the cheap metal, stuck with desiccated crumbs. Adrienne clutched it in her fist like a treasure and shouldered past Gabriel's men to exit the trailer.

She could see Tara's footprints in the snow outside the trailer, the same size as the clunky boots in the cabin. She followed the footsteps, pressing her own larger feet over the tracks. It gave her a sting of satisfaction to see them obliterated by her own steps.

If only it was that easy to wipe out their owner . . .

The footprints led to a mash up of vehicle tracks . . . a large truck, she guessed. It would be a small task to determine which vehicles were registered to the old man. The larger task would be determining where Tara was going. Whether or not she had the girl with her was inconsequential to Adrienne, but an additional kill would be a bonus for her employer.

Twirling the fork in her fingertips, Adrienne strode out to the tree line, past the pines laden with snow. She walked until she was out of sight of the cabin, until the tracks of deer were the only ones that intersected hers. The shadows of birds flickered overhead, interrupting the shafts of sunshine streaming through the trees.

She crouched down to the ground, brushing away snow until the bare, frozen earth was visible. Her fingers were red and ached with cold, but she paid them no mind. From her jacket pocket, she withdrew a creased map of the region and smoothed it over the ground, orienting the compass rose to true north. Adrienne didn't need to look to find it; she sensed the cardinal directions as easily as the others around her sensed the demarcation between day and night.

From her jacket, she pulled the bottle of earth she'd collected from Tara's cabin. Nestled close to her body for days, the glass felt warm in her hands. Adrienne unscrewed the cap and dumped half the contents of the dirt in her left hand. She breathed her intention on it, to find its owner.

She closed her eyes and scattered it on the map.

The dirt settled in a sinuous line, curling and drawing in upon itself. It slithered like a snake across the paper, as if it were composed of metal filings drawn by a magnet. The soil spiraled, unsettled, trying to draw itself in two directions at once.

Adrienne placed the fork on the map, twirled it like a child turning the spinner of a board game. The earth congealed, wrapping around the fork. When it stopped spinning, the earth coiled around the tines of the fork, gathered around one location, in the middle of nowhere. The legend on the map pointed out a village beside the interstate, listed in the smallest typeface on the map legend.

Adrienne sat back on her heels. A place like that was close to the interstate, allowing quick withdrawal after the kill. There would be few witnesses.

It was the perfect place for an ambush.

• • • •

THERE HAD TO HAVE BEEN A BETTER WAY TO SAY GOOD-BYE.

Tara stared fixedly ahead at the road. A fine sleet filtered from the sky, and the windshield wipers flipped over the glass with the regular rhythm of a metronome, in counterpoint to the loud purr of the engine and the occasional jingle of Martin's hood ornament key chain striking the dash. She cranked the defroster as high as it would go . . . Warmth issued from that, but not from the floor vents of the old truck. She'd found an old blanket behind the seat, and Cassie had spread it over the front seat, her father's laptop open and plugged into the cigarette lighter. Her eyes flickered right and left across the page, absorbing her father's work. The truck smelled of sour coffee and sweet antifreeze.

Maggie had fallen asleep in the middle of the seat, her butt on Cassie's lap and her head on Tara's. Tara was sure the dog could sense her despondency, and was doing her best to help her feel better.

She gripped the steering wheel, making her wounded arm ache. She'd allowed herself to hope, made the mistake of thinking that Harry would be able to accept and understand her. Why couldn't she have left well enough alone? Why couldn't she have accepted the gift of last night without sabotaging it? She honestly didn't remember where she'd left the card, but it wasn't like her years of conditioning to leave such a thing available for prying eyes.

And now she was paying for it. Her vision blurred. How could she have expected Harry to understand? He lived in an entirely different world, a linear one with well-drawn boundaries and clear causes and effects. She didn't belong in it. She was a fool to think she might have found some common ground, that her fluid world of intuition could coexist and intersect with his.

But she'd had hope, last night. She wiped her dripping nose with the back of her glove. It had blossomed pure and brilliant in her chest, and she had allowed herself to follow her feelings. This time, her instincts had been wrong. How could she have expected that that sense of security, of contentment, could ever become hers?

It was done. One glorious moment, over. And for what? The use of a power that always seemed to lead to ruin. The cards had led her to ruin before, had led her to the Gardener and his tender mercies. How could she expect this would be any different? This gift her mother had given her, this talent for reading the cards, was nothing more than a curse. Perhaps her mother was well free of it.

Cassie painted on the inside fog of the window with her finger, shapes of waves and stars. Tara squelched the image of the Star card that welled up in her mind.

"Where are we going?" Cassie asked.

"We're meeting Sophia at a diner off the interstate. I don't know where she'll be taking you from there, but it will be to a safe house."

Cassie looked doubtful. "You said she was an old friend of your mother's. Is she a government agent, too?"

Tara laughed. "No. Sophia is most definitely not with the government. She's not exactly what you'd call a conformist. Think Birkenstocks, not gun stocks."

"Nonconformity is good." Cassie twirled a streak of blue hair around her finger. "I'm envisioning a survivalist? Maybe an eccentric artist? An ex-hippie?"

"A bit of all three." Tara smiled. "I think you'll like her. You two will have some interesting debates."

Cassie frowned. "You're not staying with us." Tara could hear the thread of fear, the fear of abandonment, in her voice. Her fingers clutched Maggie's fur.

Tara shook her head. "I can't. I have to get back to help Harry." She paused, thinking about this. Harry may not want her help. Harry would probably refuse to let her do anything more than take notes on the case.

That was, if he wasn't driving into a trap with DiRosa. Fear bristled through her at the thought. Her intuition tingled, and she forced it down with a bubble of anger.

"We'll see," she amended. "I may have some of Sophia's strudel, after all."

In truth, she'd like nothing better than to keep going, to keep driving until she found her little cabin in the woods once more. She could lock the real door and keep all the other doors that were opened in the middle of the night firmly shut: Magnusson's riddles; Sophia; and especially, Harry.

A DIM SENSE OF UNEASE SETTLED OVER HARRY, STRENGTHENing the closer he sped to his destination. It was like driving into a cloudy day, the gray folding around him so subtly he didn't notice when condensation began to stream from the car windows. Above, the sleeting skies had cast a thin spittle of ice on the roads, making the drive slower and more treacherous than he liked. He would be late for his meeting with DiRosa. He tried to call twice, got no answer. He hoped she would wait for him.

Darkness was falling by the time he drove into Bandelier, and he barely got in the park gate before closing time, at sunset. The mountains seemed very close to the sky, as if they scraped ice from those heavy gray clouds. The ruddy rock of the canyons was dulled by frost. In the distance, he could see the myriad holes in the red cliffs made by the Anasazi, centuries ago. No visitors, today. It was too cold for the archaeology students and the hikers to prop their ladders against the cliff face and explore the labyrinths of that lost civilization.

Harry had to admire the ingenuity of living on the face of a cliff, with this glorious panorama spread out below. No one could sneak up on you. One was intimately aware of one's environment, in complete control.

Unlike this meeting, which Harry felt was quickly slipping out of control. He tried DiRosa's cell phone again. No answer. He pulled his car to a scenic overlook, offering an incredible view of the blue mountains, rust-colored cliffs, and orange sunset pouring through the few holes in the gray sky in great columns of molten light. This was the designated meeting spot. One other car was parked in the overlook lane, a late-model Beemer with a meticulous sheen of wax. It had been there awhile; frost had accumulated over the windows, and the engine wasn't running. Perhaps it was an abandoned breakdown.

Still.

Harry parked far enough from the rear of the car that

he couldn't be boxed in by another car parking behind him. He scanned the vicinity, registering no signs of life. Bitter wind stirred blonde grasses growing at the edge of the road. A guide sign beside the overlook described in basic detail the Anasazi homes carved out of the rock below the overlook and across the chasm.

He stepped out of his car, his gun drawn. He left the engine running, the lights on, framing the frost-covered car before him. He advanced on the driver's side door, knocked on the window. No movement inside. Even after scraping away frost, he couldn't make out the interior through the tinted windows.

Heart hammering, he tried the door. He expected it to be locked, but it swung open. Harry stepped back away from the door in a crouch, aiming his gun into the cold interior.

Barbara DiRosa slipped partially out of her seat belt, her left hand brushing the gravel. Her camel-colored glove and coat were stained in rust, her highlighted blonde hair streaked with the corroded bloodstain sticking her collar to the seat. She'd been shot and left for him. Harry had walked right into the trap.

"Shit." He backed away, turning to sprint back to his car.

The bright blue-white of halogen headlights bounced over the road, the engine propelling them revving. A black SUV slammed into the back of Harry's car, forcing it forward, trying to crush Harry between the front bumper of his car and the back bumper of the Beemer.

Harry jumped out of the way, over the guardrail of

the scenic overlook. His shoes skidded in gravel, and he clawed forward with his hands, trying to correct his pitch before he went sliding down the sharp slope. Gravel chewed into his hands and face, weeds slapped him, and he managed to rip out a sage bush before tumbling over the edge.

He heard voices. A shot rang out, pulverizing gravel to his left and spewing sharp fragments into his face. He returned fire, but the angle was too steep for him to see what he was aiming for; he couldn't see beyond the guardrail. He was a sitting duck.

Harry turned, looked down. The slope disappeared into darkness. He decided darkness was a better bet than bullets, and let go of the sage bush.

He pitched into the gloom, and his stomach leaped into his chest. His feet and hands scrabbled for purchase, and he landed on his knees in a flash of pain on a stone outcropping. Hearing the crunch of footfalls above him, Harry ran downward. By the dim light, he could see a narrow crevasse splitting the red rock, and he followed it. Behind him, voices shouted, pebbles spewed underfoot, and he could glimpse the glimmer of flashlights and the red flash of a laser sight.

The striated rock he wound through was both hollow and solid, honeycombed with large pockets of darkness and air, alternating paths of positive and negative space. He flung himself into the mouth of one vault of darkness, large enough for a man. Feeling his way, he stumbled down a tunnel, slipped behind a vertical rock into a shallow depression. This deep in the cliff face, he could feel the volcanic rock radiating cold around him. His breath hissed too loud, filling the chamber with his exertion. His knee felt hot and sticky. Cold air sliced through tears in his sleeves.

Above him, he could hear the crunch of footsteps echoing crazily, growing louder. He hoped they would not find him, that they'd assume he'd jumped. But the voices gathered closer, intimate in the darkness as lovers' whispers or the murmurings of ghosts.

He gripped his pistol, counting in his head how many shots he had left in the clip. Not enough to fight. There could have been up to eight men in that vehicle, and more might be on the way. He could either stay where he was, or try to run.

He flexed his torn knee. If he stayed here, they would eventually stumble across him. More suitable cover would be likely to be found on the floor of the canyon, after dark.

The bright white of a flashlight beam washed past him, and Harry leaned as far back into the wall as he could. He closed one eye in an effort to keep half of his vision adjusted to the darkness that would come back when the light passed. He held his breath, trying to keep it from condensing into a fog that would resolve too readily in the beam of light and give him away.

The beam washed away and he let out his breath, opening his other eye. He could see the shapes of men at the mouth of the little cave, outlined as inky figures against the pale charcoal of the sky. He counted four men, armed, and heard the static hiss of radios under enforced radio silence. The lights turned away, and the men descended down a short run of rough-hewn steps, out of his field of vision.

Harry waited until the last sound of disturbed gravel drained away, and stepped noiselessly out of his pocket of darkness. He crept to the edge of the cave, looked down, and spied men milling on a step below. They communicated to one another through hand gestures, fanning out.

He heard the unmistakable click of the safety of a gun being switched off behind his ear. He cursed inwardly. They'd left a man behind to secure the areas they'd already searched. He smelled the tang of gunpowder, assumed the gun had been fired recently. Distractedly, he wondered if this was one of the guns that had shot at him, or if this was the one that had executed DiRosa.

"Agent Li."

Harry's heart thudded against his spine. He knew that voice.

"We have some issues to discuss."

Chapter Fourteen

Tara stared out the diner window. It felt good to be out of the truck, to stretch her legs someplace warm. The gravel parking lot was empty, except for the pickup and two cars Tara assumed belonged to the waitress and the cook. Inside Martin's pickup, Maggie's tail thumped against the driver's side window. The window fog showed smear tracks from the dog's nose in abstract scribbles on the windshield. The darkness was falling swiftly, and there were no parking lot lights at this place.

The diner was empty except for the smells. The waitress wasn't chatty, seeming content to stay in the kitchen and flirt with the cook. The rest of the booths were empty, peppered with duct tape repairs in the torn Naugahyde seats. It smelled like bacon and hash browns, breakfast twenty-four-seven. Across the white and gold-flecked

Formica table, Cassie wolfed down her second stack of pancakes. Tara stared into her coffee, her appetite stifled. She'd swallowed a great deal of pride to ask Sophia for help. She hoped it would be worth it.

A glossy black sedan pulled into the lot, headlights washing over the gravel. Tara narrowed her eyes. The car wasn't Sophia's old station wagon. Automatically, she reached under her jacket and rested her finger on the trigger guard of her gun.

The doors opened like the wings of a raven. Sophia stepped out of the driver's side, bundled in a thick gray poncho, her braided hair flipped over her shoulder. On the passenger's side, a short Middle Eastern woman climbed out. Her long dark hair streamed behind her, her coat brushing her ankles.

Shit. Sophia had brought the Pythia.

Tara's gut instinct was to call it all back, to flee. Perhaps she could have hidden Cassie herself. But it was too late for that, now.

The cowbell tied to the door jangled. The Pythia brushed through the door first, and the scent of cinnamon came before her. Sophia closed the door behind her and sat down beside Tara. The Pythia slipped into the booth beside Cassie, and her proximity to the girl made Tara's skin crawl. The Pythia looked them both up and down with eyes dark as sloes.

Tara nodded tightly. "Cassie, this is Sophia, and . . ."

"Amira." The Pythia smiled serenely at the girl.

Tara closed her mouth. She'd never heard the Pythia's name spoken before. For whatever reason, she was using it today. If that even *was* her real name, and not a guise she was using for the moment.

Cassie placed her fork down. Surely she was picking up some of the tension. She folded her hands in her lap. "Nice to meet you."

Tara kept her hand nestled under her jacket. "I'm surprised to see you both here," she said mildly. "I'd thought Sophia would come alone."

The Pythia gave a small shrug. "You asked her to bring reinforcements." She glanced at Cassie and smiled. "Sophia brought me for my mad dancing skills."

What strange world had she fallen into? The Pythia was cracking jokes? Tara opened her mouth to say something, closed it.

"You're a dancer?" Cassie asked.

"Among other things. I lead a belly dance troupe in Portland."

"Cool."

Tara leaned back in her seat. She wasn't sure what to do with the situation: the Pythia was attempting to put Cassie at ease, and the effort put Tara on edge. The Pythia never tried to make anyone comfortable, unless it was for something that benefited her.

The Pythia pulled an envelope out of her coat and handed it to the girl. "I have a present for you."

Cassie looked at the enveloped quizzically. "A present?"

"Open it."

Cassie pulled out a sheaf of papers. A driver's license and a passport book fell out into her maple syrup. She rescued them from the goo, wiping the plastic with her napkin. Staring back at her was her photograph on a driver's license, wearing a brunette version of her hair that Tara had to admit was a very good job of photo retouching. Below it was a different name: Astrid Cole. "What's this?"

"A new identity. If we get stopped along the way, you're Sophia's granddaughter."

Tara could see the objections forming in Cassie's face. "But I don't want a new identity . . ."

"It's not permanent, my dear," Sophia reassured her. "Just until we get this settled."

Cassie looked at Tara, as if asking for permission. Tara nodded, not taking her eyes off the Pythia. Cassie scooped the documents back into the envelope. "Um. Thanks." A thought flickered across her face. "Does this mean I have to dye my hair?"

Sophia chuckled. "Any shade of brown you like that's available at the twenty-four-hour drugstore."

"Thank you," said Tara.

"You're most welcome." Sophia folded her hands on the table, looked Tara full in the face. "How are you holding up?"

"I'm fine." Tara sipped her bitter coffee. "We're—I'm—still looking for Magnusson." She looked down at the counter.

Sophia reached over to grasp Tara's hand. "Tara . . ." Her attention fixed on the tear in her coat. Her coat was black, so the bloodstain didn't show, but Sophia still noticed. Nothing ever escaped her attention. Tara fought the urge to pull her hand away. She didn't want Cassie to see conflict between her and Sophia, wanted Cassie to trust she would be safe with the older woman. Tara's issues with the Pythia were beside the point.

And Sophia was seizing this chance. "She'll be safe with me."

But would she be safe with the Pythia? Tara bit her lip, forced herself to nod. "I know. How's Oscar?" she asked, changing the subject. She missed the furball terribly.

Sophia's eyes twinkled. "I took him home with me. He made a nest in the breadbox on the kitchen counter." She lifted a spoon from the place setting, squinted into it. "He's fine," she said, as if scrying into her reflection on the spoon confirmed it. The gesture was just subtle enough to escape Cassie's notice.

Tara was grateful they were keeping their status as oracles low-key. She didn't want to explain Delphi's Daughters to Cassie. The girl had reached the limit of what she could absorb just now, and Tara didn't want her to crack.

"Oscar's not allowed on countertops." Tara smiled in spite of herself at the image of Oscar making a den in Sophia's kitchen.

"He doesn't seem to care."

The Pythia sat back against the booth, observing the banal chatter. She seemed to be appraising Tara. She pulled a silver-inlaid lighter out of her pocket. Tara couldn't imagine the fate that would befall the poor waitress if she dared tell the Pythia that no smoking was allowed in the diner. The Pythia flipped the switch on the lighter, squinting into the flame, but produced no cigarettes. Tara had the urge to ask her what she saw in the tiny flame.

Cassie wrinkled her nose. "I'm gonna take a pit stop."

Tara slid out of the booth to oblige her.

"I'll go with her." Sophia shadowed the girl to the ladies' room, engaging her in light chatter about what a pretty chestnut brown would look like over her existing hair color.

And that left Tara alone with the Pythia.

The lighter flicked on and off, the ghosts of its image flashing in the bottomless pit of the Pythia's gaze. Tara placed her sweating hands, palms down, on the table. The heat from them left condensation marks on the chipped Formica.

Tara's lips thinned. "Just make sure that you take better care of her than you took of my mother." Her voice was heavy with threat, with unshed tears.

The Pythia's attention shifted from the flame to Tara. "I'm sorry. I'm sorry I held that back from you. But you must realize . . . your mother didn't want you to know she had cancer. She swore me to secrecy."

Tears stung Tara's eyes. "You should have told me. I could have found her help."

The Pythia shook her head, a gray tendril of hair loosening around her face. "I tried. She didn't want it."

Tara paused. "You what?"

"I tried to get her to seek treatment. I begged her. Pleaded with her." The Pythia's eyes shone with tears. "She was like a daughter to me. My successor. How could I have done any less? But she refused. It was her decision."

Tara leaned against the back of the booth, deflated. She'd felt too many losses. Perhaps she had been trying too hard to find someone tangible to blame. Sophia had been there, just as she always had since she was a child, and had gracefully accepted the brunt of her anger. The Pythia had been far distant from her adult world, and perhaps that made it easier for Tara to place the blame on her. But she wasn't ready to forgive, not yet.

"What do you want from me?" Tara hissed. "What does Adrienne want?"

The Pythia's gaze devoured her. "Adrienne wants you dead."

"And what do you want?" Tara challenged her. "Do you want me to follow nicely in my mother's footsteps? Be your puppet?"

The Pythia placed the lighter on the table. "I would not ask anything of you that you've not already given."

"Why did you allow her to come after me? Don't you have better control over your daughters?"

The Pythia frowned. "We don't foresee everything. We're not omniscient. You know that. We see bits and pieces, glimpses of a larger, unknowable, and hidden whole. And Adrienne is . . ." Tara watched a lump work its way down the Pythia's throat, "more powerful than any of us, now."

"How could you let that happen?" Tara was dumbstruck at the admission.

The Pythia shook her head. "It was a mistake. I saw, from the start, that she could be a great and powerful oracle. What I did not see was that she was incapable of forming attachments with others. Incapable of empathy. I'm sure that, if she were a child today, a psychiatrist would give her a suitable descriptive label . . . reactive attachment disorder? Whatever her life had been before she came to us, it robbed her of the ability to see people as anything other than cardboard."

Tara narrowed her eyes. "Are you sure Delphi's Daughters didn't do that to her?"

The Pythia's red mouth tightened. "We did the best we could."

Cassie and Sophia returned from the ladies' room, but the waitress never did come back. Tara laid her guesstimate of the bill on the table, and the four women jangled the cowbell on the way to the parking lot. Cassie opened the pickup door, and Maggie tumbled out, tail wagging, snuffling over Sophia.

"Can Maggie come with us?" Cassie's eyes were large with fear that she would say no. Tara understood the dog was the last piece of her former life that she had left.

"Of course." Sophia scrubbed her fingers into the dog's coat, and Maggie made awful faces of enjoyment. She followed Sophia and the Pythia to the glossy sedan, and Sophia opened the door. The interior smelled like new leather. Maggie bounded into the backseat and laid down. She looked ruefully up at Tara and whimpered. Tara tried to smooth the worried furrows on her furry brow with her thumb.

Cassie threw her arms around Tara.

"I'll talk to you soon. I promise," Tara said. She hoped she could keep her word.

Cassie nodded and handed Tara her heavy backpack. "Here."

"That's your father's laptop. He wanted you to have it."
Tara was reluctant to take it. She understood the weight
parental relics could have, these last bits of knowledge,
that, for good or ill, were power in their children's hands.
And Tara doubted that she could protect it.

Cassie shook her head. "I've read through every file."
She tapped her temple. "It's all up here in the photographic
memory cells, now." She smiled self-consciously. "I don't
understand it all yet, but it's here."

Cassie patted the bag. "I did . . . I think I did what he
would have wanted me to do with the data." Her smile
was enigmatic, but Tara thought she understood its meaning. It seemed the girl had taken on something larger
than herself, suddenly become older and wiser for having ingested her father's life work. "The laptop is just an
empty shell now. Use it to find him," the girl implored,
then disappeared into the car and shut the door.

The Pythia stared over the roof of the car to the horizon. Her reflection warbled in the paint, and it seemed a
great heat was generated from her glare. Tara followed
her line of sight, seeing a pair of headlights exiting from
the freeway.

"It's Adrienne," the Pythia said.

Tara squinted at the shape. "Run. I'll cover you."

Tara ducked into the pickup, cranked over the ignition. The Pythia's car peeled out of the parking lot, and
Tara positioned the bulk of the truck behind it. In her
rearview mirror, she saw brake lights. The SUV that had
exited the interstate realized who they were and was making a U-turn.

The Pythia's car glided onto the on-ramp like a sleek, black bird. The pickup's engine groaned to follow. The entrance ramp had been well-salted, and the deep grooves of the tires gained traction.

Tara swung the truck into a slide. It fishtailed, then turned in a half circle to block the entrance ramp. She reached into her holster for her gun and cranked down the window. The bitch was going to have to go through her. In the distance, she could hear the sound of the Pythia's car accelerating.

The charcoal-gray SUV completed its turn, picked up speed. Its lights flashed over Tara's truck.

Shit. Adrienne was crazy enough to ram her. Tara stepped on the gas. The SUV slammed into the tailgate of the truck, spinning the pickup around on the glaze of ice. Tara wrestled with the wheel as the pickup clipped a road sign. The truck came to rest on a frozen divot between the exit ramp and the interstate.

In her rearview mirror, Tara could see men in black fatigues climbing out of the SUV. She waited, slumped over the wheel, playing opossum until it emptied. Her heart hammered under her tongue. Three men, dressed in black fatigues and gripping MP-5s, advanced upon the pickup.

Adrienne wasn't among them.

Tara slammed on the gas pedal. The truck crawled out of the shallow divot with a shudder and a belch. Bullets pinged off its thick hide. Tara's admiration for the truck increased: it was like a dinosaur. It bumped over the shoulder of the road and onto the entrance ramp.

In her peripheral vision, the men clambered back to the SUV.

Alarm coursed through her. Adrienne knew where she was . . . Where was the bitch? And who else had she brought with her? Her thoughts raced to the Pythia's car. As the pickup labored up to speed, she could see the glow of multiple sets of taillights in the far distance.

Shit.

She stomped on the accelerator. The truck growled and surged forward, struggling to close the distance between her and the Pythia's car. Cold winter air lashed her face, numbing her skin. As the distance narrowed, she could see a pair of taillights, close behind the black car.

The SUV from the entrance ramp chewed up the road behind her. Tara's thoughts raced, her eyes darting around the interior of the truck cab. Somehow, she had to keep them behind her . . . far, far behind her.

Tara rolled down the driver's side window. The cold blast of air stung her face hard. She reached down on the floor of the truck. Martin kept a lot of junk down here. Hopefully, some of it was heavy junk. She fished around among empty coffee cups, candy wrappers, and newspapers. Her hand wrapped around a floor jack. She threw it out the window. The jack crashed wide, missing its intended target. The SUV plowed ahead, undeterred. Bullets peppered the tailgate of the dinosaur truck.

Tara ducked down, her right hand scrabbling among the debris on the floor again. She picked up and discarded a flashlight, then smiled in triumph as she found the cold, smooth metal of a tire iron.

She lightened her step on the gas, waited for the SUV to gain behind her, then chucked it out the window. She watched it bounce once and chip the pavement before it crashed into the windshield of the SUV, caving it. The SUV swerved, struck the guardrail, and stilled.

Tara ground her teeth. Lucky shot. It might take them a few minutes to recover, to kick out the glass, wipe their bloody noses, and get moving again. She hoped that was enough time.

Ahead, the second SUV was playing road games with the Pythia. It accelerated, trying to clip the car's bumper. At this rate of speed, contact would send the car sailing past the guardrails into the darkness beyond. Snow spat flakes into the sharp ravines below the freeway, falling free and weightless.

Tara accelerated within range of the SUV. Clutching the steering wheel with her right hand, she lowered her pistol out the window and balanced it on the side mirror. Wind whistled over the barrel with the sound of air blowing across the lip of a bottle. It was nearly impossible to aim correctly; she wanted to hit the point at which the SUV's tires met the pavement, but she had five shots. Her hand was flash-frozen numb in the cold, and the wind shook her aim. Her eyes teared.

The first two missed; the third lodged in the bumper. Her next shot exploded the rear driver's side tire in a blossom of rubber ribbon. The SUV swerved and struck the Pythia's bumper. The SUV slid away, past the guardrails, and down an embankment, out of sight.

But Tara's attention was riveted on the Pythia's car.

The tag from the SUV had caused Sophia to lurch out of control. The car swerved left, then right, as Sophia over-corrected, and skidded on the ice. To Tara's horror, the car struck the rumble strips on the side of the road and flipped, side over side. She could hear her hoarse voice echoing in the car as she clutched the steering wheel and screamed.

The dinosaur pickup skidded to a halt. Tara grabbed the heavy flashlight from the floorboards and jumped out of the cab. She sprinted to the car, turned upside down like a beetle on its back. She could smell gas leaking and the acrid stench of smoke.

She reached the back doors first, but they were jammed shut. Swinging the flashlight, she battered the glass until it cracked in a spiderweb and dented in. She pulled the sheet of ruined safety glass away from the window.

"Cassie!" she shouted. The girl wiggled out of her seat belt and through the window, followed by Maggie. Her forehead was bloodied, but she seemed otherwise unhurt. Maggie whimpered and licked her face, lashing her legs with her tail.

"Get to the truck. Now." Tara could see flames licking under the hood, see the gasoline staining the snow.

The car had come to rest on the driver's side. She crossed to the passenger's side, ready to wield the flashlight.

A thumping echoed from inside the car. The windshield flexed and caved, kicked away under the force of an Italian leather shoe. The Pythia peeled away the remnants of the windshield and leaped onto the hood of the car with the grace of a dancer. Glass shimmered on her, and Tara was struck by the raw power in her stance. Flames licked at the edge of the coat.

Tara climbed up on the hood, already scorching from whatever broken piece of hydraulics had caught fire. She reached inside for Sophia.

The Pythia caught her arm. "No."

Tara shrugged it away and crawled up the creased hood to the driver's seat. "Sophia?"

A platinum braid dangled over the steering wheel, stained pink over a limp hand. Tara reached in, grasped her shoulder. "Sophia, c'mon. Let's go."

But Sophia's head lolled to the side. Her face was a ruined mass of pulp where it rested against the broken dashboard. Tara's blood-slick fingers reached for purchase, trying to find a pulse. Her own roared in her ears. The rearview mirror dripped red onto the burled wood dash.

She felt the Pythia's hands on her like a vise, dragging her away. The Pythia's shouts were indecipherable, but the diminutive woman hauled Tara off the hood of the car, back into the snow. Tara fought her, but some part of her knew it was useless.

Flames licked up over the frame of the windshield, and black smoke overtook the wreck. She could smell burning rubber and oil with the sweet aftertang of antifreeze. Tara's bloody hands flung off the Pythia's grip, but the heat kept her from approaching the fire.

"There's nothing you can do," the Pythia told her. "We have to go."

Tara choked. Her logical mind tried to force her back to the shadow of the truck, but she remained rooted in place. Beside her, the Pythia stared into the fire. Even when Tara started the truck and limped them out onto the highway, the cab of the dinosaur pickup full of two oracles, a girl, and a shivering dog, the Pythia kept staring at the receding fire.

It wasn't until afterward that Tara wondered what she saw in the flames.

A RAVEN SCAVENGED ALONE BY THE SIDE OF THE ROAD, BESIDE a car wreck. His head bobbed as he walked. Snow stuck to his iridescent plumage and filled in his tracks. He paused over a broken taillight, admiring his image in the shiny surface. He had the attitude of an oracle scrying, turning his head this way and that, watching until the snow blanketed the fragment of plastic and blotted out his reflection

Yards distant, the door of a battered SUV opened. A woman climbed out, one eye matted with stringy blonde hair and blood.

The raven paused, watching her. She wasn't playing with anything shiny, so it ignored her, returning to forage for things in the wreckage that glittered.

She snapped the antenna off the roof of the SUV. Adrienne squatted at the edge of the road, pulled a bottle and an envelope from her coat. From the bottle, she tapped out the remainder of the earth she'd collected from Tara's cabin. Warmed by her body, the granules sunk into the snow. From the envelope, she pulled a few strands of dark hair. The strands caught on the snow and road grime at the shoulder of the road.

With the broken antenna from the SUV, she made sixteen lines of random dots, counting under her breath. The dots speckled the snow and drove the strands of hair deep into the snow. This was traditional geomancy, one of the oldest and most powerful forms. It operated similarly to the I Ching, relying on sixteen possible geomantic figures to divine the future. Figures were derived in stages from the sixteen random lines called the Mothers, Daughters, Nephews, Witnesses . . . and finally, the Judge. Each of the sixteen geomantic figures could occupy one of those positions. The figures, given traditional Latin names, represented timeless human conditions: people, paths, union, imprisonment, fortune, gain, loss, sadness, joy, passion, illumination, men, women, entry, and exit.

"Tell me where to find my prey."

She reduced the sixteen lines of dots to four geomantic figures, the four Mothers. Odd sums gave one point, and even sums gave two. She counted under her steaming breath, sketching four figures below the sixteen original lines. She summed and reduced the Mothers to four Daughter figures, and the four Daughters to four Nephews.

The raven, bored with his treasure, wandered by to see what she was doing with the shiny stick. He had little interest in her, but the shiny stick fascinated him. He wandered under her shadow, and Adrienne made note of where his tracks fell. Divination by animal tracks was an art unto itself; any input the raven would provide would be heeded.

His tracks crossed over the symbol Amissio in the row of Mother symbols, over a cluster of six dots in the shape of two nesting cups turned upside down, spilling their contents onto the ground. Amissio represented loss, things taken away from the querent, whether willingly or by force. Adrienne frowned at seeing this symbol in the Mother row.

The raven hopped over to the Daughter row, and his talons scraped a figure with dots arranged in a large *V.* Tristitia, the Latin word for "sorrow," was a marker of sadness.

That was the past. No information she didn't already know. Impatient, she returned to her calculations with the broken antenna.

From the Nephews, she derived two Witnesses. She paused when she derived the two figures: Conjunctio and Cauda Draconis. Conjunctio, a simple X formed by the dots, suggested the recovery of missing things. The figure was a sign of conjunction, the joining of two lost things. A good omen for a tracker.

Cauda Draconis was known as the Tail of the Dragon, represented by an upside-down Y. In some situations, it spoke of a way out. This was the solution she sought. But the Tail of the Dragon was considered a sign of evil, and was tied to the astrological symbol for the moon.

Adding together the symbols for the two Witnesses, she arrived at the final outcome, in the final position called the Judge. This represented the Fates' judgment of the situation. Carcer, six dots arranged into a closed shape, was her final figure. It represented imprisonment, a link in an unbroken chain.

Adrienne leaned forward. That was where she would catch Tara: where her partner was imprisoned. She had spent too much time chasing her. She needed to allow her prey to come to her.

She cast aside the antenna and reached for her cell phone. No signal, this far into nowhere. She began to walk back to the nearest exit on the interstate. If the cell phone was still useless there, at least she could hitch a ride.

The raven waddled back to the geomantic oracle. He cocked his head right and left, looking at the impressions rapidly filling in the dirty snow. When he took wing, one of his pinfeathers brushed a figure in the Nephew row: Rubeus, Latin for "red," the color of blood. The dots formed the shape of an overturned cup, its contents spilled. The figure was a warning to cease and desist, presaging destructive passion.

Unseen by Adrienne, snow continued to fall, obliterating the warning.

Chapter **Fifteen**

Y ou've lost much, my dear. But not everything."

Tara shook her head. "Pythia . . ." She focused on scrubbing the blood from her coat with a motel washcloth. She didn't know whose blood it was staining the white washcloth or the coat spread over the motel ironing board. She would have felt guilty removing it if it had been Sophia's, but she liked the illusion of not knowing.

Tears glossed her eyes. She had never forgiven Sophia for the loss of her mother. And now it was too late.

At her feet, Maggie moaned. Tara had spent a half hour brushing glass out of her fur, but the dog was otherwise unhurt. Tara suspected the groan was another complaint about the bath she'd been given. A damp spot from the dog's fur soaked into the carpet.

"You still have Delphi's Daughters, whether you want us or not." The Pythia sat on the edge of the bed. She seemed somehow elegantly incongruous with the ugly floral bedspread and the quarter slot for the Magic Fingers vibrating bed. Tara could never imagine the Pythia using the Magic Fingers. Freshly scrubbed, her hair was bound up in a towel, and she was wrapped in a robe. A cigarette twitched from her fingers into the ashtray that the Pythia had demanded from the night clerk in no uncertain terms. Worms of red light pulsed through the ashes that never quite grew cold. She stared at them. "And . . . there's someone new in your life. I can feel it."

Tara looked away. She spread her hands out helplessly before her, and her voice dropped to a whisper. "I destroy everything I touch. Everything I love is taken from me . . ."

"No." The Pythia's voice was harsh as steel wool. "Look at me."

Tara faced her, her vision blurry.

"Do not do what your mother did," the Pythia whispered furiously. "Do not give up. Fight. You are a fighter. You have the strength to see this through."

Tara gave a wan smile. "I'm not so sure." She felt weak, ineffective as dandelion fluff in a thunderstorm.

"I am," the Pythia said. She tapped more glowing ash into the ashtray. "Don't let him get away."

Tara lifted her eyebrow and opened her mouth, but the bathroom door opened. Cassie came hesitantly into the room, running her fingers through her newly brunette locks. "What do you think?" she asked. The hair swung over a cut on her forehead Tara had closed with butterfly bandages. She smelled of the cloyingly sweet smell of the hair conditioner that came with the dye.

The Pythia smiled. "You are lovely, my dear." She fished out a pair of scissors from the discount-store bags cluttering the floor: hair dye, new clothes, candy bars, first aid supplies. The Pythia herded her back into the bathroom, and Tara could hear the *snip-snick* of scissors as the Pythia cut Cassie's hair.

They were waiting. Waiting for Delphi's Daughters to come and hide Cassie. The nearest ones were still a few hours away. The Pythia had stared into her lighter and stated that this fleabag motel would be safe. Tara had parked Martin's dinosaur pickup in the shadow of tractor-trailers; there was no way it could be seen from the road.

Tara gathered up the bloodstained clothes and put them in opaque black trash bags. After a moment's hesitation, she put her coat in there, too. There was no saving it. She let herself out of the room and walked out to the Dumpster to dispose of the evidence. A lump formed in her throat; she felt as if she was losing the last bit of Sophia.

The cold lanced through her T-shirt and jeans as she walked, barefoot, to the Dumpster. Her feet crunched over the sharp ice slivers as she crossed the parking lot.

She paused before a pay phone and fished out some change.

Tara pressed the greasy receiver of the pay phone to her ear. Bitter wind chewed at her hair, and she turned against the wind to keep it from whistling across the receiver. She knew that the GPS chip in her own cell phone would be traced the instant she powered it up; her odds of remaining undetected were better using a pay phone. She transferred through three operators, hoping that would obscure her tracks, before connecting to Harry's cell phone number. It clicked immediately over to voice mail, and she hung up before hearing more than *"Hell-."* Two seconds wasn't enough time for Gabriel to trace her whereabouts, but that one syllable told her all she needed to know. She wound through directory assistance and an operator again to connect her to the number at Martin's home. She let it ring twice: no answer.

She hung up, shivering. Dread twitched through her. Had Harry fallen into a trap, or was he merely angry with her? Had Martin managed to escape, or had their pursuers taken him prisoner?

She minced her way through the parking lot to the truck, climbed in, and punched the dome light on. It filled the cab with a warm yellow glow. She fished her cell phone out of the glove box.

Resolutely, she reached into her back pocket for her cards. Tara had no choice; she had to find out. As ambivalent and resentful as she felt about her powers as an oracle, there was only one way left to her to find out the truth.

She shuffled the cold cards, thinking of Harry. She thought of the last time she'd seen him, of the look of hurt on his face, thought of last night and the sense of wholeness she feared was lost.

"Is Harry all right?" Tara whispered into the darkness, and drew a card.

Her breath froze in her throat when she flipped over the Eight of Swords. It depicted a bound and blindfolded woman surrounded by a cage of eight swords thrust, edge-down, into the ground. A castle on a cliff stood in the background with lights shining from its windows, suggesting that her keepers were watching her struggle. The card represented imprisonment and indecision, fear of extricating oneself from a situation. Seeing this, she knew he'd fallen into a trap, that he was being held prisoner.

She looked closely at the card. There was a gap between the cage of swords, and the woman's feet were unbound. She could be freed. There was still hope.

Tucking the card back in the deck, she thought of Martin. "Is Martin all right?" she asked, still hearing the phone ringing endlessly in her mind.

She picked a card. The Eight of Wands depicted eight flowering branches flying through the air over a tranquil landscape. Tara let out a breath she hadn't realized she'd been holding. This was a positive card, one that indicated travel and positive momentum. It suggested that Martin had found a way to escape. She smiled, wondering what the cagey old man had dreamed up to get away.

She held the cards close to her chest. She had to help Harry, whether he wanted her help or not. He clearly wasn't in a position to help himself.

Attempting to still her thoughts, she shuffled the cards.

"What do I do next?" she whispered, breath fogging in the saffron light of the truck. She drew seven cards and laid them out in a clockwise circle on the seat. This spread was intended to represent Ouroboros, the mythological serpent that ate its own tail. It was a powerful spread she rarely used, but it spoke to universal cycles, to re-creation of a situation.

She turned over the first card, the one at the top representing the serpent's head. This represented the distant past. She pulled the Six of Wands, showing six wands interlocked together, framed by the wings of victory. This card was reversed, suggesting treachery, betrayal by colleagues, life drawn to a standstill.

Tara rested her head in her hands. She needed more clarification, and drew another card from the deck to provide more information.

The Death card, the one she'd associated with Corvus, peered back at her from his skeletal visage. She shook her head. Corvus was ancient history, but he kept cropping up in the present. She pulled out her notebook and scribbled this down for later analysis, and turned her attention to the next card in the spread.

The second card in the spread represented the recent events having bearing on the situation. The Five of Swords depicted a cloaked man holding three swords, standing in victory over two kneeling dejected men. The swords of these two men lay on the ground, while a castle burned in the background. This card suggested defeat, cruelty, and vindictiveness. She thought of Harry being at the mercy of the men who had planned to kill Cassie.

The third card described immediate influences, the current events affecting the situation. The Five of Cups illustrated a man in a black cloak of mourning, head bowed over three spilled chalices. Red liquid stained the beach on which he stood. It suggested the sense of loss in a relationship, or an argument. Perhaps if she and Harry had parted on better terms, they might have made a better strategy that would have prevented him walking into the trap. Her fingernails dug into her palm. If she had only been there, perhaps she could have prevented this . . .

Two chalices shown in the card remained upright. This heartened her, gave her hope all was not lost.

The fourth card suggested immediate obstacles. She drew the Knight of Wands, reversed. It depicted a resolute-looking armored man astride a white horse, holding a wand like one would a rifle, over his shoulder.

Tara thought back to the card she'd associated with Gabriel, the King of Wands. This card might represent his soldiers. Reversed, this card suggested conflict and movement. His men were on the move.

The fifth card showed the immediate outlook, the short-term possibilities. The Devil card showed a fearsome horned beast, with a man and woman chained to his feet. An inverted pentacle was sketched over his head, symbolizing perversion of the elements. Tara frowned. This card suggested entrapment, fear, and the dark side of human nature. Most often, this card pointed to self-imposed limitations and fears, the bondage created through one's own actions and the need to see beyond it.

The sixth card showed future influences on the situation. The Strength card illustrated a woman crowned in a laurel wreath, closing the jaws of a lion. She wore a serene expression of tenderness on her face as she looked upon the destructive natural power of the lion. It was a look of love. Closing the jaws of the lion was an extraordinary feat, but not without cost: the woman's dress was torn open at the collar, showing claw marks in her chest. The card spoke of taming wild forces, of indomitable courage and strength of will. It was a card of mental perseverance over physical force. Tara fingered the scar at her own collar. She hoped she was powerful enough to do what the woman in the card was able to accomplish.

The final card, representing the serpent's tail, showed the ultimate outcome. She'd drawn the Eight of Cups, showing a man fleeing across a desolate landscape, leaving eight stacked cups behind.

She frowned. She'd seen this card recently. She pulled her well-worn notebook from her purse and flipped through it. Ah, yes . . . This was the card she'd associated with the photo she'd taken of the caldera at Magnusson's lab. This was the photo in which Harry had seen headlights where there was no road.

Her intuition buzzed throughout her. That place. Her pulse quickened, and she circled the card in her notebook. This was where she would look for Harry.

Her eyes flicked to the lit hotel room window, drapes drawn shut. That was where she would look as soon as Cassie was safe: back at the place where it had all began.

LIKE BAD NEWS AND THE DEAD, DELPHI'S DAUGHTERS traveled fast.

Dawn had scarcely begun to redden the horizon when Tara awoke to the sounds of engines in the parking lot. Not the large growl of semi-trucks and hissing air brakes, these were smaller engines barely perceptible over the hum of the floorboard heater.

But Tara heard them. She drew aside the drapes, watched as a collection of a dozen vehicles and their owners gathered in the unplowed parking lot. A perky blonde soccer mom piloted a station wagon with a bumper covered in stickers from her kids' schools. The kids were evidently on the honor roll and the track team. A sleek SUV with skis laced to the roof spat out a woman in a snowsuit, sunglasses perched on her head. A middle-aged woman in a plaid flannel shirt parked a pickup truck beside them, joined by a car full of women in jeans and pink hooded sweatshirts. Tara dimly recognized some of these women from her youth, but she had long since forgotten their names.

"Pythia," said Tara. "Your friends are here."

The pink hooded sweatshirts stayed on guard in the parking lot, while the others invaded the motel room. Tara was surprised to see that many of the women were armed: the soccer mom had the bulge of a .357 under her shoulder, and the skier slung a rifle across her back. In a methodical flurry of activity that reminded Tara of ants, they scoured the hotel room and began taking the Pythia's and Cassie's meager belongings to the cars.

Cassie stood in the corner, her arms wrapped around her elbows. Tara placed her hands on her shoulders. "You're going to be fine."

Cassie's lip trembled. "Can you come with us?"

Tara hesitated. "I can't right now. Harry's in trouble. I need to help him." She embraced the girl. "But I promise, once I find Harry, I'll come back to you."

Over Cassie's shoulder, Tara saw the Pythia smile, and Tara fought the urge to scowl at her.

• • • •

"I'M GLAD YOU'RE WELL." CORVUS KEPT HIS DESK BETWEEN himself and Harry. Harry slouched in his chair, tasting blood on the inside of his cheek. Corvus seemed to eye the gravel scrapes on his face and the red rimming the torn knee of his pants with a barely disguised sense of unease. How a man so squeamish and hands-off managed to be in charge of anything was a mystery to Harry. He'd bet that Corvus was a real treat to work with at a crime scene or a morgue. Back in the day, when Tara had the ill fortune to work with him, he imagined that she'd done all the heavy lifting.

"As well as can be expected." He glanced at Gabriel, visible through the dark glass on the other side of the hallway. He'd pulled some cigarettes from his fatigue shirt, had lit up. The smell of smoke began to filter underneath the door. Harry watched Corvus's nose wrinkle imperceptibly. Such delicate sensibilities. He was sure smoking wasn't allowed in any federal facility, but it didn't seem like Gabriel cared so much about the rules . . . or Corvus's preferences.

"I'm grateful that Major Gabriel found you. You've been out of touch."

Harry remained stubbornly silent. Gabriel had thrown him in the back of the SUV, blindfolded. Harry had no idea where he was, only that their location was somewhere off a gravel road. The place smelled strongly of earth, of metal, with a close, strange echo that seemed to travel through the glass and roll up to the walls. Harry thought they might be underground, given the deadening of sound, but he couldn't be certain.

"Where the hell are we?" he countered with a question

of his own. This pretending, this false civility, the talking around the fact that Harry had been essentially abducted, pissed him off.

"You know that I can't say." Corvus thinned his lips. "Where's Magnusson's daughter?"

Harry looked Corvus directly in the eye. "I don't know." He could answer that truthfully, at least.

Corvus crossed his arms, brushed some imaginary dirt from his fingers onto his suit jacket. "Is she with Dr. Sheridan?" When he spoke Tara's name, something dark, like guilt, glinted across his vision.

"I don't know where either of them are."

Corvus leaned across his desk. "Listen to me, Agent Li. You're an inch away from obstruction of justice and kidnapping charges. I can salvage what little remains of your career if you work with me." Corvus's left eye twitched, and Harry noticed his shirt was wrinkled. Signs of high stress for a fastidious man like Corvus.

"Look," Harry said. "I don't appreciate being trussed up like a pig, sandbagged, and then accused of kidnapping. You and Gabriel have been waiting in the shrubbery to pounce on whatever we can beat out of it." Rebellion scalded his throat, tasting both foreign and pure. "I'm not playing the game."

Corvus's eyes narrowed. "I don't think you fully appreciate your predicament. You can either work with me, now, or . . ." His eyes flickered to the figure blowing smoke outside the door. "Gabriel will get the information from you in a much less pleasant way. It'll be out of my hands. You saw what happened to DiRosa."

The threat slithered across the desk.

Harry weighed his options. Corvus had him backed into a corner, and there was only one course of action.

Harry stood up and approached Corvus's desk with his hands folded respectfully at his sides. He spat blood on the immaculate glass surface.

Corvus kicked back from the desk in horror, flecks of blood peppering his snow-white shirt. His chair fell backward, and his shoe tipped over the desk. It shattered in a jingling rain of safety-glass fragments on the gray carpet.

Gabriel and his men burst through the door, ground Harry's face into the carpet, and twisted his arms behind his back.

Harry could hear Corvus sputtering in panic, and smiled against the itchy carpet. *Bastard*.

His smile faltered as Gabriel kicked him over, driving the breath from his lungs, and stood on his sternum. Harry could feel the pattern of Gabriel's boot tread pressing into his flesh.

"I gave Corvus the courtesy of letting you hide behind his skirt. You're all mine now."

Chapter Sixteen

T HE SWELLING moon rode low over the desert, bleaching the earth pale gray and white. Frost shimmered with the illusion of movement as the serene light played over ice crystals. Its light burned away all but the brightest stars, casting their distant gazes on the ground below.

Tara wound the truck around the northern edge of the caldera cradling the remnants of Magnusson's lab. The moon illuminated enough of the colorless landscape that she could cut the lights for the dark, silent drive. Frost from her breath accumulated on the inside of the windshield in spidery tendrils. She paused to wipe them away with her sleeve, only for her breath to conjure them anew in minutes.

Her fingers twitched at the radio dial, trying to summon something human in the darkness. The dial grazed only static, and she wondered if it was some side effect of military technology in the area, or whether the radio was simply shot.

The cold and silence of the dark had settled into her. Her fingers fused with the radiating chill of the steering wheel, the icy metal of the gas pedal flowing through the sole of her shoe. She felt drawn, as if pulled by fishing line through the surface of cold water. Her reflection, glimpsed in the rearview mirror, seemed inhumanly surreal: winter had drained the color out of her face, the moonlight casting planes and shadows over her unbound hair and eyelashes. She looked like a ghostly figure from a fairy-tale: the Queen of Swords, the Snow Queen. She felt the power of the ancient archetype settle deep within her chest: the sorrow of loss, the resolute sense of duty, staring into a desolate kingdom.

She parked the truck at the rim above the caldera, looked down at the plastic-wrapped remains of the lab. At this distance, it seemed that a ghost paused at the bottom of the crater, shrouded in pulsing white. The figure eight of the accelerator track was merely a silver path on which that ghost might travel, retracing its steps for eternity. The pinging of the truck engine as it cooled was the only sound in this barren place.

She reached into her purse for her cold cards, shuffled them in her chapped hands. She nestled her chin into her coat. It wasn't hers; the Pythia had left it behind for her. It smelled like cigarette smoke and made her eyes itch. But itching was better than freezing.

"What do I need to know?" she asked the cards.

She pulled one card with numb and clumsy fingers: the

Hanged Man. A man was suspended by his foot from a tree. His hands were laced behind his back, and serenity glowed in his expression. The card suggested sacrifice, a transformation. Her intuition shivered over her, despite the cold.

She drew a second card, and her hands stilled in contemplation. Judgment. A man, woman, and child rose up out of coffins to herald an angel trumpeting them awake. This card suggested finality, that a permanent decision for good or ill was to be made. But the symbol of the coffin, especially the woman in it, chilled her. It struck far too close to her own experience at the hands of the Gardener.

Movement in the bowl of the caldera seized her eye. Dark violet sparks seethed into the darkness, vanished. She'd seen that glimmer before, when she'd found Magnusson's watch.

Her breath obscured too much of her view, and she climbed out of the truck. The squeak of the rusty door hinges seemed to pierce some of the crystalline silence. The image of the Magician stepped into her thoughts, standing alone with the glowing symbol of infinity drawn in the ether above his head, paralleling the track of the particle accelerator below. Was this truly where Magnusson destroyed himself?

Her eyes narrowed, and she descended farther into the field, gun drawn. Dried grass lashed against her legs. Was this some manipulation of radiation, some trace of light left behind? Or was this some aftereffect of the dark matter pulled from the ether?

She walked up to the fence, cast a pebble at it. No arc

or sparking lanced across its surface. Scanning east and west for video surveillance, she saw no signs of it. She took her coat off. The cold air cut through her shirt and skin like a slap. Digging her fingers into the fence, she climbed up to the edge of the razor wire. She slung her coat over the tangle of razor wire, clambered over it, and dropped back to the other side.

She'd half expected flashlights and men with guns to appear from the dark, to corner her immediately. But there was only silence, the cold, and the moon. Tara walked down the caldera to where she'd seen the milling fragments of light, shivering. She'd stopped feeling her face, and when she touched it with her hand, it felt rubbery, like stone. Her wounded arm ached hotly, and it seemed the cold settled more deeply into the scars lacing her body.

"Magnusson," she whispered. "Where are you?"

She felt this place was too strongly tied to him, that perhaps he had never left it. There was no other sign of him, anywhere. The last traces of him had been found here, this place with the mysterious light.

She paused, looking down. Faint specks of violet light appeared and disappeared along the grasses. They glinted very faintly, and Tara had to look slightly away from them to truly see them, as one does with dim stars. These last bits of fallout from Magnusson's experiment disappeared within the earth, then reappeared.

Tara remembered the devoured walls of the laboratory, the missing guts of Magnusson's watch. Still, she felt inexorably drawn to these faint pinpoints of light, and reached toward them with her bare hand, adorned only with Magnusson's watch. Some distant part of her mind chided her for her fearlessness of bodily harm. There were much worse things than the scars she bore, that small voice warned her.

Several tiny particles hovered over the grasses and swarmed over her hand. She held her breath, half expecting to have her flesh disassembled at a subatomic level . . .

But they dissolved into the watch, vanishing painlessly.

Tara stared at the watch, stripped it off her wrist. She turned it over and ran her finger over the engraved infinity loop on the reverse. She popped open the back with the truck keys, wanting to know where that light had gone.

She gasped. The interior of the watch glowed, the violet particles racing along the remaining bits of circuitry. In a flash, she understood. In her hands lay a battery Magnusson had created to attract and hold dark energy, cleverly disguised as a watch.

She put it back together, dousing the light trickling inside it, and snapped it back on her wrist. She stood, eye roving over the landscape. Magnusson, whatever his condition, would never have left this behind.

Some yards distant, she spied something irregular in the earth, a lump seeming out of place for this perfectly sculpted place. It looked like a buried tree branch, jammed into the ground and twisted, like driftwood. Around it, the rocks and soil had swirled in on themselves, as if a dust devil had died there.

She remembered the Hanged Man, suspended from the tree. She trudged to the spot and scraped aside grasses and loose gravel with her numb hands. The hard earth cut into her hands and drew blood. But she kept digging, driven by her own sense of magnetic north. She dug until her blood mixed with the hard soil and she'd excavated a hole reaching into the earth.

She sat back on her heels, pressing the back of her hand to her mouth and suppressing a violent shudder.

Magnusson.

Or what was left of him. She recognized the line of the physicist's jaw from his photos, judged the dark eye socket to be similar to his. But the skeleton wasn't pale bone; it was rock melted and twisted like iron in a forge. A shoulder turned in the wrong direction; an arm and part of his face were half buried in the earth, fused to the stones and rocks and part of a cactus. She ran her finger over his brow. His hair had melted into the grass, and his cheekbone melded with a piece of basalt that glittered in the night. His fingers dribbled away into pebbles that dislodged their delicate formation at her touch. He reminded her, at a deep level, of renderings she'd seen of the Celtic Green Man, at one with the earth. No wonder the investigators had missed him; even with ground-penetrating radar, Magnusson's remains had fused with the earth so thoroughly that it might not have registered to the technician. He was one with the hard-packed earth, and there was no disturbance or foreign substance intrusion for the radar to detect.

This had to be the worst way to die: buried alive.

She understood the Hanged Man and the final Judgment now. Magnusson had made the ultimate sacrifice to destroy his research. She guessed he'd been caught by one of the mini black holes he'd opened up, and when it had finally winked out of existence, the black hole didn't differentiate among the animals, plants, and minerals left behind. And the bits of dark energy remaining here . . . without the battery or a black hole to attract them . . . they were fading fast.

She stood, dejected for both the brilliance that had been lost and Cassie's loss of a father. She climbed up the slope to the fence, arms wrapped around herself, eager to leave this alien place as desolate as the heart of space. She clambered gracelessly over the fence, managed to swipe down the tattered remains of her coat.

She turned the key in the pickup's engine. To her dismay, it failed to turn over. It seemed the silent vacuum had claimed it, as well. She tried again, willing it to start, but the key only clicked in the ignition, creating no spark to warm the cold metal.

Slinging her purse and Cassie's backpack over her good shoulder, she opened the creaking door of the pickup into the frigid night once more. Putting one foot in front of the other, she walked down the moonlit dirt road. The moon above drew her on, exercising its magnetism over her. She could feel its cold, soft light settling over her, settling into her frozen skin.

A coyote crept out of the sage on the road before her, its shadow cast long over the frost-hardened dirt. It disappeared as quickly as it had appeared, sauntering into the shadows. Tara's eyes followed its path, glimpsing a dead scorpion lying in the dirt, its glossy black claws raised up to the moon.

Symbols from the Moon Tarot card. She could feel their power mingling with her unconscious mind, shaking awake her intuition, even as the cold splintered her thoughts. She nearly walked past a tiny path branching to the left of the road, and she thought about the white and black pillars depicted in the card: a choice. The right-hand road stretched out broadly, smeared with the impressions of tire marks. The tracks were broadly spaced; Tara guessed military jeeps or trucks. There had been traffic, here. The left-hand path was narrow, a footpath dropping away over a slope. Anyone driving through here in a vehicle would easily miss it. She took the left-hand path, the way the coyote had come. The coyote was alive, and she accepted that as a good omen.

The narrow path pitched down into a shallow ravine. Brittle sagebrush raked against her clothes as she walked. Once or twice, she glimpsed the wash of headlights on the horizon . . . The destination of the other path, she guessed. The path Tara had taken circled around, avoiding that light. Tara guessed it might have been made by deer or other animals wanting to avoid human activity.

The path dissolved before a wall of rock and earth. An opening roughly the size of a man pierced the jagged stone surface. Old timbers supported and bracketed the uneven doorway. This doorway had been made by men.

Tara pulled a small flashlight from her bag and switched it on. Deep inside, she could see traces of guano, broken wood debris, and ropes. It was an old mineshaft. She guessed miners would have been searching for silver in this part of the country. Judging by the litter, this place was long abandoned.

Tara sat back on her heels. There was no way of knowing how big the mine was, or where it led. She dared to hope the traffic she'd seen on the main road had been leading to another arm of the mine—one modified for current covert use—and that she could find her way to it through this passage. Her intuition pulled her to this place, and she strongly felt Harry was somewhere near.

But fear trickled through her. The last time she'd been underground, she'd been imprisoned by the Gardener. Since that time, she'd even avoided subways and tunnels. The thought of entering the mine made sweat trickle down the back of her neck, as she felt the stirring of claustrophobia uncoiling in her gut. What if the passage narrowed, and she were trapped? What if she couldn't find her way out? *What if—?*

She took a deep breath, steadying the shaking flashlight, and approached the crevasse in the rock. Harry was in danger and needed help, whether he wanted her at his side, or not. Her feelings, and his, were beside the point.

The shadow of the earth fell over her, and she immediately missed the illuminating light of the moon in that sudden eclipse. She supposed some fragments of it still existed in the traces of silver in the mine, and she tried to imagine that some bit of silvery moonlight remained hidden just beyond her reach, embedded in this total darkness. It wasn't hard to imagine how the ancients believed that the moon's rays created silver. But she could detect none of that comforting light now. Gravel crunched underfoot, and her flashlight beam wavered, casting angular shadows against the debris: discarded, bent metal tools; splintered wood beams; an abandoned shoe.

Her breath scraped the inside of her lungs, and her pulse thudded too quickly in her throat. She could feel it hammering against the shoulder strap of the backpack. The passage narrowed, and she took deep gulps of air to steady herself. She was alone, she reminded herself. The Gardener was long dead. Her flesh was whole, and she was perfectly capable of running back into the lighter darkness of night. She was in control.

Breathe, she told herself.

The ceiling of the shaft scraped her head, and she shivered. It smelled too much like earth here. Not the Gardener's fresh, upturned loam fortified with humus, but stale, forgotten dirt broken into pieces and cast aside.

She forced herself to move forward for what seemed like hours, the flashlight slick in her hand. The beam flickered and yellowed, and the fear of being alone in the darkness nearly turned her around. Sweat slid into the wound on her arm, stinging, reminding her of the smell and taste of blood.

Just a little farther, she told herself. *Just another hundred steps . . .*

She played the game, over and over again. Another hundred steps. That was a manageable goal. Another hundred. Another. *One, two, three, four, five . . .*

Breathe.

She could hear voices ahead. Clutching her dying flashlight in her hand, she nearly broke into a run. The distant sounds seemed to emanate from her right, down the narrowest part of the shaft. It had fallen in on itself, leaving only a space the size of a child between the roof and the ceiling.

Tara clambered over the debris, rattling stones into the dark. She shoved her bag and backpack ahead of her and wormed her way through the opening. Her breath quickened in her throat, and a panic attack washed over her. She clawed through with her hands, earth pressed against her cheek. She dragged herself forward on her hands and knees, sharp stone tearing against her skin. Her flashlight quivered and died, leaving her stranded in the makeshift grave.

Furious panic charged through her, as it had years before. She dug, she fought, she kicked and dragged her way through. Her fingernails ripped and bled. She tasted dirt and sweat in her mouth, and she struggled against it, against the earth and the rock and the feel of suffocation pressing down on her ribs. She kept focusing on the voices, on what must be ahead . . . She thought she glimpsed light . . .

She burst through the blockage in a shower of gravel, spilling her out into a larger cavern in a sprawl of light. Blinking, she tumbled onto her hands and knees, backpack and purse slamming to the ground.

She'd fallen into some kind of storage room. Electrical wires were strung overhead, dangling utility lights like lanterns at a festival. A massive stainless steel box dominated one wall of the room, spreading sheet-metal tentacles above and over the sheetrock walls. It was warm, at least. Her ears and fingers began to ache in the presence of warmth. She guessed it was an incinerator, by the orange labels warning not to touch the feed panel without proper safety gear, and by the traumatized look of the stick figure who fell in. Voices echoed from beyond the walls, from what could have been a hallway or another room.

Boxes were stacked neatly along the walls, and she ran her fingers over the labels. The original delivery addresses were to Major Gabriel. This place must be one of the facilities under his jurisdiction, as well . . . but one not on any map. Many were studded with bright radiation warning stickers. Lifting the lid of a banker's box, she saw they were full of paper . . . e-mail, mostly benign correspondence and scientific chitchat. Some open boxes contained deflated radiation suits, limp gloves grasping at air.

She lifted the unsecured flap of the nearest large box, the one closest to the incinerator. It was marked for destruction. She peered inside, and recoiled in horror.

The smell was unmistakable. Tara turned away, covering her nose with the back of her hand. Bent in on itself on several impossible angles was a clear plastic bag with a body in it. Barbara DiRosa's sightless eyes peered back at her from a contorted neck.

The door to the incinerator room opened, and Tara scrambled back, crablike, on her hands to safety behind a tower of boxes that smelled better than the one she'd opened. She hoped the spew of dirt and gravel from the far wall would remain unnoticed.

Two men, one dressed in combat fatigues and the other

in a white radiation suit, clomped into the room. One of them donned a set of welder's gloves and opened the mouth of the incinerator, while carrying on a conversation with the other about weekend plans.

"Did you pick up some OT this weekend?"

"Nah. Going to go visit my mother for her birthday."

"I don't see how you could turn down double-time . . . Special teams have been busy."

"It's Mom. What am I gonna do?"

"Tell her you'd rather be chasing down the bad guys in a canyon than eating quiche at brunch."

"Whatever."

Tara leaned forward. Harry had been set to meet DiRosa at Bandelier National Monument. There were canyons there. Her heart felt sick, wondering if one of these other boxes held Harry's discarded remains. If this room was where her intuition had led her, it could be the end of her search.

The box scraped forward on the stone floor, and then there was a soft thump as it hit the incinerator. Tara wondered if the men had even looked inside it to see what had happened to one of the "bad guys." The men heaved two more boxes of something that rattled like paper into the incinerator, and she could hear the snap and crackle of the papers as they turned to ash. The lid on the incinerator door squeaked shut.

"Seriously. There's overtime to be had in the detention block."

"What? Now that they've got an actual prisoner to work over?"

"They're going to get that guy to talk, sooner or later . . ."

The door to the incinerator room slammed shut, disturbing the utility lights enough to cause them to swing slightly overhead, shaking the shadows. Tara crept out from behind the wall of boxes. Hope flared within her. Perhaps that prisoner was Harry.

Tara looked down at her filthy street clothes. She'd be spotted in an instant. Backtracking to one of the boxes she'd opened earlier, she pulled out a crumpled radiation suit and zipped it on over her clothes. Better. She pulled the hood up over her hair, finding it didn't bother her nearly as much as it had before. She smiled grimly. Perhaps her time in the mine had overcome lesser forms of claustrophobia. It sure beat cognitive-behavioral therapy for results.

Slinging her bags over her good shoulder, she opened the door and stepped into the buzzing white light of Gabriel's den.

CHAPTER **Seventeen**

TARA FORCED herself not to stop and gawk, tried to shuffle along as if she knew where she was going. Gabriel's den was vaster than she had anticipated: the hollowed-out mine housed computer servers buzzing along in a honeycomb of glassed-in rooms, connected by arterial hallways leading to vast work spaces the size of aircraft hangers. She glanced in the door windows, seeing figures in suits like hers, standing over shining white vats that hummed like refrigerators, insulated with layers of shiny foil. Copper tubing and wires extended from control panels, lights blinking softly.

She thought about the purpose of this place . . . Why an old silver mine? She remembered what Cassie had said about scientists trying to trap dark matter in an old gold mine in Minnesota . . . That made sense, but the extreme secrecy of this place still bothered her. What else could be going on here that was hidden from view?

She slipped down labyrinthine corridor after corridor, passing an occasional soldier or white-suited researcher. At this hour, there were few. She suspected she'd crossed back on her tracks more than once, and fear of discovery and frustration sucked at her. The corridors, bleached in fluorescent white light with drop ceilings, were identical to each other, designated only with cryptic numbers.

She paused before the eighth corridor. She'd been running into the number eight over and over, in her readings, in Magnusson's cryptic symbolism, in the infinity loop of the accelerator. She turned down this way, listening for footsteps.

This hallway was different. These doors were solid steel, pierced by a window embedded with wire mesh, each one locked as she brushed her hands over them. Absent the smell of bleach and urine, this looked identical to the secure wing of every mental facility Tara had interrogated prisoners in. All the windows were dark and opaque, except one at the far end. She could hear voices on the other side. What they said was indistinguishable, but she could hear the angry swell and fall of speech.

The door burst open, and Tara involuntarily took a step back. A cart littered with syringes, an IV bag deflated like a beached jellyfish, and blood-speckled pieces of gauze barreled through. The technician pushing it stopped before her, startled, and gestured at her bags with his chin.

"Did you bring the liquid nitrogen he asked for?"

Tara nodded, voice stuck in her throat. The technician jabbed a thumb over his shoulder to indicate the room, rattling away. "He's waiting."

Tara pulled her hood closer over her face and strode purposefully past the room. In her peripheral vision, she glanced through the door swinging shut, and her breath jammed in her throat.

A man Tara guessed was Gabriel presented his back to the door, kneeling over a figure prone on the tiled floor. She couldn't see the figure clearly, but she recognized Harry's spit-polished shoes.

She swallowed, her hand reaching reflexively in her bag for her gun. She could pass by, wait for Gabriel to finish what he was doing and leave, then rescue Harry. But Harry might not have that much time . . .

Her heart won out over stealth. She jammed her foot in the door as it swung shut, and she invaded the room. She drew her gun in a fluid motion, aiming it at the back of Gabriel's head.

"Put your hands behind your head." Her voice rang with quiet authority in the tiny room.

Gabriel laced his hands behind his head. "Thank you for joining us, Dr. Sheridan." His voice was smooth, entirely unruffled. "You're about to make my life much simpler."

Tara swallowed. "Get on your knees." She circled around to check on Harry, heart hammering. *Please be alive,* she thought.

Harry lay crumpled on the floor, his face a swollen mass of bruises. One sleeve was rolled up, and she could see the wounds made by needle marks. Mercifully, she could see the rise and fall of his chest.

"Tara?" he mumbled. "Hi, babe. Did you meet the purple dragon on the cheese wagon, yet?"

"What did you do to him?" Tara demanded.

Gabriel shrugged. "We interrogated him. He's proving rather obstinate, so we resorted to a sodium thiopental cocktail with a zolpidem chaser."

Tara tried to haul Harry upright. He was limp as a fish, stumbling on his feet.

"Hey, are we gonna go nick some tubers? I like cheese."

"Yeah, Harry. We're gonna go get some cheese." Supporting Harry's weight as much as she could, she kept her gun trained on Gabriel, who looked upon her with the serene patience of a Buddha.

"Nachos. Nacho blaster with tinfoil."

"Open the door." Tara gestured at Gabriel with the gun.

"No." Gabriel smiled beatifically at her. "Get bent, ma'am."

Tara cocked the hammer on the revolver. "It would be a lot easier for me to shoot you and then search you for your access card. Open the damn door."

"You're not going to shoot a man on his knees."

Tara wavered for only a moment. She was enraged beyond all reason by what he'd done to Harry. Gabriel deserved some retribution, and she was more than happy to give it to him.

She stepped to his side, took aim, and pulled the trigger. Gabriel tumbled back, howling. "You bitch!" He clutched his foot. Blood seeped through his fingers, staining the shiny leather of his boot. He stared at her in amazement. "You shot me!"

Tara cocked the hammer. She'd given him only a glancing blow, but she wanted him to know that she wouldn't play by the good-guy rules. "I'll do it again. I'll take out your left knee and work my way up. Now, unlock that damn door."

Gabriel reached in his jacket pocket, tossed his ID badge on the floor. It skittered to a stop by her toe. "Do it yourself. And you won't get far. Every soldier in this place will be on you."

This was a classic trick: distract your enemy long enough to get her to stoop down, then attack when her center of gravity is at its weakest. Keeping Gabriel in her sight, she told Harry, "Harry, pick up the badge."

Obligingly, Harry reached down for the badge. It took him three tries to grasp it. "Fish sticks."

"Hand it to me." Harry did as he was told.

She told Gabriel, "Give me your radio."

He lashed it across the floor, bouncing it against the wall. Tara crushed the radio's faceplate with a well-aimed strike of her heel. As drop-proof as walkies were, none of them could withstand broken keys. She just hoped it wasn't one of the models with a man-down alert that would summon help when an internal mercury switch detected that the radio had gone horizontal.

Tara kept Gabriel in front of her, moved with Harry toward the door. She didn't take her eyes off him, swiping the card behind her back. It took a few tries, but she succeeded in getting it through the slot. The door opened with a metallic clang of bolts being reeled back, and she backed out of the door. She kicked it shut on Gabriel's glowering face.

"Harry, I need you to walk with me, as fast as you can."

Harry valiantly tried to shuffle along, but he was too slow. Tara tried to take as much of his weight as she could, wounded shoulder screaming, and she felt a stitch or two pop. His limbs were simply too floppy to move the way he wanted them to. They were going to draw too much attention. She looked up and down the hallway, fervently hoping the technician had left his cart here, somewhere . . .

They rounded the corner to meet the staccato click of a half dozen handgun safeties being released. Tara skidded to a stop before a line of soldiers, her jaw tightening as a female figure shouldered its way through them. Though she'd never met her as an adult, Tara recognized the woman with eyes like agates. A bandage was stuck to her temple, and her stringy blonde hair was scraped back from her elegant brow. Her dark clothes were covered in dust; she smelled like earth.

Tara recognized her instinctively. "Adrienne."

"Hand me the gun." She extended a gloved hand. The other was in a makeshift sling "It's over."

She had no choice. She placed the gun in her palm, bracing herself for the soldiers to slam her to the ground. As they surged forward, she spied a familiar figure at the back, a figure just removed enough to keep from getting his hands dirty.

"Corvus." She had wanted to be wrong about his involvement with Gabriel, but the cards had been too right.

"Meatball licker," said Harry. "Corvus is a meatball-licking emu."

Tara paced the perimeter of the tiny cell, staring up at the ceiling. Harry guessed she was trying to figure out how to climb up, to see if there was a way through the drop ceiling back out to the hallway. It was too far up for her to reach, and trying would be dependent upon Harry sobering up enough to lift her.

That was not going so well.

Harry sat with his back to the wall, hands in his lap. She gave up and sat down beside him. "How are you doing?"

"Still fuzzy." He shook his head. "I can think pretty clearly, but my coordination's shot." He tried to run his hand through his hair and stabbed himself in the ear with his finger.

"Just rest," she said.

"You shouldn't have come back for me." His tone bristled with anger, and Tara shrank away. "Now, they have the laptop, and they have you."

Tara's mouth hardened. "I wasn't going to leave you."

Harry snorted. "Now, they're going to have the technology to harness dark energy . . . Not a good trade. And they'll kill us anyway." Why couldn't she have left well enough alone? Why couldn't she have stayed away? Now, they were well and truly fucked.

Tara wrapped her arms around her knees. She didn't say anything, just rested her chin on her knees. "I wasn't going to leave you," she said finally, stubbornly. "You may not want me here, or want me in any fashion, but leaving you behind was not the right thing to do."

He blew out his breath, reached to touch her shoulder, but she shrugged his hand off. "It's only a matter of time until they hack that thing."

"We'll see. I'm not as convinced about their competence as you are."

"You haven't spent the night getting the crap beaten out of you in a drug-induced stupor. They seem pretty competent at that, to me."

They hadn't made a move to interrogate her, yet. By throwing her in the same cell as Harry, he knew they were listening, hoping that one or the other of them would slip up and let out some information about Cassie's whereabouts or the computer password in casual conversation. Harry knew Tara knew it, too. He deliberately hadn't asked about Cassie at all.

"Your arm's bleeding again," he remarked. It bothered him to see her hurt, and he knew it would hurt him even more when they killed her.

She shrugged. "It's all right. It's not like I got the crap beaten out of me while in a drug-induced stupor."

Awkward silence settled over them.

"Trust me, it could be much worse." Her mouth thinned. "Gabriel is an amateur."

"That so?" A note of challenge rose in Harry's voice. "He doesn't hold a candle to the Gardener, does he?"

Her knuckles whitened on her elbows. "No, he doesn't."

Harry was angry at her for coming here, was lashing out. She'd take it, let him open that wound, and he felt instantly guilty for it.

"I'll tell you my bedtime story about the Gardener." Her tone was bitter, and she tried to control it, succeeded in flattening her voice to a dull recounting. Harry imagined this was the disinterested, emotionless voice she used in court testimony, or when patients with psychological issues reclined on her couch and confessed terrible sins. But she couldn't look at Harry while she told the story. Instead, she looked up at the light from the fluorescent tubes.

"Once upon a time, there was a guy in the kingdom of Missouri, a botanist. You would think that would be a pretty sedate profession, but not for Amos Dalton. He had a fanatical devotion to his plants, to his research. He even developed three new species of irises.

"But sadly, he was a pain in the ass to work with. Total diva. He was let go from his position with a major bulb and seed producer because he got into a fight with his supervisor over patent rights to his darlings . . . That's what he called them. His darlings. He stomped off in a hissy fit. Unfortunately, his reputation preceded him, and he couldn't find another job in his field. He went to work at a florist shop to make ends meet.

"But he was determined to feed his darlings. In his mind, it took a great and terrible sacrifice to make these delicate specimens flower. He began looking at the women he delivered flowers to as nothing more than the sum of their biological parts, as plant food. He'd convinced himself that there was something special about the blood of women's wombs that would give life to his plants, that they would give them something he couldn't: a creative spark, a bit of primal fertility that would wrap his seeds and bulbs in life."

Harry saw that her eyes drifted to the side in unfocused memory. Her pupils dilated, and Harry could glimpse the darkness growing there.

"A dozen roses from a paramour . . . a get-well bouquet of daisies . . . They led him to women who opened up their doors to him in delight, overjoyed to become part of his project.

"It was the bridal bouquet that made me most suspicious. I was working on his profile and drew the Eight and Nine of Pentacles from the Tarot, reversed. The Eight represented sour fruits of labor, the Nine suggested danger to a woman in a garden. A bride went missing on her wedding day, taken right from the church. Corvus and I arrived on the scene, and all that was left behind were white rose petals, a symbol of Death."

She paused, and there was an audible click in her throat.

Harry touched her hand.

She shook her head. "I'm recently associating Corvus with that card, sorry." She blew out a shaking breath, continued. "There was no bouquet, none anywhere. I was focused on the flower petals, where they'd come from. I took them to the lab, found that they were laced with ether. The bride's credit card receipts showed the name of an internet company that rerouted orders to local florists, and I tracked down the address from there."

"Did you go alone?"

She nodded. "I tried to call Corvus for backup, but he was not to be found. As usual. He said later that he hadn't gotten the message. There was no time to wait if I hoped to find the bride alive.

"The florist's shop was closed, but I could see a light on in the back. I circled around the back alley. The door was open. I went in.

"It was . . . a fairyland. All leaf-shadow and roots suspended in glass vials, white Christmas lights in the darkness. It smelled cloyingly sweet, the kind of artificial scent they added to hothouse roses to enhance their naked smell.

"I didn't see him coming. He kept his ether in a plant mister. I got one shot off, I think. Last thing I remember was the furious look on his face when I fell and broke some of his rhizome vials, shattering those plants and water all over the floor . . . all that beautiful, fractured light.

"I woke up in the dark. Not the kind of dark you encounter in your house, on the street, or even in the forest. Total, utter darkness. Instead of the smell of artificial roses, I smelled irises. I was covered in them. I could feel their softly rippled petals, the fine hairlike texture of their stamens, sticking to me. I smelled earth, and the resin of pine. I was lying down, and I could feel splintered wood above me. I could feel there were holes in the floor of the wooden box—in the coffin—he'd put me in to keep me still, keep me from tearing up the bulbs.

"And I smelled blood, that metallic smell mixing with the sweetness of the flowers. I felt numb, and I realized I was the one bleeding. He was bleeding me out, letting the soil drink me in. The perfect fertilizer for his delicate irises. I found out later that his favorite tool was something called a Hori-Hori knife. It's a traditional Japanese weeding knife with a sharp, concave blade. It leaves very distinctive marks. It's very useful for transplanting bonsai and other delicate plants . . . and for perforating a human's internal organs. Dalton liked to use it to aerate bodies to allow for maximum blood flow into the soil." Her fingers unconsciously slipped to her hip and her belly, to the scars crossing her skin. "I knew then, I think, what he'd taken from me. I could feel . . . I could feel the possibilities draining away. Not just my own life, but the life I could have contributed to, once upon a time. But in Dalton's sick and twisted way, I was the mother to his irises, to his 'children.' "

Harry's grip tightened on her hand, and she did not pull away.

"I thought about giving up, but I heard a voice. I think it was in my head, some part of my psyche urging me to fight. I took off my belt, used it as a tourniquet. I dug the buckle into the ceiling of the box, over and over again, until I could feel it splinter. I jammed my hands into it, felt an avalanche of dirt that choked me and stung as it poured into my wounds.

"Fortunately, he'd buried me shallowly in a raised flower bed, so as not to waste any blood. I came up out of the box, breaking through a mass of bulbs and half-grown irises. I was in a greenhouse, and it was night. All around me, I could see other raised beds, dotted with irises . . . striped, speckled . . . I couldn't see any color but gray. But that night in the greenhouse was so brilliantly bright . . . It was nothing like the darkness in the box.

"I broke out of that greenhouse, soaked in blood and flowers and glass. Thank God the bread truck driver on his early run saw me on the side of the road and stopped. Dalton killed himself once he realized who I was, and that my resting place was open."

It was then that she looked at him, the pupils of her eyes so dark they eclipsed her irises. It was such a pale expression of transcendence that it made Harry's chest ache. "So when I tell you that there's not much Gabriel and Corvus can do to hurt me, I mean it."

He pushed a strand of hair behind her ear. "I'm sorry."

"Whatever else happens, I thought you deserved to know." Her voice was small and sad, and Harry had the fear he'd lost her entirely. He felt such in awe of her, of her strength, her courage, and that enigmatic stillness that ran counterpoint to all his restlessness.

He reached for her, and the back of her neck felt cold. He kissed her, and her lips yielded to him.

He rested his forehead against hers. "I'm sorry."

"Me, too."

The bolts of the door clanged back, and Corvus stepped into the cell, two soldiers at his back. Gabriel's shape filled the door. He limped into the cell, his bandaged foot crammed in a swollen athletic sock. He looked like he'd jammed his foot into a giant marshmallow. His expression was one of controlled neutrality.

"Ms. Sheridan. I trust that you find the accommodations to be comfortable."

"I've had worse. I'm sure you heard."

"I did." Gabriel's smile split his face, and it even crinkled his eyes. "I have to say, Ms. Sheridan, I do admire you. You're a worthy adversary, and I'll be sorry to see this finished."

"What do you want now?" Harry contemplated how far he'd have to reach to kick Gabriel in the wounded foot.

"That computer you were carrying. It's toast."

Harry glanced at Tara. Had she sabotaged the computer? Had she destroyed all that valuable research?

She raised her chin. "I've been having problems with it."

Gabriel shook his head. "It's not yours. It's got Magnusson's fingerprints all over it. What did you do to it? The hard drive is completely destroyed."

"I didn't do anything to it."

"That's a shame." Gabriel leaned against the wall, favoring the sock monkey attached to his leg. "It seems that you would be of no further use to us. And I don't like wasting my time."

"I'll make you a trade," Tara said. "Let Harry go, and I'll show you where Magnusson is."

Gabriel's eyebrow crawled up his shaven head. "All right. But then, I give you to Adrienne. She's been chomping at the bit to get a piece of you."

Harry pulled himself to his feet, but he stumbled and fell in a rubbery heap. "No. Nobody's giving anything up. If anyone's walking out of here, it's her."

Tara put her fingers to his lips, smiled that sad little smile. "'Bye, Harry."

Chapter **Eighteen**

A T LEAST she'd been able to make a more proper good-
bye to Harry this time.

Tara watched as cars gathered at the mouth of the
mine in the pink brilliance of dawn. Harry was led to
one of the sedans. Rentals, she judged by the plates. She'd
refused to help without seeing him freed with her own
eyes, had watched as they cut the zip-tie handcuffs around
his wrists and handed him a set of keys. He looked at
her for a long moment, and it seemed he beseeched her
to change her mind. She smiled at him. She knew Harry
would try to do the right thing, to go get help, but it would
be far too late for her by then.

But at least he knew now. Telling him her story felt
like a weight lifted from her chest. It had been years since
she'd told another living person the full account of what
had happened to her. Though she knew Gabriel and Cor-

vus had heard it, too, their intangible presence didn't matter to her. The darkness had fallen from her heart, and she was at peace with what would come next.

She climbed into a Jeep with Gabriel, Adrienne, and Corvus. Thankfully, the heat was cranked up as it bumped over the dirt road. Corvus and Adrienne sat in the backseat, silent. Corvus was pressed to the far side of the seat, away from the dirt covering Adrienne's clothes. Tara could feel Adrienne watching her, but wouldn't give her the satisfaction of showing it bothered her. She stared out the window at the molten gold coming over the horizon, not yet high enough to melt the frost. She wanted to believe Corvus was merely following orders, that he wasn't taking any personal enjoyment from this. Adrienne . . . well, Adrienne would enjoy it.

"Stop here," she said when she saw the abandoned pickup. She climbed out of the Jeep with Gabriel's gun at her back, and a caravan of two other cars stopped behind her. While a squad of men opened the truck to search it, she led a phalanx of men down the slope to the fence.

"You want to go through, or over?" she asked.

Gabriel pulled a multi-tool out of his jacket pocket, limped to the fence, and cut out a seam. He pulled the mesh back, motioned for her to go through.

"Ladies first."

She ducked through the fence, and the men followed her like insects, down the slope into the caldera. The dawn light illuminated the infinity loop of the particle accelerator in washes of pink and gold. Tara followed her footprints, still visible in the frost from the night before, to the broken tree and Magnusson's remains.

"Here." She turned away, and Gabriel's men descended on the location like ants on candy. Corvus, disgusted, kept his distance. He pressed the back of his hand to his nose.

Adrienne, however, seemed fascinated. She squatted beside the remains. Something like jealousy seethed in those flinty eyes. Tara didn't understand the covetousness she saw there. Surely she didn't seek the power of dark energy, as Gabriel and Corvus did?

Adrienne reached out and touched Magnusson's brow, an odd little gesture of reverence.

Gabriel nodded appreciatively at the find. He seemed satisfied to see Magnusson dead, and that rankled her. "Good work, Dr. Sheridan."

"We had a deal," she reminded him. Gabriel seemed to have his own twisted sense of honor; she hoped that by fulfilling her end of the bargain, that he wouldn't send men to retrieve Harry.

"We did. And I'm keeping my end of it," Gabriel said. He fished in his pocket for a cigar and lit it. "Agent Li is free. But our deal, regretfully, does not make any conditions for your freedom."

Tara bowed her head.

"Corvus, take her back."

Adrienne wrested her attention from Magnusson and stalked up to Gabriel, standing toe-to-toe with him. "She's mine. That's part of the deal."

Gabriel was nonplussed. "You were supposed to get the girl for us. There's no girl."

Adrienne's hands balled into fists. In a throw down between Gabriel and Adrienne, Tara wasn't sure who would be the victor

"You'll get a crack at her. Don't worry. But not until we get the information we need."

With something like cold pity in his gray eyes, Corvus walked Tara back up the slope to the fence. They trailed three of Gabriel's men, guns ready. Tara considered running, knowing she'd be shot, and that it would be over quickly.

"Do you love him?" Corvus asked quietly.

Tara stopped in her tracks. "What the hell are you talking about?"

"Agent Li." A wrinkle deepened above his eyes, and Tara could see she'd somehow wounded him.

Tara closed her eyes. He'd been listening to them in the cell. Who knew what kind of sick obsessions roiled behind that bald forehead.

"Yes," she said.

Corvus looked as if she'd slapped him. Wordlessly, he stalked away. The search team met Corvus at the fence. They'd emptied the truck's contents into black plastic garbage bags. One soldier was busily cutting into the seat cushions with a knife, searching the stuffing. Another grimaced as he pulled the petrified remains of a sandwich from under the seat.

"What did you find?" Corvus asked them. "Anything?"

"Mostly trash, sir." The team leader handed Corvus a small folder of papers and Tara's purse. "We've got the truck registration to follow down. And this."

Corvus peered into the purse, stirred for a moment. Tara closed her eyes when he pulled out the deck of cards wrapped in her mother's scarf.

"What's this?" he asked her.

Tara shrugged. "Souvenirs."

Corvus unwrapped the parcel, fanning the worn cards out. Tara clenched her fists. Her skin crawled at the idea of Corvus handling him, of his malignant energy sinking into her mother's cards.

He could see her attachment to these things. With a small, cruel smile on his face, he severed that attachment. He threw the cards to the wind as if they were garbage. Tara watched helplessly as her mother's cards spiraled away, down into the caldera. Some stuck to the fence, trapped. Others blew across the road. It was as if someone had released a flock of brightly colored birds. Her heart sank. There would be no retrieving them.

But at least Harry was free. She sucked in a breath, stilling her emotions with that knowledge.

Corvus must have read it on her face; he knew her too well. "There is no deal for Agent Li," he told her quietly.

She spun on him, hands balled into fists. "Gabriel said—"

"Doesn't matter what Gabriel said. I still have people under my own command, and they'll intercept Li before he gets to the interstate."

Fury boiled away her sense of resignation. Perhaps she could appeal to the past. "Corvus, we were partners once. I'm asking you to honor that by—"

"Honor what?" Corvus made a self-deprecating snort. "Tara, that was broken a long time ago."

"I don't know what you mean."

He leaned toward her. "I have to confess something. It's been eating me alive, but this situation has given me the opportunity to . . . assuage my conscience." His smile was small, guilty, like a kid who'd stolen candy and savored every moment of it. "When you went after the Gardener . . . I got your call for backup."

"You what?"

"I got your message. I knew where you were, where you were going. And I chose not to go, not to send assistance."

Her brows drew together in horror. "Why?"

"I wanted you out of the way. I wanted this." His hand sketched his domain around them, his invisible power. "You were in the way. I thought it best to let the Gardener solve my problem for me."

Tears stung her eyes. She had had no idea of the depths of his professional jealousy, that it had become personal. And she couldn't believe she hadn't seen this darkness in him. She was a profiler . . . too busy profiling the criminals around her, and never turning her attention to the greatest threat standing right beside her. "You let the Gardener abduct me, cut me up, bury me? You left me for dead? You *let* that happen?"

Golden dawn light washed over his glasses. "I did. I'm sorry it had to be that way, but . . ."

She swung at him. Her fist slammed into his jaw, flinging his glasses from his face. Immediately she was tackled by Gabriel's men, tasting frost and dirt on the ground.

From the corner of her eye, she could see Corvus plucking up the remains of his shattered glasses from the grass.

"Take her back to the mine." He knelt before her, and she felt a twinge of satisfaction at seeing the worm of blood trickling down his nose. He tried desperately to staunch it with a handkerchief. "Tara, my dear, enjoy this moment. It's the last daylight you'll ever see."

They hurled her back in the cell, kicking and howling.

Then they turned the lights off.

Tara heard the click of the electricity being cut to the wing, saw the lights winking out, one after another, down the hallway, until she was left in rapidly cooling darkness. She pulled the Pythia's coat around her body, wondered if they intended to leave her here, in this isolation, until she starved or went mad.

Corvus had a sense of irony. *Bastard.* In hindsight, she could see how all the pieces fit together, why she'd pulled the Death card to represent him . . . and the white roses. The Six of Wands in conjuction with that card . . . representing betrayal by someone close . . . Why had she not seen it? And most recently . . . the Devil card, imprisonment. Her blindness had caused her to be bound by her own fears, in the cold and the dark. Just as Corvus was bound by his own avarice.

She pressed her hand to her forehead. She'd been too wrapped up in her own experience, too focused on healing and withdrawing from the world to suspect him of any wrongdoing. Now, it was too late. And too late for Harry.

A lump rose in her throat. More than anything, she

wanted Harry to be free. And she'd failed. And she'd failed Martin and Cassie . . . Surely, it was only a matter of time before Corvus and Gabriel combed through the barren landscape and found them. She wondered if even Delphi's Daughters could keep Cassie safe, if there was any fighting the fate that seemed so inevitable.

A small voice tickled the back of her mind: *Fight.*

Magnusson's watch scraped her eyebrow, and she stared at it.

Perhaps there was still a way to fight. Tara took off the watch and felt for the smooth back of the case, for the etched infinity sign in the metal. She dug her fingernails into the edge of the steel casing, succeeding in working the cover free with her torn nails.

Bits of dark energy glowed soft violet, spinning through the circuit of the battery. Precious light. She breathed into the fragile tangle of wire, trying to remember what Cassie had said about the properties of dark energy, how she could use this to her advantage. She examined the battery, the circuits turning in on themselves. Cassie had said the circuit could be interrupted, shorted out, by something as simple as crushing them . . .

And then what? Tara thought of the destruction of the laboratory. Such a small amount of power, such a terrible result . . .

Violet sparks milled peacefully along the tiny circuit, deceptive in their tranquility. No telling what would happen when the energy discharged. Might be nothing, might bring the whole place down around her ears. Either way, it was her only bet to stop Gabriel and Corvus.

She took a deep breath. She had regrets, many of them: blaming Sophia for her mother's death; not seeing Corvus for what he was. Most of all, she regretted how things had turned out with Harry. She wished she could have had more; more conversation, more lovemaking, more time.

But none of these things were left.

She heard footsteps approaching. She concealed the watch under the heel of her shoe in enough time to see the glint of a flashlight, hear the grate of a key in a little-used lock. Tara was surprised these doors even had old-fashioned keys, other than the electronic key cards. She heard the heavy bolts dragged back, squinted at bright light beaming in her face.

"I thought we could use some quality time alone. Just us girls."

It was Adrienne's voice. She could see her tall silhouette above the halo of light. She threw something on the floor before her, something that smelled cloyingly sweet . . .

A clutch of irises. They lay on the concrete floor like a bouquet tossed at a wedding that no one had caught, unwilling to tempt fate.

"Those are a present from Corvus. He wanted me to bring you something to keep you company in the dark. Something familiar." Tara stared up at Adrienne. "He is one sick son of a bitch.

"They won't give you to me until I get the girl's location from you." Adrienne circled her, the heels of her shoes bruising the flower petals and opening more of their dusky fragrance to the stale room. In the dim light, her eyes shone like a cat's. "And I will enjoy getting it."

"Why me, Adrienne? What've you got against me?"

"The Pythia has chosen you as her successor. The title should be mine."

"The Pythia knows you've been stalking me. Do you think she would willingly give the title to you now?"

"Not willingly, no." Adrienne's white teeth gleamed. "The Pythia is old and weak. If I challenge her, she will yield."

"I wouldn't be too certain about that. The Pythia is a pretty determined bitch."

"What would you know about it?" Adrienne's eyes narrowed. "You haven't been among us in years."

"I don't *want* to be among you! I left Delphi's Daughters," Tara snarled. "I have done everything to get you people to leave me the hell alone."

"The Pythia has never forgotten you. She has always watched over you, though you were too stupid and rebellious to see it."

"The Pythia hasn't done shit for me."

"She saved your life, you ungrateful wretch." Hate glowed in Adrienne's marble-like eyes. "When you were taken by the Gardener, when you were imprisoned in the ground, the Pythia knew. She was the one who whispered to you, with the diluted power she had left, to fight. She lent you her strength, and suffered for it. Her power diminished exponentially after that . . . She is a weak shadow of her former self."

"I don't believe you." Tara's mind reeled under the weight of the possibility.

"Like you said, the Pythia is a pretty determined bitch.

No one ever leaves Delphi's Daughters . . . for any reason other than death." Adrienne balled up her fist. "And I will be happy to release you from that obligation."

"It's good of you to keep me company, Adrienne." Tara lifted her foot and stomped down on Magnusson's watch with all her strength. She felt the crackle of the circuit breaking, a low hum almost beyond the range of her hearing thundering through the floor.

Light swelled up under her foot. She backed away, staring in fascination as the violet light escaped the confines of the watch, pushed her out in a shock wave, ripped open the air in a terrible weal of sound . . . and exploded in a cold flash of dark brilliance.

It was still dark. Always dark.

The darkness weighed heavy and cold against Tara's body. She smelled the dreaded scent of earth, crushed irises, and the warm copper tang of her own blood. Her nose and mouth were packed with dirt, and the weight of the earth kept her aching limbs from stirring.

Despair and panic overwhelmed her. She had been here, before: buried alive. She was stuck in an infinity loop, sucked over and over again into this situation, like a Tarot card coming up in draw after draw, unable to escape. It seemed this was her destiny, to be committed to the earth, to feed it with her lifeblood. Her judgment in this life. This unavoidable knowledge paralyzed her. She could feel her heart pumping faster, wasting air and shoving blood through wounds that burned brightly in her flesh.

"Fight."

This time, she could distinguish the voice. It was clearly the Pythia.

No. This was not her destiny. She squeezed her eyes shut, thought of the Judgment card she'd drawn, just hours before, how it depicted a woman rising from a coffin into the daylight, into the embrace of an angel. She remembered the Strength card, the slight woman taming the jaws of the lion. And she remembered the Knight of Pentacles, Harry, how much she wanted to see his face again. And Cassie, the Star, whom she'd promised to protect.

"Fight."

Her mother had raised her to be a fighter. She would not allow Corvus and his sweet-smelling Death to win.

She wiggled her fingers in the dirt, forming an air pocket. She worked her hands back and forth until she could feel her wrists move, then her elbows. Her bad arm howled in protest, sending shock waves of pain to the soles of her feet. She worked against the gravel, the weight of the earth, until she could shrug her shoulders, turn her head. She clawed her arms up over her, as if she were swimming, pulling clods of earth up, opposite the direction where gravity seemed to tug the debris. She imagined this was how Strength felt, struggling against the jaws of the lion, ignoring her own wounds.

Up. Up. She kept that thought foremost in her mind. She glimpsed fading sparks of the violet dark energy as they slid through the earth, unencumbered by the mass of the soil. She envied them, how quickly they moved out and away, as easily as fireflies navigated air.

But she was not like them. She was bound by mass and form, and couldn't phase through matter at a wish. Her energy flagged. She was buried much deeper than she had been in the Gardener's flower bed, hopelessly deep in a mine. She forced herself to continue, promised herself she would go as far as she could until she ran out of air.

Something compressed the earth above her, shook the gravel. Through crusted-shut ears, she could hear the rain of dirt, the sluice of earth moving. She reached up for it, feeling furtive scraping, movement, shouting . . .

And she was being dragged free of the debris. She cried out in pain, her leg twisted beneath her, dirt crusting light that was suddenly agonizingly bright.

"Shh, babe. It's okay." She felt Harry's arms around her, wiping dirt from her face. "Just breathe . . . long, slow breaths."

She sucked in lungs full of air and stared up at his swollen eyes. Gabriel had given him one hell of a shiner. "How did you find me?" she asked, spitting around the dirt in her mouth.

Harry gestured to the scene around them. The mine had partially collapsed in on itself. Emergency crews scurried around the sunlit site, hauling people and precious bits of metal out of the disaster zone. The land was littered with scraps of paper, torn pieces of insulation, candy wrappers, chunks of concrete . . . the lightweight random litter of an explosion. In this area, though, at the northwest edge of the mine, she could see it was scattered with the torn debris of Corvus's iris petals, glinting white in the sun.

"I found this, right over where I found you." He showed her a torn and filthy Tarot card, the one depicting the wounded woman closing the jaws of the lion: Strength

THE EARTH KNEW HER. IT KNEW HER LIKE A MOTHER KNEW a child, lovingly wrapping its arms around Adrienne. She felt the rumble of the pulse deep within its breath, sensed the weight of the earth's love as it drew her near.

She'd come home.

Her lungs filled with blackness, and she sensed metal twisting and breaking below her. A ley line trembled somewhere far below. She sensed the cold veins of silver, still sleeping miles underground. The glitter of quartz and geodes shimmered in her sight, as they shifted and settled. Dirt dug into her skin, permeating it. Fragments of silver and dark violet light melted and flowed through her veins, scorchingly cold. The border between her body and the earth dissolved, and she and the ground became one. Distantly, she wondered if Magnusson had known this bliss when he fell in the field at the bottom of the caldera.

Home. Synthesis.

The roar of silence suffused her. After hours, days—she couldn't mark the passage of time in this still place—she felt the rumble of earth-moving equipment above her, the scrape and sloughing of shovels. She shrank away from the sounds of digging, burrowing deeper into the cool black.

But the machines found her, eventually. Daylight washed over her, burned her eyelids.

She howled.

Leave me here.

Men stood over her in white suits, Geiger counters clicking and zinging. Their voices fell over each other in alarm. A man she recognized as Gabriel bent over her; she could see his horrified eyes behind the mask.

"Dig her up," he said.

Other voices buzzed. "How in the hell are we supposed to do that?"

"Do it," he ordered savagely. "Uproot her like a turnip."

The blade of a shovel cut into her body, fused with the earth, and she screamed.

Chapter Nineteen

On a visceral level, Tara understood the principle of dark energy . . . understood it to be the natural, polar opposite of the solid matter comprising her world, that it was not subject to any of its laws, save gravity. For every action, a reaction; for every thing, an equal and opposing force. Magnusson had left a scrap of it behind, to balance the equation he'd set into motion. But it still didn't make things easier for Cassie.

Tara had come to tell Cassie about her father in person. It had been nearly a week since she'd seen her, but it seemed much longer. Tara drove up the long, straight road to Sophia's farm with empty hands and a heavy heart. Spring had begun to touch the fields . . . The earth would be turned in the coming weeks, waiting for seed. Blades of new grass had begun to prickle through frost. The apple trees were studded with pale green leaf shoots, and a touch of fickle warmth had begun to permeate the March Tennessee air. She had not been here since she was a child, with her mother, and she wondered what it would be like to see this familiar landscape without Sophia in it.

The farmhouse was the same as she remembered: a yellow two-story house sprawling under the weight of slate shingles. Chickens milled through the yard, muttering to themselves, as Maggie stalked them around the corner of a shed. Tara pulled up in the driveway before the barn. Maggie thundered up to the car, claws scraping against the door. She fell upon Tara in a hail of doggie kisses and snuffling.

To her delight, Oscar sauntered down the porch steps and pressed his body up against her leg. Tara kneeled down to scoop up the cat with her good arm as he purred like a chain saw.

"Oof. Oscar, you've put on some weight."

Oscar nipped her ear, kneaded her wounded shoulder with his claws. She shifted him over her shoulders, where he lay like a stole, well out of Maggie's reach. His purring vibrated through her skull.

On the porch, the Pythia sat in the swing, smoking. Her bare feet pushed her colorful skirts back and forth, and her ankle bracelets jingled in time with the squeak of the chain suspending the swing. In the shade, the bright gleam of her cigarette burned like a star.

"How are you feeling?" the Pythia asked. She frowned at her cigarette, as if it told her something she didn't want to hear. She stubbed it out and lit another.

Tara frowned at her arm in a sling. "Better." She was

sore all over, bristling with stitches and bruises. And her radiation sickness had returned, perhaps retriggered by the explosion of Magnusson's watch. She felt weak and pale. But it felt immeasurably good to breathe the fresh, open air. It even wiped away some of the uneasiness of the truce between Tara and the Pythia. "How's Cassie?"

"She's in the shower. I told her you were coming for dinner." She shrugged. "My cigarettes say so, anyway." There was a twinkle of humor in her eye that Tara had long forgotten.

Tara hesitated. "Is there dessert?"

"Of course. The Daughters of Delphi know how to bake. Most of them, anyway." The Pythia blew a smoke ring to the ceiling of the porch, like a wizened dragon. Tara sat down on the other side of the porch swing.

"I am glad you are safe," the Pythia said.

Tara rubbed the sweat from her hand on her jeans. "Is it true?"

"Is what true?"

"What Adrienne said . . . that I'm to be your successor? The next Pythia?" Words fell over each other. "I don't want it. No way in hell. You'll have to pick someone else."

The Pythia looked at her and burst out laughing. It was not the reaction Tara had expected.

She took a drag on her cigarette and touched Tara's arm, bracelets jingling. "You are not my successor. You're good, but you're not *that* good."

Tara blinked. "But . . ."

"You never were," the Pythia said mildly. "Cassie is the one I want for Pythia."

Tara's jaw dropped, dumbfounded. "But she's not an oracle . . . She's a scientist . . ."

The Pythia smiled. "We are all many things. I wanted Sophia to bring you back to the fold, in order to guard her and bring her here. I foresaw that the next Pythia will need to guard the secrets of darkness, to keep that knowledge safe from the hands of men. And Cassie has that knowledge, the power of dark energy.

"You're a warrior, at heart, Tara. Fighting is what you do best . . . whether it's with men in the outside world or with me."

Tara stared at her. "Was that you talking to me . . . in the Gardener's box?"

The Pythia wouldn't answer, just smiled like the Sphinx with an unanswerable question.

"This Pythia business. Cassie can't see the future . . ." Tara sputtered.

"Not yet. Not well, in any case. But she's got an aptitude for astrology, for reading the stars. I could feel it when you brought her to me in the trance. She's a few years behind in training, of course, but she'll catch up."

"Hang on." Some part of her wanted to protect her, to keep her safe from the Pythia's grasp. "How the heck does Cassie feel about this? We're talking about her like she's a thing."

"She hasn't made her mind up yet. She wants to talk to you about it."

"You're not going to force her into it?"

The Pythia shook her head. "I can't force anyone into anything. Even when I see the future, as you do, it's a possibility that never trumps free will. She can stay with me, or she can go."

"That's generous of you."

The Pythia ignored the dig. "You have news about Cassie's father?"

Tara nodded. "It's not good."

"I'm sorry to hear that. Sorry for Cassie, especially."

"You don't seem surprised."

The Pythia swung for a moment, her painted toes moving across the floorboards of the porch. "I think Magnusson's time had passed, but he gave what he needed to give to his daughter. It was . . . his legacy that was important."

The screen door banged, and Cassie thumped down the whitewashed steps. Tara was startled at her transformation. The dark makeup had been scrubbed from her face, and a few pounds had been added to her too-gaunt frame . . . the Daughers of Delphi did, apparently, know how to cook. With the light-brown bob, she reminded Tara of her own mother, beautiful and glowing.

Cassie threw her arms around Tara, and Tara smiled into her embrace. Tara saw how her eyes slid to her empty car.

"Where's Harry?" Cassie asked.

"Harry's back in New Mexico, being deposed by the state's attorney."

"Is he in trouble?"

Tara's mouth thinned. She hadn't seen Harry since she'd been discharged from the hospital. He'd come to tell her Corvus was dead, but that no trace of Gabriel or Adrienne had been found. At least he had enough sense not to send her flowers. "I think the Pythia has set him up with a very good attorney. He should be fine."

"And Martin?" Tara could see Cassie was working herself up to the big question, warming up to ask about her father.

"Martin's back home. When Gabriel's men came for him, he faked a heart attack, then wound up in a psychiatric hospital. He faked dementia all too well, and Harry had a hell of a time getting him released." Tara smiled. "But while in the psych ward, he apparently managed to set himself up as the dictator of an imaginary empire of followers who worshipped him as a god."

Cassie's eyes were anxious, and her voice was lower than a whisper. "And my father?"

Tara rubbed the girl's arms. She hated to be the bearer of bad tidings, but it was best it came from her. "Sweetie, I'm sorry, but your father died in the explosion. He destroyed his research to keep it from falling into the wrong hands."

The girl's face crumpled, and she buried her face in her hands. "I thought so," she whispered, through tears.

"Why did you think that?" Tara asked, stroking her hair.

Cassie sat down heavily on the step. "He had been so secretive about his work, as if he was trying to protect me from it. When it was clear that he gave the laptop to me, I knew something was terribly wrong."

"You destroyed the laptop's hard drive."

Cassie nodded, wiping her nose. "Yeah. I just felt . . . that was what he wanted me to do. And it's all in my head, anyway."

The Pythia came to stand beside the girl and put her arm around her shoulders. "That knowledge is your father's legacy. It will live and grow through you."

But her eyes were on Tara when she spoke.

THEY DUG HER UP AND PUT HER SOMEPLACE BRIGHT, A PLACE that smelled like chrome and piss and disinfectant. A place full of the chatter of people and machines, far removed from the soft, organic silence of the ground.

Adrienne was furious.

Through eyes taped shut, she could sense the shadows as they stretched over her bed. Some came to stare at her—she could feel the weight of their gazes on her. Others brought blessed oblivion in the form of drugs . . . but it was an incomplete oblivion. She always woke with pain and fury. The crinkle of plastic, the beeping of machines—nothing could disguise the wariness she heard in their voices. And the pity.

"Poor thing," she heard a woman say. "They should just let her die."

Pages on a chart flipped like a deck of cards being shuffled.

"No," another voice responded. "They're going to keep her. Study her. No one's ever seen anything like it."

"It just seems inhuman."

"Well, she does look horrific, but . . ."

"Not *her*. Keeping her alive is what's inhuman."

Adrienne felt a needle slide under her flesh. Another drug that brought the false darkness.

When she awoke again, she smelled tobacco. She

flexed her fingers, feeling them curl against the sheet. At least she still had fingers.

"Gabriel," she whispered, with malice. Her throat was raw, perhaps from the scrape of a feeding tube. Her mouth tasted like dirt and blood.

She opened her eyes. Something was wrong with her vision . . . Her field of view was speckled with fragments of tiny prisms and dirt. Her brain struggled to adapt, to frame Gabriel's image in her wobbling perspective. He stood over her in a white hazmat suit, head cocked to one side like an inquisitive bird.

"Did you sleep well?" he asked.

"Where the fuck am I?" Her mouth felt numb and warped, and her tongue swelled. The word came out sounding like "thuck."

"In the isolation wing at Los Alamos Medical Center. You took on some dark matter." He said it as casually as if she'd taken shrapnel, his eyes tracking up and down her body. "Now that you're stable, our scientists can't wait to get their hands on you."

"Take me back," she pleaded. She wanted nothing more than to be returned to the earth.

"I'm afraid that's not possible."

He gestured somewhere beyond a clear plastic curtain, and she could hear the wheels on her bed being unlocked. Someone pressed an oxygen mask over her face, and white-suited men zipped a plastic bubble over her. With the clatter of IV poles, they began to wheel the gurney out into the hallway. Through the warble of plastic, dingy ceiling tiles and fluorescent lights flashed past. Adrienne's thoughts were sluggish with the aftereffects of drugs. She struggled to focus, to pull the head-clearing oxygen deep into her lungs. She had to think of a way to escape. She would not be their science project.

They wheeled her into a service elevator with padded walls. Gabriel crowded in with two nurses, and the numbers blurred on the way up. The elevator ejected them into fresh air and blue sky. The roof of the structure, Adrienne guessed.

The sounds of helicopter blades sliced the air, thrumming at a low whine. A black Huey perched on a helipad like a giant black mosquito, ready to whisk her away to an unpleasant fate, under Gabriel's microscope.

Adrienne took a deep breath. The plastic bubble over her rattled. She felt something dark and lightless roiling in her chest. Something strong. She reached up for the zipper as men in camo uniforms rushed forward to pull the gurney into the gaping maw of the copter. They were going to devour her.

For the moment, she let them. Her bed was lifted into the back of the copter, IV poles and machines trailing like the tentacles of a squid. Adrienne took a head count: a pilot, two guards, a medic in white, and Gabriel. Her odds were improving.

They milled around, securing the gurney and blinking equipment. One of the cabin doors had become jammed open by a rock. Gabriel gestured for the men to secure themselves, and to leave it. Adrienne waited for the sickening lurch that told her the helicopter had lifted off, waited for it to bank left and peel away into the sky, before she struck.

The zipper ripped open, and the wind from helicopter blades snagged the plastic bubble like a kite. Adrienne twisted and reached for the gun at the hip of the nearest man in camo. She felt IV lines tear out of her arm and the oxygen mask rip from her face. She grasped the cool metal, flopped like a fish on land, and pulled the trigger.

Blood spattered on the outside of the bubble.

Wind ripped through her hair, nearly blinding her. She heard Gabriel shouting for them not to shoot her. Must've been part of his latest mission: bring back the dark matter without damaging it. She wondered what he was willing to sacrifice in order to do it. Adrienne launched herself out of the egg of the plastic-covered bed, feeling cold air skimming through her hospital gown against her raw skin.

Her . . . skin. She hesitated for a moment, glimpsing mottled, warped skin that glistened like granite.

But only for a moment. She rolled beneath the cart, ripped away the Velcro straps holding it anchored to the helicopter frame, and kicked it as hard as she could. The cart slammed into the medic and kept rolling. Both tumbled out of the open cabin door of the helicopter in a rattle of plastic and white sheet.

"Adrienne." Gabriel said something more that she couldn't hear; she just recognized the shape of her name on his mouth.

No more words. No more stupid, simpering, deceitful words. She was tired of people talking to her.

She shot the remaining guard.

The pilot pitched the helicopter forward, trying to throw her off-balance. Adrienne skidded in bare feet, snatching at a cargo strap. She leveled the 9mm at Gabriel, saw he'd drawn down on her.

He'd not killed her so far, when he'd had the chance. His mission must be too precious for him to lose her.

"What do you want from me?" she screamed at him, and the wind shredded her voice.

"The dark matter," he shouted. "It's in you."

She shook her head, lashing hair around her face. She wasn't going with him. She pulled the trigger. The wind muffled the pops chewing into his chest. He fell onto the floor of the copter, sliding precariously toward the open door.

The helicopter pitched forward in a dive. Adrienne advanced to the cockpit. She wouldn't let him ditch the copter. She had places to go.

She skidded forward and pressed the gun barrel to his helmet. "Level off."

He paused, then pulled up. Good man. Perhaps the pilot had more of a sense of self-preservation than Gabriel.

"Where to?" he shouted.

Where, indeed? Adrienne slid into the copilot's seat. She had none of her usual tools of geomancy to guide her: no stones, no dowsing rods, no handfuls of earth to scatter.

No. She did have the earth. She could feel it singing in her bones. It was inside her. She listened to it. It grew and filled her with a sense of magnetic north. From this great height, she could see the blue spiderweb of ley lines crossing across the distant ground, could feel the energy of earth as never before. Unraveled threads of wrath and unshed tears rose in her.

She pointed to the horizon. "East. Take me east."

Her quarry was there, gathered with the rest of Delphi's Daughters. She could feel it, as surely as she could feel gravity or hate.

Knowledge was a living gift, passing from one generation to the next. It could be a boon or a curse. Tara wasn't quite sure which it was that Cassie had inherited from her father.

Tara sat on the porch swing at Sophia's house, looking out toward the yard into the darkness, one of Sophia's sweaters wrapped around her shoulders. It smelled like sage and jasmine. Maggie stretched out at her feet. Oscar had emerged from Sophia's breadbox to grace Tara with his presence, tucking himself under her arm. Cold chills rippled through her, though her brow was glossed with sweat. She'd eaten little of the sumptuous dinner Delphi's Daughters had prepared. She was afraid to imagine how deep the radiation sickness went, and had slipped out into the darkness to allow the stillness to permeate her, to allow some equilibrium to sink in. Inside the house, a half dozen of Delphi's Daughters bustled about. Someone was playing music, and by the laughter and creak of the floorboards, she guessed they were dancing. Polka, followed by the Electric Slide, from the sounds of it.

She remembered the apple trees in the yard from when she was a child, when she and her mother and Sophia would gather them in laundry baskets to make pies. She remembered her mother's easy grace, her love, and the gift of knowledge she'd passed on to Tara. Tara's mother had never treated her abilities with cartomancy as a curse. Strange that Tara had come to look upon it as such.

Tara looked at the tattered Tarot card she held in her hand. Strength. Her mother's cards were gone. Her mother was gone. All she had left was the ability to honor her memory, by being of service.

Tara turned the card over in her hands, thinking of Harry. He'd saved her life, in many ways. She wished she could tell him how grateful she was to him for pulling her out of her shell, for breaking her exile and helping her to feel again. She frowned. Perhaps she and Harry were too different to make a relationship work, but she still owed him a debt.

The screen door slammed, and Cassie slipped out onto the porch.

"Hey."

"Hey."

"Mind if I sit with you?"

Tara scooted over to give Cassie room on the swing. The girl vigorously rocked it back and forth with her sneaker, making Tara queasy.

"About this thing with the Pythia . . ." Cassie began.

Tara waited, laced her hands in her lap.

"I'm not sure what to do. Everything's happened so fast, and I . . ." She leaned back and looked at the stars. "I don't know."

Tara followed her gaze to Cassiopeia rising on the horizon. Without her cards, Tara's intuition was stubbornly silent. For an instant, she felt as if she were missing a limb, unable to accurately advise or see around corners.

She was surprised at how easily she'd fallen into her old familiar patterns, and how much she missed them.

"No matter what happens," Cassie said sadly, "I'm gonna have to leave everything behind . . . school, my name . . . everything but Maggie."

The military might still be looking for her, and Cassie would have to shed her old identity, whether or not she stayed with Delphi's Daughters. Tara suspected one of the hardest parts of her grieving process would be losing her father's name and taking on a new identity. But as long as she kept her father's knowledge close to her heart, Tara was convinced the girl was stronger than even she knew.

"The most important thing," Tara said slowly, "is to make sure that you're safe. The rest are simply choices that can be altered later on."

Cassie smirked. "You think the Pythia would let me change my mind? Join later? Or drop out of the Daughters of Delphi?"

Tara shrugged. "Why not? I did. And she hasn't eaten me alive. Well, not yet."

"It wouldn't surprise me to find out that the Dragon Lady eats people."

Tara snorted. "Dragon Lady. I like that." Her expression sobered. "Look, I've got very little love for Delphi's Daughters. But I do believe they can keep you safe. So . . . it's your choice. Just tell the Pythia that you reserve the right to change your mind at any time. And keep my number handy. I'll come get you, no matter where you are."

Cassie smiled. "I believe you. Thanks." Her eyes shone with reflected starlight. Tara guessed that if she looked deeply enough into her eyes, she might see galaxies unfold. "When did you join Delphi's Daughters?"

"I was initiated when I was about seven. Yeah, that sounds about right. That was the year my mom made me the Wonder Woman birthday cake and the year I discovered comic books."

"Your mom was in it, too?"

"Yes. You might say she was the Pythia's favorite. Like you."

"Why did you leave?"

"I'm not much of a joiner." She thought about it. "That's not exactly true . . . I wanted to save the world. And I didn't think that I could do that within Delphi's Daughters."

"Wow. Delphi's Daughters seem . . . to have so much power."

"They do," Tara agreed, trying to be objective. "But that's just not where my path lies."

Cassie leaned back again in the swing to stare at Cassiopeia, and Tara wondered exactly what she saw in her future. Without her cards, she had no way to know which route the girl would choose, but she hoped it would be the right choice for her.

Tara straightened when she heard the crunch of gravel and a dust plume rising from the road. The porch swing stilled with a squeak.

"Go into the house, Cassie," she ordered, reaching for her gun. No more of Delphi's Daughters were expected tonight. Cassie obeyed, running into the house.

Barefoot, Tara walked down the gravel driveway. The

gravel was sharp and cold on the soles of her feet, and the grip of her gun was slick in her left hand. The headlights washed over her, clicked out as the car engine shut off. Tara lifted her chin, still dazzled by the light.

When her vision cleared, her breath caught in her throat. Harry opened the car door. Some of the swelling had gone down in his face, but he still had a hell of a shiner and a few stitches over his eyebrow. He jammed his bandaged knuckles in his jacket pocket and smiled at her. As beat-up as he was, he looked incredibly good to Tara.

Maggie bounded down the porch steps and plowed into him, nearly knocking him off his feet. She pinned him to the car door, slurping all over him, tail wagging.

"Hey," he said.

"Hey, yourself." Tara put the gun away, surprise writ all over her face. "How did you get here?"

"Someone named Amira called me."

Tara glanced back at the house, was sure she saw a flicker of movement in the lace curtains of one of the upstairs windows. "Oh."

Awkward silence stretched.

Harry rubbed his hand through the back of his hair. "Did you tell Cassie?"

"I did. She's . . . she's doing okay."

"And how are you doing?"

Tara looked up at him. "Better. Did you get deposed?"

He made a face. "Yes. For days."

"Sorry." Tara jammed her hands in her pockets. "How did it go?"

"On the bright side, it looks like I won't get fired. But

there's not much evidence to back up what I say. Much of it seems to have been destroyed, disappeared, or is classified."

"I'm sorry." Tara didn't seem to be able to stop apologizing.

Harry reached for her hand. "There are other things I want to focus on right now." He leaned forward and kissed her. It was a sweet kiss, full of hope.

Tara looked down at her hand in his. It felt good, right.

"I brought you something."

"Not flowers, I hope." She wrinkled her nose.

Harry laughed. "No flowers." Reaching into the jacket pocket, he handed her a small box, wrapped in shiny red foil that glinted in the porch light.

"What's this?" It felt heavy.

"Open it."

Tara pulled apart the paper and opened the box. It was a deck of Tarot cards, beautifully illustrated, displaying a midnight-blue pattern of stars on the verso. They were edged in silver leaf, the figures drawn in a delicate hand that reminded her of Art Nouveau works, shaded in vibrant watercolors.

"I, uh, was in the bookstore, and I didn't know if these were the right kind, or anything . . . but I knew you lost the ones you had . . ." He scrubbed his hand at the nape of his neck in that nervous gesture she'd come to love.

Tears welled in Tara's eyes. She'd felt the loss of her mother's deck powerfully, hadn't even begun to think of how she'd begin again. She laid her fingers on his lips and kissed the corner of his mouth.

"Thank you," she whispered.

CHAPTER Twenty

LATER THAT night, Tara and Harry lay awake, entwined in each other's arms. The Pythia had given them the old guest room at the top of the house that Tara had occupied during the summers when she was a child. It hadn't changed. The same shade of pale yellow paint covered the walls, and the bed was dressed with the same quilts she remembered. Some of Tara's old Nancy Drew books stood at the top of one dresser, and a lump rose in Tara's throat whenever she saw them.

"Hey." Harry brushed her hair from her shoulder. "You okay?"

"Yeah." She rested her chin in her hands. "Just remembering. I spent summers here when I was a kid, with Sophia. I wonder what's going to happen to the house, now that she's gone." There were too many memories associated with this place. She wanted to wrap them around herself like a blanket one minute, and run away from them the next.

"It seems like the house is well-occupied," Harry said circumspectly.

Tara looked into his almond eyes. "I should probably tell you who all these crazy women are." The time had come to tell him the truth.

"I assumed they were crazy relatives of yours."

"Well, that's partly true." She took a deep breath. "These women are all like me. They call themselves oracles."

"They can tell the future?" Harry's eyebrow crawled up his forehead.

"In their own ways, yes. They're a society of women that can trace their intellectual lineage back to the time of the Oracle of Delphi in ancient Greece. They call themselves Delphi's Daughters."

"This is the chick version of the Freemasons?"

"Yeah. Pretty much. The woman who called you, Amira . . ." The name still tasted foreign on her tongue. "She's the head oracle, the Pythia. My mother was her successor. My mom died, so . . . the Pythia's been without someone to train."

"She didn't train you?"

Tara shook her head. "No. I left when I was an adult."

"Sounds like a wise move."

"But one of the other Daughters of Delphi thought I was in competition with her for the title. She wanted it. She went rogue, and was working for Corvus and Gabriel. Adrienne . . . killed Sophia. She was with me, in the cell . . ." Tara swallowed, and Harry rubbed her good shoulder.

Harry leaned back and stared at the ceiling. Tara was reluctant to continue without some sign of positive feedback from him. "What do you think?" she asked after some minutes had stretched.

"I don't know," he admitted. Tara felt him slightly pull away from her.

She decided to plunge ahead. Better to get it all out into the open. "The Pythia wants Cassie to be her successor. She's willing to hide Cassie for as long as necessary."

Harry turned over to look at her. "Wait a minute. I can accept that you used to belong to a . . . a cult. But you've got no business handing Cassie over to them."

"Cassie is an adult. She'll make her own decisions." Tara could scarcely believe that she was defending Delphi's Daughters. But she couldn't disagree with Harry's assessment: they were a cult.

"Christ, Tara . . . you're a psychologist. I don't have to tell you how emotionally weakened Cassie is now. This is seriously bat-shit crazy." His voice rose, and Tara wondered who else in the house heard him.

"Harry, we can't keep her safe. Do you really think the military is going to just stop looking for her?" Tara whispered furiously, hoping to draw down the loudness of his voice. "It's the lesser of the two evils."

"Maybe. But it's still the wrong thing to do. There may be another option we haven't considered. Witness protection. Moving Cassie to another country. Something."

Tara shook her head. "Delphi's Daughters are all over the world. They will find her."

Harry rolled over, sighed, and lapsed into silence. Tara rested her head on his shoulder, listening to the rhythm of his breath. Neither of them slept, but Tara could almost hear the thoughts rattling in his head as he considered possibilities and discarded them.

Finally, he slipped out from under her and sat on the edge of the bed. He scrubbed his hand in the back of his hair and reached for his shoes.

"Where are you going?" she whispered. She bit her lip, afraid that he heard too much need in her voice.

"I need some time to think about this. I know you've gotta do what you've gotta do and you're doing the best you can. But I've gotta clear my head, make sure I haven't missed anything. I've got to be sure that there's no other option."

She nodded, swallowing. "I understand."

He leaned forward to kiss her on the forehead before he gathered his shoes and left, closing the door behind him. Tara could hear the car engine turn over and the crush of gravel as he drove away.

She stared at the ceiling, blinking back tears. She refused to go to the window and watch him leave. The swords of Harry's logic hung too heavily over her.

"DID YOU GO THROUGH THIS BULLSHIT WHEN YOU WERE INITIATED?"

Cassie wrinkled her nose as Tara braided the short strands of the girl's hair around the crown of her head. She stared down at the simple gauze dress she wore, crossed her arms self-consciously over the sheer fabric.

"Mmm-hmm. But that was back when shoulder pads were big, and dinosaurs roamed the Earth. Imagine how hot this looked with tarantula mall-chick bangs."

Cassie looked down at her purple toenails peeking out from under the gauze hem. "I think I'd take the big shoulder pads. But maybe not the bangs."

"Delphi's Daughters have a somewhat . . . eclectic ceremonial aesthetic," Tara muttered diplomatically as she tucked bobby pins at the nape of the girl's neck.

"It sucks."

"Yeah. It does suck," Tara agreed. "But it's a big deal to them."

Tara glanced out the window at the driveway. The driveway and the yard were full of cars. None of them were Harry's; not that she had expected him to come back. Delphi's Daughters had descended upon the farmhouse all day, crisscrossing the grass in bare feet, toes curling against the chill of the ground. Delphi's Daughters loved to party, and the drink had already been opened. In the kitchen below, she could hear the clank of pots and pans. Outside, some of Delphi's Daughters crowded around roast pig, encased in a drum leaking smoke. One of Delphi's Daughters advanced on the drum with a paint bucket full of what looked to be barbecue sauce. Oscar followed in her wake, stalking a string of sauce drizzling from the bucket.

Cassie sniffed her bare arm. "Yuck. What is this crap I had to bathe in?"

"It's bay laurel. The tree is sacred to Apollo."

Resigned, Cassie stood still as Tara tucked the last loose strands of her hair behind her ears "What other indignities can I expect to be subjected to today?" she asked crankily. But Tara could read the anxiety under the snark.

"There's nothing to be afraid of. There's no bloodletting or dead goats." Tara sat down on the edge of the bed made up with a sunshine-yellow quilt. She traced a calico butterfly on the worn fabric. "They're not crowning you Pythia today. This is just like . . . the pledge of allegiance for oracles."

Cassie sat beside her. "I just wish I knew whether or not this was gonna work out."

"Tell you what. I'll read your cards." They had time to pass before the rite began; no one was dressed, the pig was still half-raw, and the woman weaving the floral head-dresses had run out of crocuses and tulips and was raiding the herb cabinet for something else to use.

Tara pulled her purse out from under Maggie's slumbering belly. The dog barely so much as twitched. She pulled her new deck of cards from the crinkly red wrapper. They felt stiff and blank and new. She held them to her hands, warming them with her skin and her breath.

She was nervous using them, and not just because of the pang in her heart she felt knowing they were a gift from Harry. She'd never used any other deck than her mother's. Part of her suspected the new cards wouldn't work, that the magick had been inherent in those worn cards, and had nothing to do with her. What if these cards made no sense, were random scraps of cardboard? What if her ability to see into the future was lost to her forever?

Would that be so bad? Her power had brought her little joy, but she was reluctant to lose it entirely. Before, she'd been secure in the knowledge that if she ever decided to peer into the future, she could. Though the cards had been tucked away in a drawer, she could touch them any time she wanted. But now . . .

What if it was all gone? Used up? Adrienne had intimated that this is what had happened to the Pythia, that the well had run dry on her power. Why couldn't it happen to Tara?

"Okay." Tara handed the deck to Cassie. "Shuffle the cards until they feel right to you. Take as long as you want."

The cards bristled together and apart as Cassie worked through the deck. After a few minutes she handed them back to Tara.

"The reading I'm going to do for you is called a Tree of Life spread."

She drew the first card and placed it on the center of the bed. "This is your significator card. It represents you in this reading."

Tara turned it over, revealing the Star as Cassie's significator. It showed a serene young woman dipping a pitcher of water in a spring. Relief washed over her. The tool didn't matter. She had her mother's legacy, and she would use it.

Tara dealt the remaining cards around the significator: north, northeast, northwest, south, east, west, southeast, and southwest. The significator was the center of the compass rose of her fate. The cards formed the shape of a tree, with the last two cards placed in a straight line at the bottom as the trunk.

Turning over the card north of the Star, Tara said, "This card represents your aims and your purpose in the situation. It deals with your higher ideals."

The Magician. A man stood before a table containing symbols for all four elements: air, earth, fire, and water. He held a wand to the sky as he transmuted the elements into spirit, and his violet cloak furled out behind him.

"This represents your father," Tara told her. "You've embodied his knowledge and ethics, as well as his power to create. His goals are now your goals . . . When you seek to hide the secret of dark matter, that was also his will."

Cassie hugged her knees to her chest. She fingered the gilt edges of the card. "I hope so."

Tara flipped over the card to the northeast of the Star. "This card represents the sphere of immediate influences on your life, what's taking most of your attention."

The Priestess stood in flowing robes, holding her scepter. She was crowned with a diadem shaped like a crescent moon. In this deck, she was holding a pomegranate. Tara associated that with the myth of Persephone in the underworld, absorbing it as a symbol of polarity, of bargains.

"This is a card I associate with the Pythia, with hidden knowledge. Since she appears close to the Magician, it suggests that their aims are similar. She can help hide you and your father's knowledge.

"The card positioned to the northwest of the significator sheds light on the general nature of the issue facing you. This may be a facet of the situation you haven't considered." Tara turned over the Seven of Pentacles. A farmer leaned against a garden hoe, watching seven pentacles blossom in the fertile earth. "The Seven of Pentacles represents the fruits of one's labor, a commitment. You will, literally, reap what you sow. You're making a decision about your life's work. I'd anticipate that since it appears so close to the Magician, that you may eventually wish to continue your father's work in some form or other, after a period of respite or withdrawal."

Tara glanced at the pentacles. "They're stars?"

"Actually, the suit of pentacles represents earth, material life, career, and stability. They're often depicted as coins in other decks."

"So . . .being Pythia isn't a career?"

"It's a calling, which is different from a career. You'll notice that even the Pythia has a day job."

"It's possible, then, that I could continue his work?"

"Anything's possible, Cassie."

Cassie smiled at that.

Tara pointed to the card immediately south of the Star. "This is the key to your situation, the key to making your decisions and helping you move forward."

She turned over the Ace of Wands, a flowering branch thrust up to a brilliant sunny sky. "This is one of the luckiest cards in the deck. The suit of wands is associated with fire, passion, movement. This card shows you have a groundswell of enthusiasm beneath you, that you are in touch with the creative life force."

To the east of the Star lay the Six of Cups. It showed a young boy handing a cup overflowing with flowers to a little girl. "This card deals with times past, and with childhood. These are things from your past influencing the present. It can signify a happy childhood, or it can indicate one is living too much in the past."

Cassie bit her lip, and Tara moved to the next card.

"West of the Star is the near future." She revealed the Three of Cups, depicting three women in beautiful dresses dancing, holding gold chalices aloft in the air. "The Three of Cups is a good card—celebration, joy, and unity. It's a card of growth. Cups deal with emotions, with water. These women are sometimes interpreted to be the three Graces, or the three classical Muses. Overall, it's a good sign."

In the kitchen below, a pan crashed to the floor. The sound was immediately followed by raucous female laughter.

To the southeast of the Star, Tara picked up the Three of Wands. It showed a man flanked by three wands staring out at the ocean to a ship on the horizon. The weather was calm, and the waves even. "What do you see in this card?" she asked Cassie. "Just go ahead and free-associate whatever comes to mind."

Cassie turned it to get a better look. "This guy looks like he's waiting for the ship."

"Is the ship approaching the shore or moving away?"

"It looks to me like it's approaching."

Tara nodded. "A ship is coming in, and the card marks the completion of a first stage in a plan or a successful first part of life."

Cassie wrinkled her nose. "Does that mean I've got to look forward to being an adult?"

"You've been an adult for quite some time. This is moving forward to a new phase. You've got a lot of wands in this reading, which are suggesting a great deal of forward momentum and movement toward your goals. I think you have more autonomy than you realize."

Tara plucked the last card from the tree's foliage, positioned to the southwest of the Star. The Wheel of Fortune showed a sphinx holding a wheel between its paws. In the clouds around it, symbols of the four elements perched: a bird, a man, a cow, and a lion. "Another card of endings and beginnings, new cycles. Whatever is past is falling away, and the future is rolling in. The Wheel of Fortune also speaks of taking risks and accepting the consequences, whether good or bad."

Tara turned over the first card in the tree's trunk. "The Four of Pentacles illustrates your hopes and fears. In this case, it's reversed." The card showed a woman sitting under a tree in a meditative posture. She cradled three pentacles in her lap and was crowned by the fourth. "It suggests you're in deliberation, but that you will need to take action or a risk to move forward. It's a card of complacency and miserliness."

"Does it mean I shouldn't take any action now?" Cassie's brow wrinkled.

"Not necessarily. It just means that if you don't act, nothing will be gained, and you'll remain in the same position." Something tickled Tara's memory about the card, and she grinned. "Traditionally, the reversed Four of Pentacles can sometimes herald being sent to the nunnery."

Cassie stuck her tongue out. "Screw that." She paused, reflecting. "Wait a minute."

Tara lifted a brow. "Oh?"

"I haven't seen any men around here. Besides Harry."

Tara avoided the insinuation. "Yes."

"Does that mean . . . ?"

"Does it mean what?"

"Does that mean that joining Delphi's Daughters means I have to take a vow of celibacy?" Panic crossed the girl's face.

Tara laughed out loud. "No. I think you're safe."

Cassie sat back. "Whew. I mean . . . I wondered there, for a moment, if that was the real reason why you'd left Delphi's Daughters."

Tara shook her head. "No. That wasn't any part of the equation. That 'wife of Apollo' stuff wasn't even strictly adhered to back in the time of sandals and togas."

Cassie nodded. "Okay. I'll try not to panic at the rest of the reading."

"The last card is the final outcome of your question," Tara said. She was heartened by the positive flavor of the reading, and expected the final card would seal the reading.

The Page of Swords. A woman armored like Joan of Arc stood against a gray sky with sword lifted, peering into the wind with wariness. Her green cloak curled around her, hiding something.

Tara's finger rested on it. She'd encountered this card recently, when Gabriel and Corvus had sent the assassin for Cassie. Then, she'd associated the card with the shooter, with a puppet of Gabriel and Corvus, but hadn't quite been able to get the feminine taste of the card out of her mouth.

"This card cautions you to be clearheaded and quick-witted. It also suggests the need for discretion. Be cautious and enter the situation with your eyes open."

She circled the configuration of cards with her finger. "Overall, I'd say that the cards predict an auspicious beginning to the next part of your life. You have many allies, though you have some emotional business to attend to. Joy is on the horizon. But be vigilant, and guard against complacency."

Cassie nodded. "Understood. Thanks, I do appreciate it."

From the other side of the door, a knock rattled. "Cassie, it's time for flowers . . ."

Cassie made a face. "Ugh."

Tara smiled. "Go get tarted up like a parade float. I'll check on you in a bit."

Cassie dragged her feet going to the door. When she closed it, Tara picked up the Page of Swords. She turned it over in her hands, observing the cold expression in the Page's eyes.

She'd seen that cold expression before, in Adrienne's agate gaze.

"Shit," she breathed.

She shuffled the deck, cut the cards, and began a reading for herself. "What's coming next?" she muttered at the deck. She did a simple three-card spread.

The first card she drew was Strength: the woman holding the jaws of the lion closed. A runnel of blood traveled from her collar where the lion had bitten her, soaking the front of her gown. But the woman held fast, her expression serene.

The Ten of Swords depicted a man lying prone on a beach, his back pierced by ten swords. Blood drained into the water of the nearby lake. It was the sign of a painful and inevitable ending.

The Page of Swords brought up the last position, vigilant and staring back at her with eyes the color of the gray sky behind her. Adrienne again. The young upstart, seeking to dethrone the Queen of Swords.

Could she have survived the mine collapse? Tara steepled her fingers at her chin. The cards were insisting she was a proximate factor. Drawing the card twice in two different spreads went far beyond chance.

There was an ending to be had between Tara and Adrienne. And the cards predicted it would be bloody.

HARRY DROVE THROUGH THE COLD HOURS OF NIGHT UNTIL the stars burned out.

He felt guilty for leaving Tara, but he needed to sort this shit out. There was clearly some bat-shit craziness going down at the farmhouse. Asking him to believe in Jung's synchronicity was a far stretch for him, and this cult stuff . . .

He felt guilty for leaving Cassie behind. He wondered how much brainwashing Cassie might be subjected to. So far, all he had to go on was Tara's word that she'd be safe. Several times he picked up his cell phone and started to dial the local FBI field office. It would take some doing to get agents to descend upon the farmhouse, but he might be able to pull enough strings to get it to happen. Each time, he hung up without completing the call. Tara was right; Cassie's life was safer with Delphi's Daughters than in any witness protection program he could place her under.

But it bothered him that there seemed to be nothing he could do about the situation. He was accustomed to being able to act and solve problems . . . and there was no good answer for this situation. It was merely a choice between two evils. And it was Cassie's choice.

Dawn reddened the horizon before he stopped along the interstate, at a small town near the edge of the state line. Few lights were on as he cruised down the main street. Convenience stores and restaurants were closed, not to open for another hour or more. He doubled back down residential streets, searching for caffeine or a place to piss.

Spying the inviting red glow of a vending machine in the distance, he pulled off the road. He'd take his caffeine any way he could get it. He drove through an open gate in a chain-link fence, through a deserted county fairground. Parking the car before the seductive red glow of the pop machine, he emerged from the car. He jingled change in his pants pocket as he perused the selections.

Choosing a high-octane energy drink, he fed a handful of change into the humming machine and punched the button. The machine rejected his change. Harry growled and fed it to the machine again, one coin at a time. The damn machine spat them out again. He kicked the machine.

Harry snatched the change from the coin slot, sifting through it. Maybe he'd accidentally picked up a slug somewhere. His fingers counted out two quarters, a dime, a couple of nickels, and . . . a weird coin that was the wrong shape.

It figured that the damn machine wouldn't take Canadian money. Harry turned to go back to the car. Perhaps he could scavenge some more change from the seat cushions. But something tingled in the nape of his neck, and he opened his hand again to look at the strange coin.

It wasn't Canadian. It was British money. One side of the golden coin showed a portrait of the Queen. The other side showed the words *Ten Pence* above a crowned lion.

Harry paused. The coin reminded him of the Tarot card he'd found where Tara had been buried: Strength. The tattered image of the woman holding closed the jaws of the lion had inspired him to start digging.

He'd driven away from the caldera, as she'd wanted. But as soon as he'd pulled out of the compound, he'd picked up a tail. Through some harrowing turns down two-lane roads in the desert, Harry had succeeded in ditching the tail. He called the nearest field office for reinforcements, then turned back to the caldera. The only thing on his mind had been rescuing Tara. Halfway back, he heard a roar that jangled gravel on the road and shook the lines on the overhead telephone poles. He could feel the shudder of the earth through his foot jammed to the gas pedal, and his heart lurched into his throat. He arrived at the old silver mine just behind the local volunteer fire department. Sheer luck had led him to Tara.

Perhaps not luck. He flipped the coin in his hand, weighing it.

Movement behind the building caught his eye. The morning sun illuminated a grand old carousel. Filled with horses and fantastical beasts, the immaculately maintained paint shone brightly. It was closed down for the winter; tarps covered the control panels.

But someone still imagined riding it. Astride a brightly painted lion, a woman in a long coat sat sidesaddle. The lion's mane was painted orange, and he was captured mid-roar, with white fangs glistening. She stared up at the sun, while a dog snooted around the base of the carousel. The woman held a leash in the hand that rested on top of the lion's head as she waited for the dog to finish his business.

It was the scene of a simple morning stroll, but it hit Harry hard, hard as the shredded Tarot card perched in the dirt.

Harry climbed back into the car, started the ignition. He turned the car back down the way he'd come.

He couldn't shake the irrational sense of impending danger. He was certain that Tara needed him, whether she knew it or not.

"YOU'RE NOT WEARING THAT."

"I am."

The Pythia planted her fists on her hips, jingling the gold bracelets over her thick gauntlets. She was dressed in a scarlet dalmatica with gold trim and a matching girdle strung with tiny bells that tinkled when she moved. The overall effect was of having one's pissed-off fairy god-mother cast in a Bollywood flick.

"You are," Tara growled, "not my mother." She folded her arms over her button-down shirt and black jacket. She was wearing jeans, period. There was no way to hide a gun in a toga.

"This is an initiation. Have some respect."

"Yeah, well . . . I'm a guest. I'm not in the club, remember?"

The Pythia rolled her eyes and threw up her hands. She flipped on the burner of the gas kitchen stove to light a cigarette. On the kitchen counter, Oscar poked his head out of the breadbox. He fixed Tara with a baleful look and disappeared back inside.

"Pythia." Tara tried to change the subject. "I read something in the cards that has me worried. About Adrienne."

That got her attention. The Pythia glanced sidelong at her. One of the flower petals from her headdress drooped precariously over one eye. "What about her?"

"That she may still be out there, somewhere, and in revenge-seeking mode."

The Pythia plucked a bay leaf from her headdress and dropped it into the burner. Tara's stomach rumbled as the sweet smell of bay leaf smoked up to the flame hood. The Pythia watched the blue fire catch it, burn yellow, curl it, and reduce it to ash.

"There is nothing here that can be changed," she said.

"But there is no immutable future," Tara protested.

The Pythia made a slicing gesture with the hand not

occupied with a cigarette. "Let it play out the way it's meant to."

"But . . ." Tara began.

The Pythia poked her in the ribs with a sculpted fingernail. "Go get something to eat. You're too skinny."

"Radiation sickness will do that to you."

The Pythia snorted.

Cassie stomped into the kitchen, flower petals flying in her wake. Two of Delphi's Daughters twittered after her, trying to tuck the errant flowers in place. The girl looked like a maypole. Flowers covered her: a chaplet of bay leaves curled around her head; wilting crocuses were tied to her arms with ribbons; orange and yellow tulips were garlanded around her waist.

Cassie sneezed. "Is this all really necessary? I'm allergic to this shit."

The Pythia raised her eyebrows. Cassie fell into a sneezing fit that dislodged her chaplet and blew a handful of tulips off her toga. She stood in the kitchen floor, miserable, wiping her nose with a paper towel. Tara went to her and started plucking the worst of the flowers from her clothes and hair.

The Pythia threw up her hands again. "Let's just get down to the spring." She stalked out the back kitchen door.

Cassie looked at Tara. "Is she pissed at me?"

"No. She's really mad at me. Don't worry. You'll get used to it."

"Used to her being mad at you or me?"

"Both."

The Pythia was calling for Cassie. Delphi's Daughters were beginning to flock together on the front porch. Like extras from *A Midsummer Night's Dream,* their pale dalmatica robes were white, and the women had braided flowers and herbs into their hair. Tara smelled incense, and someone yelped as Maggie's nose scooted up an unsecured skirt.

Cassie rolled her eyes and dragged her feet to the door. "You're coming?"

Tara set her mouth in a grim line. "Wouldn't miss it for the world."

She just hoped the guest list was under control.

Chapter Twenty-one

THE PYTHIA Parade began shortly before noon.

Tara resolutely fell in line behind the uneven line of women spewing rose petals across the field. She stubbornly refused to change clothes, and stuck out like a sore thumb among the women dressed like the Muses' crazy old aunts. The drinking had already begun, and some were already none too steady on their feet. Sophia's chickens followed them for a short distance before losing interest, but Maggie bounded through the freshly plowed field to catch up to Cassie. Mud began to sully the edges of their skirts, and claimed more than one sandal.

Tara scanned the edges of the field and the tree line of the forest. Between the flower petals and the tracks in the mud, they'd leave a trail easy enough for a child to follow. She reached self-consciously for her gun. She remembered the Page of Swords, with her sword upraised: the Page did not enter any conflict without being well-armed. Neither would Tara.

They crossed the field into the shade of the forest, following a winding overgrown footpath downhill. Tara remembered this place from her childhood. Delphi's Daughters were versatile: they didn't fight to possess locations for permanent oracles, like the Temple of Apollo. Their ancestors had wasted too much energy on places. Delphi's Daughters could play a pick-up game of magick wherever they found themselves.

But this place was one of Tara's favorites. She remembered when her mother had led her by the hand down this labyrinthine dirt path, years ago. Tara had stepped on a honeybee, and her mother had carried her down into the deep, shaded ravine to the place where a spring bubbled before a shallow sedimentary cave. She remembered the way the sandstone glistened, the cool feel of moss under her feet, and the sharp taste of the iron-laced water. Improbable trees had wedged their roots into crevices in the stone, clinging to the sides like spiders, reaching up toward the sun.

It was almost the same as she remembered it, but smaller. The cave seemed less deep, and the trees were still mostly bare this early in the year. Pale sunlight shone down onto the spring, which bubbled and gurgled like a half-open tap on a water hose. This early in spring, it smelled like moss and leaf-rot.

The Pythia delicately stepped onto a flat rock overlooking the spring. A fissure had formed in the rock decades ago, splitting it halfway. Below and behind it, darkness stretched, and the spring ran beneath. Tara's mother had never allowed her to play there, warning her away from the steep sides.

Delphi's Daughters busied themselves with building a fire in a brazier on the flat rock and arranging the Pythia's tripod chair. They kept a few affectations of the old order of the Oracle of Delphi. Tara appreciated the fire aspect of it (the Pythia was a pyromancer, after all), but thought the small, tippy chair looked terribly uncomfortable. Perhaps it had been designed to keep the original Pythia from getting too comfortable and falling asleep after long sessions at the temple of Apollo. Tara was wholeheartedly glad she'd never be Pythia.

Two of the women led Cassie down to the pool at the edge of the spring. Tara heard Cassie exclaim shrilly, "What? I've got to take my clothes off?"

It was a tradition going back to Delphi: initiates had to be ritually cleansed in pure water. In ancient Greece the Castalian Spring had been used, but Pythia's modern daughters would use any handy source of water. In an emergency ceremony, she had once seen the Pythia use a garden hose wrestled from a kids Slip'N Slide game.

But using the spring had much more gravitas. And the Pythia loved ceremony.

Maggie bounded ahead of her into the water, splashing mightily. She took two small circular laps, jumped up to the shore, and shook herself off. Frigidly cold water peppered the assembled women, who squealed in dismay.

Cassie shyly pulled her tunic over her head. She crossed her arms over her body, and Tara could see her cheeks flaming red. She hissed as she was led into the water and her foot connected with the chilly surface. Modesty won out over goose bumps, and she waded to her neck in it to obscure her body. Tara could hear her teeth chattering from her stance at the edge of the circle of women.

After a few false starts, Delphi's Daughters managed to get a decent fire going with some scrap wood brought from the house and a couple of fire bricks. The Pythia gathered her robes and perched on her ridiculously little chair. She popped a few laurel leaves into her mouth to chew. Unlike in times past, hallucinogenic vapors were not required to have a ceremony. The Pythia maintained that hallucinogenic substances were for poseurs. She looked out over the women, and her voice echoed off the walls of the gorge. "Sisters, we assemble today in great sadness and in great joy. We come to mourn the passing of our sisters and to welcome a new initiate. Time passes, and times change. Sophia and Adrienne are lost to us, but our lineage begins anew, in the veins of Cassie Magnusson. She will carry our line forward into the future."

Cassie shivered in the pond so hard water droplets were shaken off her laurel wreath. Tara was thankful that her own initiation had taken place in July, when the spring had been warm as bathwater.

"We mourn the passing of our loyal sisters from our sight, and we ask Apollo to bless their memories."

A voice from above rattled down, thin and reedy. "So easily out of your sight and out of your mind. Is that right, Pythia?"

Tara reached for her gun. Footsteps creaked in the

leaves above the crevasse. This place was too much of a natural trap, with blind sides and echoes, and she couldn't tell where they originated from. She scanned the ridge of the landscape over the sight of her gun, skimming that high horizon for any sign of movement.

"Everybody get down," she shouted.

Delphi's Daughters scattered, pressing themselves to the walls of the cave. Cassie sucked in a deep breath and ducked under the surface of the water. That was a temporary hiding place; she was far too open. Maggie stood at the mouth of the spring and barked. The Pythia climbed out of her contraption of a chair and drew herself up her full five feet in height.

"Adrienne," the Pythia bellowed. Tara was amazed that such a mighty voice could come from such a tiny woman. "You've dishonored yourself. Come here and face judgment."

Bitter, rusty laughter squeaked overhead. "I've dishonored myself? You've dishonored the lineage by your own weakness. You've squandered your power on the ungrateful. And the successor you've chosen? A girl with no power of her own? Unimaginable."

"I do not answer to you," the Pythia shouted.

"The Daughters of Delphi are dying, old woman. And I am happy to help consign you to history."

A hail of bullets cracked into the gorge. They split the surface of the water and spattered shards of sand from the stone. Tara returned fire blindly, unable to see, much less hit anything over the outcropping of rock. She glanced back at the spring in her peripheral vision. She didn't see

Cassie. Maggie plunged into the water after the girl. The Pythia had pressed herself against a wall, hands balled into fists. Her tripod chair was shattered by the bullets, lying like a broken insect on the stone. One of Delphi's Daughters lay, bleeding and twitching, on the ground.

"Haul your ass down here and face me, Adrienne," Tara shouted.

The footsteps echoed overhead, receded. A figure appeared at the mouth of the gorge, and Tara froze, momentarily stunned at the sight of her.

Stringy blonde hair brushed the shoulders of a too-baggy military flight suit. She held an MP-5 in her hands, even as some part of Tara's brain tried to figure out how many shots she had left in the clip. Cold gray eyes glared with searing malevolence.

But that was all that remained of Adrienne. Her pale skin had warped like glass under too much heat. It sparkled like quartz at her temple and on her warped lips, but blackened to the color of rich prairie soil on her chin and throat. A vein the color of silver pulsed behind the zipper at her neck. She looked like a rough-hewn diamond, just pulled from the ground, uncut and without polish. She limped toward Tara, and Tara could see that her foot was pigeon-toed in her boot. She couldn't imagine what else was ruined beneath that flight suit.

"What the hell happened to you?" Tara breathed.

Adrienne tipped her head to one side. "Gabriel said I got too much dark matter. Particles of the earth fused with me."

"You survived what happened to Magnusson."

"Adrienne." The Pythia moved forward. Her almond eyes were widened in horror. "Come back to us. We will take care of you, get you the help you need."

"Help?" Adrienne spat. "You'll take care of me like you took care of me as a child? You'll shuttle me from place to place, never having a true home?"

"We were training you," the Pythia said. "I had high hopes that—"

"Not high enough to give me the title of Pythia, no matter how hard I worked." Tara could see tears glittering in those inhuman eyes as she paced forward, onto the Pythia's dais.

The Pythia met her eyes. "I had hoped that for you, yes. You were a brilliant student. But there was too much coldness in you."

Behind them, the surface of the water broke open. Cassie's head burst through the surface to gulp a lungful of air. Adrienne spun to shoot, presenting her back to Tara.

Tara lunged forward and opened fire. The bullets struck Adrienne in the throat and below the ribs. Adrienne pulled off two shots that shattered the surface of the water before she fell, growling, at the edge of the rock.

Maggie paddled, whining, in the crystal-clear water. Tara dove in behind her. The shock of the cold water against her chest was like a slap in the face, driving the breath from her lungs. She grabbed for the arms of the pale figure suspended beneath the water and hauled Cassie to the surface. The Pythia, looking like a drowned rose in her soaked robes, helped her drag the girl out of the water.

A gunshot echoed through the tiny gorge.

Tara turned to see Adrienne aiming at her with the MP-5. Tara instinctively shielded Cassie and the Pythia with her body. She tensed, anticipating a bullet tearing into her.

Another gunshot echoed, and she flinched. But the gunshot wasn't from Adrienne's hands, and it didn't strike Tara.

It came from above, and struck Adrienne in the eye, the last human part of her. Red blossomed on Adrienne's cheek, and she fell on her back to the rock. The MP-5 clattered away into the water.

Tara looked up at the ridgeline. Harry stood on a rock outcropping, gun in hand.

He'd come back.

"She's not breathing," the Pythia shouted. Cassie's head lolled limply on the Pythia's shoulder, and she'd turned blue.

Tara shoved the Pythia out of the way. She performed the Heimlich maneuver on Cassie. A trickle of water emanated from her mouth.

"C'mon." She jammed her doubled fist into Cassie's diaphragm again. This time, water gushed from her mouth as if poured from a pitcher.

Cassie coughed and sputtered. She leaned over and vomited up water.

"Are you hurt?" Tara demanded, shoving her wet hair back from her face. She could see no sign of blood on the girl's body, quaking from the cold.

She shook her head but couldn't form any words under the force of her teeth chattering. The Pythia wrapped her cloak around her, and one of Delphi's Daughters retrieved the girl's toga to wrap around her shoulders.

Tara climbed back to the flat rock for Adrienne, but she had disappeared. A smear of blood extended from where she'd been shot to the dark crevasse behind the spring. She'd gone to ground. The darkness below was thick, black as the Gardener's graves.

But Tara felt no residue of panic when she lowered herself into the space between the rocks. She landed in cold water splashing up to her knees. There wasn't enough room to stand upright, and Tara hunched over. Water dripped from the ceiling, and the enclosed space smelled like iron. Light poured in a jagged shaft from the fissure above, enough to distinguish a human shape, curled into the fetal position in the farthest, darkest part of the tiny cave.

"Adrienne?"

She sloshed forward and warily touched the woman's shoulder. There was no movement, no rise and fall of her chest. Tara couldn't be sure, but in the dim light, it seemed a smile played across Adrienne's swollen lips. Adrienne had chosen a familiar grave. The geomancer had gone back to earth.

And the close earth held no fear for Tara, now. She took a moment to marvel at that, at the sharp contrast between dark and light in this place, at the sound of water and the breath rattling in her throat. Her fingers brushed the wall of the tiny pocket cave. It felt safe, womblike. She knew then that her ordeal at the hands of the Gardener had been cleared from her psyche; she had no lingering fear.

"You all right down there?" Harry's head and shoulders were outlined at the opening of the cave.

"Yes." She grinned up at him. "What brought you back?"

Harry shrugged. "Your cards."

She looked up at him quizzically.

He shook his head. "Long story. I'll tell you later."

He extended his arm to pull her out, and she reached up to take it.

SITTING IN SOPHIA'S PORCH SWING, TARA LEANED BACK TO stare into the starry sky. Her cards lay in her hands, and she shuffled them over and over without drawing one. She wasn't sure that she wanted to know the future, what lay ahead. There was too much to contemplate: Cassie's initiation, the Pythia's intentions, whether Harry would stay.

And Tara had to decide where she wanted to go next. Being thrust out into the world like this . . . It had felt good to break exile. To be useful again. The last few days, she'd been contemplating what it would mean to go back into practice, if the world of profiling was necessarily closed to her.

Unlike so many of the others, she had options and a mutable future. One of Delphi's Daughters was killed in the firefight. She had no surviving blood family, and the Pythia was having her buried nearby. Delphi's Daughters had moved a large stone over Adrienne's rocky grave, and showed no interest in retrieving the body.

Even Harry showed no inclination to do anything other than leave the body there. DOJ had summoned him back to the New Mexico field office to file a mountain of reports, and she'd reluctantly let him go. She knew she'd see him again, but the bed in the upstairs bedroom felt much too large without him.

But there was still unfinished business to attend to.

A match flared in the darkness, as the Pythia walked through the screen door, patched with duct tape. Tara watched her, waited.

The Pythia didn't speak. She stood beside Tara, dragging on her cigarette.

Tara was first to break the silence. "You knew this would happen. You knew that Adrienne would come back, and that Harry and I would be forced to kill her."

The Pythia tapped ash from her cigarette. "You know as well as I do that seeing the future only shows possibilities."

"You grew that monster in your own backyard. Here." And Tara feared for what that meant for Cassie. Under the watchful eye of the Pythia, would she grow into a monster, like Adrienne? Or would she become a hollow shell, like Tara?

The Pythia seemed very old to Tara, as the tiny ember outlined the sagging skin under her chin, the kohl smeared under her eye. "No matter into what fire I looked, I saw that Adrienne would grow into a powerful oracle. You have no idea how much I wanted her to follow in my footsteps." She shook her head. "No idea. I felt her turning away, moving into the darkness, and I was powerless to stop it. We all were."

Tara glared at her. She wasn't buying it.

"What about Cassie? What are you going to do to make sure she doesn't follow in Adrienne's footsteps?"

The Pythia puffed out a ring of smoke. "Cassie will be a wonderful Pythia. Someday, she will turn that title over to your daughter."

"What the hell are you talking about?" Tara growled. "I can't have children. The Gardener saw to that."

The Pythia snorted. "You're not the type of woman who believes what she's told."

Tara reviewed her cryptic conversations with the Pythia. "You said I would be the one to bring you the new Pythia."

"And you will."

The Pythia faded back into the house, leaving Tara alone in darkness. She considered what the Pythia had told her. The future was about possibilities. Perhaps the Pythia had been right, and some new ones had been opened to her.

Her emotions reeled. She had taken a long time to forgive her mother for dying, and to stop blaming Sophia. It would take even longer to forgive the Pythia. If that ever happened.

But she now had good reason to forgive, to stop fighting destiny.

Butt-kicking Urban Fantasy
from Pocket Books
and Juno Books

Hallowed Circle
LINDA ROBERTSON
Magic can be murder...

Vampire Sunrise
CAROLE NELSON DOUGLAS
When the stakes are life and
undeath—turn to Delilah
Street, paranormal
investigator.

New in the bestselling series from Maria Lima!

Blood Bargain
Book Two of the
Blood Lines Series

Blood Kin
Book Three of the
Blood Lines Series

"Full of more interesting
surprises than a candy
store! —**Charlaine Harris**

Available wherever books are sold or at www.simonandschuster.com

22186